SAVE ME

SAVE ME

**The Wolf Hotel Mermaid Beach
Book Two**

K.A.TUCKER

ISBN 978-1-990105-57-9 (paperback)

ISBN 978-1-990105-59-3 (ebook)

Edited by One Love Editing

Cover design by Shannon Passmore

Published by K.A. Tucker Books Ltd.

Manufactured in the United States of America

1. Ronan

If the dictionary included pictures, Henry Wolf's smug face would be right next to the definition of a prick.

If Satan were searching for a human host to possess, he would look no further than the evil specimen seated next to me, humming along like a fucking pioneer woman at a washboard on a sunny spring day.

If we were on a sinking ship with only one lifeboat, this motherfucker would shove past women and children to—

"You're quiet." Henry interrupts my brooding.

"I'm always quiet." I deftly maneuver our golf cart past the small army of staff unloading linens from a delivery truck, my foot crushing the pedal.

Okay, so maybe Henry wouldn't strong-arm children —Abbi would never marry a guy like that. But he is a Grade A douchebag. And maybe I am unusually quiet, but it's because I'm struggling to keep my cool about the bomb he just dropped on me.

He is intent on destroying Sloane's life.

How long has he been planning this? If he's talking about eminent domain, then it's clear this is not an overnight grudge he's indulging. He had to have set wheels in motion months ago, and he has the right people in his pocket to make it happen.

There's no doubt it'll happen because Henry Wolf always gets what he wants.

My hands hurt. Probably because I'm choking the steering wheel. I ease up on my grip and force indifference into my tone. "These big plans for Mermaid Beach ... what do they look like?" I didn't have a chance to ask before. He took a call and directed me to drive back to the hotel with a dismissive wave of his hand, like I'm Jeeves, his chauffeur.

"New harborfront, definitely. The one here is dated and lackluster."

I frown. "You want to put in a new *harborfront*, right next door?"

"Hell no, not there." His chuckle is condescending. "We'll tear down the docks and replace them with a new system. Build a new boardwalk, widen the road, add dozens of restaurants and shops. Make it a true destination for people visiting. It'll bring millions in revenue. The chains are dying to get in, especially now that the hotel is here."

"And there's space for all that?" I ask, but the uneasy tingle along my spine tells me I know where he'll find the space.

"There will be once all those shacks are gone."

Shacks like the Sea Witch, he means. Fuck me. He's

not just after her home. He wants her business too. "Eminent domain can't be used for private corporation land grabs." I don't know much, but I know that.

A smug smile answers me. "I'm not after the land, just the atmosphere that'll draw in more people's wallets, and I've spent many months and millions with my architects, designing exactly what people want."

Sloane doesn't want it. "So you're not after that?" I jut my chin toward her property.

"I was," he admits. "Seemed smart to have it for future expansion. But a new road will work too."

"A new road," I repeat. Henry's going to tear down and pave over Sloane's entire life. That's his big plan.

"An access point for the hotel. We'll benefit from that. When we revitalize the harbor and the boardwalk, congestion will only get worse. The local planners agree, and they're willing to do just about anything to please me."

"I'll bet," I force out. All hail to the great and powerful Oz.

"With all that space, they're pushing the idea of a public beach and conservation area, but I'm not keen on having that so close to my hotel. We'll see." He shakes his head. "Sloane Parker would have been smart to take my offer. It was a hell of a lot more generous than what she'll get with this new deal."

"Clearly, she didn't want the money."

"And now, she'll have no choice. The Mermaid Beach council and I are unveiling the design on Friday. It's going to modernize this entire town. I'm sure the meeting is in your schedule."

"Can't wait." Archie has stuffed my calendar like a piñata at a five-year-old's birthday party. It's ready to burst. But that's not my concern now. My stomach stirs with nausea. "A lot of locals live and work around here. Do you think they'll have a problem with you coming in and blowing everything up?"

"Of course they will. People don't like change," Henry scoffs. "Locals tried stopping Wolf Cove too, and now look at them. All the shops in nearby towns have quadrupled their seasonal business. They're building two new strips for stores and a supermarket. The growth has only started too. Wait until the ski runs are completed. A lot of those people complaining are also the first ones in line to benefit." He scrolls through his phone screen as he murmurs, "Nothing stays the same forever. The sooner people figure that out, the better."

"Sloane's not gonna benefit from this. Short of a fat bank account she's not interested in. This is a dick move, even for you." I can't help the bitterness in my tone.

There's a long pause, and then ...

"You son of a bitch." Henry sighs heavily. "You went against my orders and fucked her anyway."

I school my expression. "I don't know what you're talking about—"

"Don't bother denying it. You're as predictable as that Florida sun." He points at the glowing ball in the sky.

I briefly wonder what my tell was. Whatever. I'm not going to embarrass myself by continuing to deny it. The hotel's main doors are coming up ahead, and Belinda is loitering, waiting for her supreme commander. So I lift my foot off the pedal and bring us to a halt. It's best we finish this conversation here. "What I do on my own time is my business."

"I own you." Henry snorts derisively. "I gave you the opportunity of a lifetime, and you couldn't even keep your dick in your pants long enough to reach opening day."

I don't miss the past tense in that sentence. Is this him firing me? If I'm going down, I might as well do it swinging. "Funny, didn't your father say the same thing to you?" Abbi once let slip that William Wolf had all but threatened to take the hotel from Henry if he couldn't stop sleeping with his assistants. Of course, enter Abbi stage left, and what Daddi-O wanted didn't matter.

Henry's gaze narrows. "What the fuck did you just say to me?"

Okay, I'll admit, bringing up his late father was a douche move. "Look, it's not a big deal—"

"The hell it isn't! You are senior management now, Ronan. What you do reflects on this company and on me," he barks.

And Henry is all about image. Again, I'll bet he had this exact same conversation with his father when he was fucking around, but I bite my tongue this time. He hasn't officially fired me yet.

"When did it happen?" he demands. "Before or after she agreed to take the signs down?"

"Why the hell would that matter?" I'm not giving Henry or anyone else details about my time with Sloane.

"Because I need to know if I'm going to have a PR mess on my hands because of this."

"Why would you ..." My words drift as I clue in.

Does he think I used sex as a negotiating tactic? That I seduced Sloane into getting what I want out of her? Pieces of shit like Cody do that.

I don't fucking do that.

My teeth grind as I fight the urge to defend myself. Admitting that what happened with Sloane was way more than just an opportunity to get laid, that I'm developing feelings for her, is not what Henry wants to hear. "Any PR mess you have won't be because of me. Bulldozing half of Mermaid Beach will earn you that."

"That's business. I can deal with that. What I can't have are sexual harassment headlines tied to this hotel's name."

"Jesus, are you kidding me right now? That's not how it happened! It wasn't anything like that," I snarl, my typical even keel vanishing with a rare flare of temper. "That's not me, and you fucking know it!" I've never laid so much as a finger on a woman without her being crystal clear about wanting it. "Honestly, what kind of situations have you gotten yourself into that your brain thinks this way?"

"That's not the point!"

Pieces are beginning to click together. Is this what Belinda was hinting at that day she warned me off the "unhinged neighbor?" Because this can't just be unhealthy paranoia on their parts.

I doubt many people have the balls to raise their voice to Henry.

I brace myself for a yelling match that I will gladly participate in, but instead, Henry's answer comes in a calm and collected tone. "Sometimes, when people are hurt or angry or embarrassed, they lash out in unexpected ways," he answers vaguely, and then his brawny chest sinks with his exhale. "You know, what? It's done. Those stupid signs are down. That's all that matters."

I falter at the unexpected and quick course correct.

"She is a complication for me, and I don't need complications. Find someone else to entertain yourself with. Go to the beach, go to the bar, go to the fucking Piggly Wiggly, I don't give a shit where you pick them up, as long as I don't hear another word about Sloane Parker that involves you ever again. And we can pretend like you didn't take a piss all over my wishes. Deal?"

Wishes? More like demands. And who does he think he is? Vito Corleone?

But it doesn't sound like I'm looking for a new job yet. "Sure thing, boss." Whatever I need to say to end this conversation.

The electric golf cart whirs as I set it in motion again.

We're almost at the front door when Henry adds, "And just in case you're tempted, let me remind you that you signed a confidentiality agreement when you accepted this position, which means you better keep your mouth shut about this revitalization project, or I will gladly bankrupt you."

"I can always count on you for a threat." As if I want to be the bearer of that news.

Belinda meets us at the hotel's front doors with a cautious expression. "Enjoyable tour?" She couldn't have overheard our conversation, but I'll bet our body language told a convincing story of two men inches away from choking each other out.

"Peaceful one. I'm looking forward to early morning rounds," Henry says, playing it off. "Happy to see our problem has been dealt with."

I wish I'd never convinced Sloane to take down those signs.

"Yes, your director worked his magic." Belinda's sharp blue eyes dissect me, reminding me of her not-so-subtle proposition not even an hour ago. We've been working well together lately. Too well, I guess. "Dorian is looking for you, Ronan."

"Again?" Dealing with that guy and his mustache more than once a day is too much. "The sprinklers still?"

"I have no idea and no interest in knowing until it's resolved. Henry? We'll have our meeting outside, at Seraphina's." She gestures toward the revolving door, leaving little room for negotiation.

With a secretive smirk, like he could remind Belinda who's boss but finds this role reversal "cute," Henry slides out of his seat. "Keep up the good work, Ronan."

"Yup."

They stroll into the hotel without a backward glance.

"Fuck you," I mutter under my breath as soon as they're gone. And fuck me. I squeeze the bridge of my nose as I weigh the impossible position he's put me in. Do I warn Sloane about his plans for decimating her life? I don't even know when it's happening, but if he's presenting models on Friday, I imagine someone official will be knocking on her door sooner rather than later.

I wouldn't be in this position had I listened to him in the first place and stayed the hell away from her. Had I not gotten to know and like her. Now what? How can I look Sloane in the eye and pretend everything's fine?

But maybe it's a nonissue. The way we left things yesterday at the end of our little tiki booze cruise, it's likely she's already written me off. She all but called me a man whore, and it's been radio silence since.

I dig out my phone to confirm: still no response to my update about Katie's twisted ankle, which is surprising. I would have thought Sloane more considerate than that, as a business owner. I guess that solves the problem of her hating me once the local government forces her out with a fat check because I don't see how my association with Henry won't be another black mark on my name.

And yet, the idea of giving up on whatever this is between us stirs a feeling harsher than disappointment. Sloane's different, and the way my pulse spikes when her jade-green eyes are on me, the intoxicating smell of her hair, her soft skin beneath my fingertips, the sound of her laugh, her playful smile ... I can't pinpoint what it is, except to say that I can't get her out of my head.

My phone rings in my grip, startling me from my daydreaming.

Chester's name appears, and I groan. He wouldn't be calling me if there wasn't a problem with my name written on it.

2. Sloane

"**Y**ou are *so* incredibly stupid." I cradle my forehead in my palm as I stare at the two pink lines on the stick. They match the lines from the first test I took. There's no doubt about it.

I am pregnant.

How could I have let this happen? I'm thirty-one years old. I've been on birth control for almost half my life. I'm smarter than this! And way too responsible. Then again, the last few months have been chaotic and stressful. Sure, I was late taking a pill. Or a few. I didn't think it would matter.

I didn't think, period.

And now, I am pregnant by some guy I barely know, who I swore off just yesterday because we are not a good match in any world. It's clear Ronan sleeps with every female who crosses his path. Am I the first he's managed to knock up? Does Ronan have children with other women?

I have no idea because ...

I don't know him!

I let out a strangled sound, my anger and frustration impossible to contain. All we had to do was put on a condom. One stupid condom that was surely sitting in his wallet. That's it, and that day would have been nothing more than a lapse in judgment that we can both move on from. Now, though?

A clattering sound carries from the kitchen, announcing that I'm not alone in my house. Not surprising. During the summer season, there's a constant stream of people parading in and out of the kitchen, bringing groceries, grabbing a snack, starting a meal. Everyone has the door code—even Ron, the wannabe traitor.

Stuffing the test and its packaging deep into the wastebasket, I pull myself to my feet.

On impulse, I lift my Sea Witch T-shirt to study my flat stomach. Is this really happening to me? Is there truly the spark of a human being growing inside there? It seems impossible.

There were fleeting moments in the past where I wondered what it would be like to be pregnant. I thought I was heading that way once Cody proposed.

What the hell am I going to do?

Not hide out in the bathroom until people get suspicious, that's for sure.

Shock grips me as I emerge. Rebel's back is to me, her jet-black pixie cut styled to messy perfection. She's focused on whatever she's washing in the sink. Grocery bags clutter the counter, and the slow cooker is waiting to be filled.

"What's on for tonight?" I ask, hoping she can't hear the strain in my voice.

"Oh, hey! I thought chicken enchiladas and a side salad. The greens in the garden are looking good." She peers over her shoulder at me, her smile bright even as her face shows worry. "You feeling okay? You were in there for a while."

"Oh, I'm fine. Just ... too much coffee on an empty stomach, I guess." I stumble over my excuse. "How was the shop when you left?"

"The usual. Nothing exciting. I ran to get groceries after the morning rush. Skye's training Lara."

"Oh, good." I forgot about the new employee. "How's she doing?"

"Quick learner and funny. A lot better than that last one."

"Well, that's a low bar. But good. I was hoping she'd fit in."

"She's great! I'm going to get this all going, and then I'll head back before Skye leaves for the cruise shack."

"Right. What time is it?"

As if in answer, Gigi's teal-and-yellow cuckoo bird pops out of its box to announce the eleventh hour. It instantly brings me back to the last time it so poignantly announced its presence, that fateful day when Ronan and I stood in this exact spot, naked and breathless—the whole reason I'm now in such a mess.

Hell, if I'm being honest, though, I was doomed the day he walked into the Sea Witch. Maybe that was Henry Wolf's plan all along, though. Maybe Ronan is a plant, come to seduce and destroy me.

I swallow against a burst of nerves and resist the urge to touch my stomach. "I should get back to the office."

Rebel's brow furrows. "Are you sure you're feeling okay? You seem off."

"Yeah, I'm fine. Just ..." In shock is what I am. Thank God Frank is taking the cruise shift. I don't think I could play fun captain right now. "I didn't sleep well."

She jerks her chin toward my room. "Take a nap. You're the boss."

"I wish, but I have so much to do. Payroll and accounting stuff, inventory orders, next week's schedule for bookings." And I'd just stare at the ceiling while mentally berating myself anyway. No, keeping my mind busy and off my dire situation is the right move.

"Okay, well, dinner's taken care of for tonight." Rebel waves her hands around the kitchen to prove her point. "One less thing to worry about, right?"

"You're the best." Though the last thing on my mind is food, and I doubt I'll have much of an appetite later either.

"Of course. We're all in this together. We're family." With a wink, she sets back to her task.

"Exactly. *Family*. Not a commune." I grab my purse and the keys to the Cherokee off the hook and head out the door.

3. Ronan

"Do you hear that?" Chester holds up a crooked index finger, aimed at the floor-to-ceiling aquarium in Opal Reef.

I pause and listen intently as a cluster of tropical fish glides past. "That weird whirring?" It fades in and out, a repetitive sound.

"Ray said it wasn't doin' that yesterday during his daily inspection, and it's getting louder by the hour. Staff noticed it this morning." The facilities manager frowns at the tank. Back in his day, I'll bet Chester was a sturdy guy, but his cheeks have hollowed with age, and his lanky arms are more bone than muscle. "That there could be a big problem."

I imagine every problem with this enormous fish tank is a big problem. It might rank up there with the most expensive feature in this entire hotel. "What does that mean?"

"Don't know yet. Ray checked for clogs in the filtration systems and didn't find any, so he's pretty sure it has to be a faulty part, but he needs the manufacturing company to confirm. They're sending someone in tomorrow. Then we may need parts."

"How long will that take?"

Chester shrugs. "They come from overseas."

"You're fucking kidding me right now."

"Wish I was."

I shake my head. "Why does it seem like every system we have in this hotel is giving up on us before we've even opened?" First the sprinklers, now this?

A second shrug. "I worked at the Aspen Wolf when it opened after the remodel, and I remember three hot-water tanks blowin' the hell up one morning. Not the first time that's happened either."

"Something to look forward to is what you're telling me?" I mutter.

"Let's hope we're in the clear." He reaches out to knock on a wooden wall panel.

Potential hot-water issues are not our concern now, though. "We can't have this aquarium going down on us, this week of all weeks." Belinda expects our mermaids to make the front cover of every major travel magazine.

He holds up his hands in surrender. "I know, boss. We're doing everything we can. Just thought you should be in the know, in case it outright quits on us before we get it fixed."

"And what happens if it quits? I mean, what about all these fish? And can the entertainers still use it?"

He scratches the top of his thinning hair. "We need the system to clean the water, or it'll get funky real quick. How quick? I'm not an expert on giant fish tanks, but I can't imagine any of those girls will want to get in murky water. Pictures probably wouldn't look ideal either." He cringes at the thought. "Hopefully, it doesn't get to that, and I'm on it."

I sigh. "Thanks. I appreciate it."

His phone chirps, and he scans it. And curses. "That's because you idiots connected the kegs wrong."

My eyebrows arch in question. "Problem?"

"Just foamy beer. Better go deal with that."

"Better you than me." I think I'm beginning to see how this director thing works—these guys do all the problem-solving and running around and only loop me in when there's something they can't solve without it costing, in which case I get to take the heat from the higher-ups.

Commotion sounds from the kitchen, and a moment later, a man dressed in a white chef's uniform plows through the swinging door, his hand wrapped in a tea towel, his face pinched with pain.

"That can't be good," Chester declares as a petite woman in a peach-colored manager's uniform chases him out Opal Reef's doors.

"No, but that's Lena's problem." I have enough to worry about, and it's not even noon. I'm pretty sure I'm supposed to be in a meeting somewhere. "Call this tank manufacturer back and get someone here today. After hours if they have to. Drag them out of a hospital bed, I don't care. A system like this going down on our opening week? Unacceptable. They should be jumping through hoops to please us."

"Will do, boss."

I grit my teeth. "Call me Ronan." I don't need anyone kissing my ass.

He salutes me and takes off.

With one last look at the enormous tank, I head back to my office, my mood growing more acerbic by the hour.

———

BRITT:

Do you have featherless pillows?

Define featherless

I'm not kidding! I have allergies, remember?

You're all good. No feathers.

Okay …

I'm so excited.

See you soon.

I SET MY PHONE DOWN. My baby sister and I have always been close, and I don't mind admitting that I've missed her. Still, I wonder if inviting her this weekend of all weekends was the smartest move. I won't have time for her.

"Fourteen stitches," Lena confirms, reading a text from her phone before leaning back in the plush armchair, the oversized umbrella above our table providing shade against the sweltering afternoon sun. "And he's lost part of his finger."

"We haven't even opened our doors yet," Belinda

muses, setting her fork on her plate to mark her salmon salad finished. The server hovering over us like a seagull swoops in to collect. "I thought chefs were trained to not maim themselves."

Lena snorts.

I unfasten a button at my shirt collar, wishing I'd chosen a golf shirt. I wasn't expecting an afternoon meeting at Seraphina's. I'll admit, the view over the gulf is a million times nicer than staring at the frosted glass walls of the meeting room, but we're on hour two of comparing notes about all the ways we're still not ready for guests, and I'm minutes away from stripping down and diving into the pool on the other side of the privacy wall.

"Does this mean no dinner party tomorrow night, then?" I was looking forward to it because Abbi will be there, but now I'd rather eat a bag of tacks than be around her husband.

"You're kidding, right?" Belinda counters. "We have an *entire kitchen* of chefs. Besides, he's the master chef. You don't need a finger to give orders."

"Good to know everyone has their priorities straight," I say under my breath.

"Is that dinner mandatory?" Lena asks, her tone reluctant.

"Is it mandatory that you accept an invitation from the CEO of Wolf Hotels?" Belinda arches an eyebrow. "I'm going to pretend you didn't ask me that."

Lena's shoulders sink. "That's not ... I mean, who else is going to be there?"

"Your boss and his wife, which should be enough,"

Belinda begins with forced patience. "Henry wants to celebrate the opening of the hotel. Besides, it's a good trial run for the servers in a less stressful environment."

"Serving Wolf is supposed to be *less* stressful?" Ten bucks says they don't get through the night without another blood-letting injury.

Belinda's lips purse. "It's a more casual atmosphere. His people will be there. Preston and Merrick, for one. You remember them from the wedding, Ronan?"

"How could I forget?" They were both groomsmen. Two richer-than-thou bastards—one a pompous hedge fund executive from England, and the other one a guy who runs a hotel in Vegas and may or may not be tied to a crime family. The whispers are loud but inconclusive.

I got along well enough with them regardless, so I guess it's not the end of the world.

"And, of course, Margo," Belinda continues.

I stifle my inward groan. That changes things. Wherever that woman goes, chaos and debauchery follow. "Are we positive this dinner is mandatory?" I echo Lena's question.

"Yes." Belinda's voice is laced with annoyance. "You can bring your sidekick if it makes you feel better. Gary is coming, right?" She stares expectantly at Lena.

"Yes, though Daniel has a soccer game that one of us *should* be at." Lena studies her fingernails while her passive-aggressiveness seeps into the conversation.

Belinda's phone rings. "I need to take this." She smoothly vacates her chair as she answers, leaving Lena and me alone with our tablets and our thoughts.

I check my watch. It's almost three. What's going on

with the mermaid tank? And have they figured out the sprinkler situation yet? I punch out quick messages to Chester and Dorian, checking in. What I really want to do is get the hell out of here and go find Sloane. It's been twenty-four hours since I've seen her, and I think I'm suffering from withdrawal.

But what the fuck do I say to her? *No, you've got me all wrong. I'm not a fuckboy, I promise.*

And now, there's this whole eminent domain bullshit that I have to either play dumb about or tell her, in which case I can basically kiss my job goodbye.

I feel Lena watching me.

"So ... Daniel's your kid?" I knew she was married on account of the flashy ring, but I know nothing else about my counterpart. Maybe I should attempt to be friendly. And, hey, at least then I can honestly say I haven't slept with *every* woman in my life.

"Yes. My twelve-year-old son, who is very angry about his mother taking this job and forcing him to move away from his friends. You'd think the beach would be more enticing than Chicago's suburbs, but apparently not." Her smile is tight.

"That's where you're from?"

"Charlotte, originally, but we were living in Chicago for the past decade." She smooths a hand through her auburn hair. I note the faintest hint of gray at her temple. "It's all Daniel knows."

"I'm lucky, I guess. I didn't have to think about a wife or kids when Wolf told me I had three days to get here." No one to pack up except for a giant man-child. Speaking of, I should check in to see how Connor's knee is doing.

Though I'm sure Katie and Rachel are taking *really* good care of him.

Lena's golden-brown eyes narrow as she regards me.

"Something on your mind?" I ask guardedly.

"I still can't figure out how you ended up in this job."

"Besides my sharp intellect and vast experience?" I quip. Me, an outdoor crew guy with no real management experience. Everyone knows it. It's a fair statement, and yet I can't tell if she's genuinely curious or if it's an attempt to insult me. "I must have skills you haven't seen yet." I wink.

The simple move seems to startle her. She clears her throat while refocusing on her tablet, her cheeks pinking.

I smile. Lena may be as uptight as a bridezilla working on a seating chart, but I could bend her my way if I wanted to. Thankfully for both of us, I don't. She's attractive, but there's nothing appealing about wrecking a marriage. As soon as that ring is on a woman's finger, a giant "do not enter" sign appears. I won't let myself so much as imagine what they look like naked.

Except for Abbi, of course, but that's different.

Belinda returns then, saving us from our awkward conversation. "Okay, I think we've covered off everything we need to for today, unless there are any other pressing matters?"

"Besides my housekeeping supervisor stumbling upon two staff members having intercourse on a freshly made bed?" Lena frowns at her screen. "Connie is asking how we would like to proceed."

"What do you think, Ronan?" The corners of Belinda's painted lips crook upward with a secretive smirk.

"Should staff caught in compromising positions be terminated?"

If so, then I sure as hell wouldn't be here, and neither would Belinda.

I haul my sweaty body out of the seat, dying for air-conditioning. "I say let them fuck and get it out of their system, but ask Mike. He's the HR manager, and I've already fired someone today." I feel bad for that girl who fell for Sloane's ex and lost a promising career.

If I ever see Cody again …

My fist clenches with the thought.

Belinda's gaze rakes over my chest, settling on where my collar sits unbuttoned. "Minnie sent you both decks on every person invited to the media open. Spend the next thirty-six hours memorizing them, especially those whom you have scheduled time with. I expect you to know the names of every person before they introduce themselves to you."

I plaster on a wide, fake smile. "You got it." Fat chance.

"Favorite flower is the daffodil. She has two Shih Tzus named Rocky and Noodles," I read out loud, scrolling through Shelby Singer's bio from the comfort of my desk. "Are you kidding me? This has to be illegal." There's a dossier on every journalist, politician, and corporate bigwig coming, and they include far more than their credentials and a professional photograph. This one in particular is a fifty-three-year-old congress member in a pantsuit with two American flags in the background.

Archie lounges in the chair across from me, squeezing an orange stress ball that matches the color of his hair. "It's all public stuff. The GMs make us do it for media days. It's helpful, according to Belinda."

"It's helpful that I know Shelby enjoys competitive duck herding in her spare time? What the fuck even is that?"

He grins. "It's when you guide ducks through obstacles using dogs."

"Why would someone do that?"

"Sport? I don't know. I had to look that up."

"And why do I need to know all this? Am I supposed to pretend that I, too, herd ducks through obstacles on my days off so I can bond with Shelby Singer?" I pat my chest for embellishment.

Archie's grin widens. "I don't know, man. I just do what I'm told. Belinda scares me."

"You and me both." I flip through the other bookmarked dossiers. "The ones with the stars are all the people I have one-on-one meetings with?" Three travel magazine journalists, two news reporters, two politicians, and three company CEOs.

"Yeah, but Belinda wants you to read through all of them."

"Not just read. Memorize." I flip through the starred ones. "All of my meetings are with women," I note.

"And all of Lena and Belinda's meetings are with men."

Doubt that's a coincidence. "Fucking diabolical."

How *exactly* does Wolf want me to impress these VIPs? Because there were rumors aplenty about his relationship with one of these media open travel journalists at the Alaska location. In fact, that woman played a big part in Henry and Abbi's breakup. I guess I have her to thank because Abbi would never have given me the time of day otherwise.

My phone chirps with an incoming text, and I dive for it, holding my breath against hope that I'll see Sloane's name.

TASHA:

> So ... Two nights seems like such a short trip. Any chance you have an extra room at your place in case I wanted to stay until Sunday?

Fuck me, I should have seen this coming. Connor did, back in Miami. Can't wait for him to grind me about it. I guess it's fine, though. The house is big, and Tasha is not the woman I'm pining over anymore. Plus, I have a door lock on my bedroom.

> Yeah, lots of room. I won't be around much but Britt and Dani are staying there too.

They can hang out together if they want. I sure as hell don't have time to entertain anyone. With that taken care of, I flip over to my calendar to see where all these kiss-ass meet-and-greets fit in. "You have me booked for two breakfasts on Friday."

"Order something light?" Archie counters.

I frown. "And three coffee meetings at the Coral Cafe on Wednesday afternoon." The hotel's coffee shop is quaint but small.

"You love coffee."

"Yeah, but are you trying to kill me with caffeine?"

He tosses his stress ball in the air and catches it. "Drink decaf."

"Screw that." I note 7:00 a.m. tee-off times on Wednesday *and* Thursday. Worse, with Henry on my team. As if I want to spend all morning with him. "What's Axis Core?" Because we're golfing with a pair from there the first day. Thursday is a media open tournament that runs all day.

"A global consulting firm. They hold their yearly meetings at Wolf locations."

Two rich assholes who probably golf seven days a week while conducting business. Can I get out of that? Highly unlikely. "Do you know anything about golf?"

"I can hold my own." The way he says it means he knows his stuff.

"Okay, good. You're gonna be my caddy. Memorize whatever's in these two dossiers. Also, I need you to book me with the golf pro tomorrow morning." Maybe that'll give me a fighting chance of not embarrassing myself.

Archie stiffens, his demeanor shifting to business in an instant. "Any time in particular?"

"The earlier, the better." Less chance of my session getting derailed by problems.

A knock sounds on my office door.

"Come in," I holler.

Dorian and his mustache appear. "Sprinklers are all sorted. Our guys had to dig up some lines, but—"

"Perfect," I cut him off. I really don't care how they fixed it, just as long as it's one less problem to end up on my plate. "Anything else to worry about?"

"For you? No. Got the replacement beach equipment in today, finally, for everything that arrived busted. I sent you the labor report for the month, plus the updated projections for next month, as well as the equipment list. Ten percent higher than the budget. I prioritized what I think is necessary."

I sigh. Can't wait to be lectured by Henry's CFO for overspending. "Thanks, Dorian."

With a wave, he ducks out.

Now is the perfect time to escape, before anyone shows up to drop a new problem in my lap. I quickly collect my laptop and tablet. "I'm going home to digest all of this in peace. Don't call me unless it's an emergency."

"Sounds good. I'll get you in with the pro first thing and update your calendar."

"Good man." I rush out before he's even out of his seat.

It's all a ruse, of course. Home is not where I'm aiming to go.

———

My pulse races as I pull up next to the old blue Cherokee wearing a Sea Witch bumper sticker. That has to be Sloane's, which means she's here. Thankfully, it doesn't look like Frank or anyone else is. The row of colorful trailers sits quietly between the line of trees, no vehicle to be seen.

The hens greet me as I step out of my car, flocking to my shoes as if I've dropped kernels for them. When they realize I've come empty-handed, they strut away, clucking.

"Hey, Ralph," I call out to the hulkish rooster loitering a few feet away. I haven't seen a lot of roosters in my day, but I didn't know they came that big. "Don't shit on my hood this time, okay?" It took two rounds in the car wash to get off.

He spreads his tail feathers as if in answer.

"Yeah, you're definitely gonna shit on my car again," I mutter, dismissing him as I make my way past the fenced-off garden. A set of gloves rests next to a pitchfork and a pile of weeds. A basket nearby is filled with lettuce, cherry tomatoes, and radishes. It looks like someone gave up harvesting halfway through.

I take a moment to absorb the entire idyllic view. Even though the hotel is right next door, you'd never know it from this spot. It's a kitschy little oasis of brambly trees and colorful buildings, personality in every corner you look. And Henry wants to pave over this. Tear it down and turn it into a road. It's wrong on every level.

I climb the quaint little teal-blue beach house's porch steps, hit with a flash of the last time I was here, armed with my laptop and good intentions. I can't believe how quickly things between me and Sloane got out of control. I wouldn't change a thing about that day, though.

Scratch that—I would change one thing: I would have made sure it lasted a hell of a lot longer.

The glass pane rattles under my knock, and then I wait.

And wait.

I knock again, stealing a glance through the window. Movement catches my eye. It's not inside the house, but through the back doors. A figure in a hot pink string bikini strolls up the beach, a towel wrapped around her shoulders, her wet hair pushed back off her forehead.

My pulse races at the sight of Sloane, even as I chastise myself for not thinking through this impulsive visit. What am I supposed to say to her, now that there's this giant secret hanging in the air, these plans that are going to upend her entire life that I know about. That I can't tell her about without risking my career and her wrath.

Sloane veers to her left.

I take quick steps down the porch and to the far side of the house, following the stone path around to meet her.

4. Sloane

The towel is unnecessary in this heat, but I wrap it around my shoulders anyway as I stroll toward my house. I needed that swim. Something about the warm gulf water and the lapping waves and the endless blue sky above always calms me. But it didn't assuage the disbelief that still grips my every thought.

I nearly took a third test when I got home from the Sea Witch after an afternoon of bumbling through paperwork, but distracted myself with the garden instead. That led to sweating under the hot sun, which led to the need to cool down.

But none of these diversions change the fact that I'm as pregnant now as I was this morning.

What do I do?

Do I keep it?

That's not a question I ever thought I'd be asking myself, but I always pictured reaching this milestone when I was happily married or at least in love, not accidentally and by a guy I barely know.

I need to talk to Gigi is what I need to do. She's the least judgmental person in my life. She'll have good advice. I'll go tomorrow morning. I was planning to anyway.

Right now, though, I need to rinse the briny seawater and clinging sand off before I attempt to make a salad for dinner.

I follow the path to the outdoor shower at the side of the house.

And jump as I come face-to-face with Ronan.

"Hey." His voice is deep as his gaze drifts over my bikini-clad body. "Sorry, I didn't mean to scare you."

"You didn't." I swallow against my suddenly racing pulse, fresh memories of what we did on the tiki cruise yesterday—what I allowed to happen out in public—hitting me like a forceful gulf wave. "What are you doing here?"

"I thought I'd stop in to see you since you didn't respond to my text." The corner of his mouth kicks up with amusement.

He's direct, I'll give him that. And with everything else going on, I forgot to call Ryan. *Shit*. I'm a terrible business owner. "I'm glad to hear Katie's ankle isn't broken."

"Yeah. Flying home tomorrow might be a challenge, but she's got crutches and help." His pace slows until he stops next to the outdoor shower stall, his polished shoes sending loose gravel skipping. He must have come from work, but his dress shirt is unbuttoned to reveal the delicious ridges of his collarbone and his thick, columnar neck.

I wasn't sure how I would feel when I ran into Ronan again, given the present circumstance. But now that he's standing here, he's as jaw-droppingly attractive as before. And I'm still feeling that physical pull toward him, the urge to be close, that keeps getting me into trouble. In fact, it might be stronger now, this connection I feel. Because we are truly connected, in a way he has no clue about.

What would Ronan do if he knew I was pregnant with his child? Surely he would not be looking at me the way he is—like he's deciding which string to pull on this bikini. No, he'd likely hightail it out of here as if I were a ticking bomb. And I guess I am. Or rather, this cluster of cells growing inside me is—a bomb that will blow up Ronan's life as he knows it.

I couldn't really blame him if he ran—this is not what either of us was aiming for—and yet the thought disappoints me far more than it should.

A furrow wrinkles his brow. "You okay?"

"Huh?" I realize I'm staring at him. I'm *always* staring at him. "Yeah. I'm fine. Just ... today didn't go as planned." My entire life just swerved toward an unknown and chaotic road ahead.

"Your captain spilled?"

I frown. What is he talking about?

"Your tiki captain, Jeremy. Did he tell the others they got blacklisted from the hotel?" he clarifies.

"*Oh.* No." I pause with the reminder. I hadn't given that a moment's thought since this morning. "Jer promised he wouldn't say anything, but Cody probably will. Who knows when." Great. Now I get to worry about being pregnant *and* staffless in high season.

It's shady beneath the canopy of the trees and beside the house, and a chill runs through me from standing here in a wet bathing suit. I duck past Ronan and drape my towel on a hook before stepping into the shower stall.

"Wish I'd had a chance to punch that fucker in the mouth yesterday," Ronan murmurs as he sizes up the bamboo walls and river rock floor and the brass taps that give the outdoor shower an upscale feel. Frank cursed those stones while he was installing them like Gordon Ramsay berating his cooking contestants, but the end result is one of my favorite parts of the entire thing.

"Consider yourself lucky. Knowing Cody, he'd sue you. He'll do anything for a fat paycheck. Trust me, I know. He tried to sell this place out from under me."

A troubled look flashes across Ronan's face. "Yeah, well, his source no longer works for Wolf."

"You fired her? I mean, you figured out who it was?" Which poor, foolish woman joined the ranks of those who fell under Cody's spell?

"Wasn't hard. And yes, I did." More to himself, he adds, "At least I can do that much."

"You didn't have to."

"I wanted to."

Though it doesn't change the reality that Cody can still ruin my reputation, that Ronan did that for me is ... something. "Thanks."

His gaze roams my face, settling on my lips. "You're welcome."

Any second now, I'm going to forget everything else

except how good that mouth feels on mine. Needing a distraction, I crank the faucet and wait for the water stream to turn warm before stepping under the rain showerhead.

"You use this a lot?" Ronan leans against the support post, pinning the bunched curtain with his shoulder. His pose suggests he has no plans on leaving.

"Probably more than the shower inside." Everyone staying here does. There's ample privacy. Normally I would peel my suit off, but doing so in front of Ronan is an invitation for a repeat performance of our last two encounters, and now is not the day for that.

I will admit, though, I like having his attention, and it is certainly rapt, his green eyes heated as he watches me. But what's more, I'm happy he's here, despite everything.

I reach for my loofah. "So, Henry Wolf arrived today, right? How's that going?"

"It's ... going."

"That good, huh?" A big part of me is curious about the billionaire CEO. Is he truly as indomitable as the newspapers and magazines make him out to be? Ronan doesn't seem to like him much. Based on what Connor was saying on the cruise yesterday, it sounds like Ronan may have earned his plum job because of Henry Wolf's wife. What is the dynamic there? How did he end up being such close friends with her?

And how does Henry Wolf feel about that friendship?

I have *so* many questions.

Ronan's throat bobs with a hard swallow. I may be out of sorts, but he seems on edge today too. That casual, detached swagger is missing. And that expression he wears now, he looks almost pained.

"Seems like you had a tough day too."

"Yeah, I guess you could say that," he answers gruffly.

Warm water sluices over my head as I turn away from him, afraid he'll somehow read the secret on my face. *Believe me, your day could get a whole lot worse with just two words out of my mouth.* I close my eyes and let the salt water rinse off. I'll have to have a proper shower later, when I don't have an audience.

Keys jingle behind me.

I turn back around in time to see Ronan emptying his pockets onto a nearby shelf. "What are you doing?"

He kicks off his shoes and socks.

My heart pounds as his intentions become clear. "I'm not really in the right headspace for ..." My words drift as Ronan steps into the shower stall, still dressed in his work clothes.

"Why does everything have to be about sex with you, Sea Witch?" Grabbing the nearby bottle of shampoo, he squirts a dollop on his palm, seemingly unfazed as the water soaks into his clothes. "Why can't we just talk?"

I can't help but laugh. "Because ..." My voice falters as his strong fingers seize either side of my head. "We don't seem to know how to do that."

"We haven't tried."

"Fair enough." I study the hard lines of his jaw as he works the shampoo into a lather, a heady mixture of coconut and pineapple combined with his masculine cologne. "Is that what this is? You, trying to talk to me?" Because his overwhelming presence in this tiny space has my half-naked, traitorous body forgetting all my current troubles and eager to find new ones with my back pressed up against the wall.

"*I'm* trying," he whispers, his touch sending a wave of shivers through me. "I'm not sure what you're angling for."

"You wish." The way his fingers massage my scalp is both soothing and teasing, and a moan escapes me unbidden.

The corner of his mouth kicks up. "See? I'm just a guy trying to have a conversation, and then you go and make sounds like that."

God, his voice is so grating and deep. This is all so overwhelming that, for a moment, I'm afraid I'll lose my balance. My hands find their way to his waist, resting gently against his sculpted body. I barely know this man, but I'm positive that he's all wrong for me. Positive! Still, I could fall for him so easily, and that is a dangerous reality I'm struggling to come to terms with.

"I can tell you what I'm *not* angling for, and that's a fuckboy."

His fingers stall a moment on my scalp before continuing. "Neither am I."

"You're not looking for a fuckboy?" I quip, unable to help myself.

He chuckles. "You know what I mean."

"But do *you* understand what *I* mean?" That came out patronizing. "I'm not sure we're looking for the same thing." I want a man I can sit next to on the beach and watch the sunset at night. *Every* night. From what Ryan alluded to, Ronan is looking for willing orgy participants.

His lips curve into a wry smile. "I was in a relationship for four years, so yes, Sloane, I understand."

His admission catches me off guard. Four years is longer than any relationship I've ever had. "How long ago was that?"

"We broke up a little over two years ago."

"What happened?"

His minty breath skates over my face with his sigh. "She wasn't ready for a commitment."

I can't help it—I snort.

That earns a sexy smirk. "What? You don't believe me."

"No. I don't. What actually happened?" I watch his face closely. Will he be honest? If he cheated, would he admit to it?

"She's younger than me, and she wanted to experience other people before she settled down."

That isn't the answer I was expecting. "Settled down like—"

"Marriage. Yeah, we'd talked about it."

This guy? That's ... unexpected? "Did you love her?"

"I did. Yeah." He reaches up to adjust the showerhead and then angles my head back with a finger under my chin.

Water rains down, rinsing away the suds with the help of his fingers as I process this new bit of information —acutely aware of his gaze on me. So, Ronan is capable of commitment. But from the sounds of it, he can also fuck his way through a cheerleading squad. "Do you still love her?"

"No." No hesitation. Not for a second.

"Not even a little?"

"No. I did, for months after we broke up. That's when I moved down to Miami and met Connor. And Ryan."

Pieces in the Ronan puzzle are beginning to click. "That's when you two hooked up?"

"Yeah, for, like, two weeks. If that. We were both freshly broken up, and neither of us was looking for a relationship. She hated my guts at the start, but we ended up being good friends. Then, Connor and I left for Alaska, and yeah, I'll admit, maybe I took full advantage of my single status."

Meaning he fucked around. A lot. That part doesn't surprise me.

"So, what Ryan said about you and Connor..." I let that question drift.

"Ryan said a lot. You'll have to be more specific." By the twinkle in his eye, he knows damn well what I'm poking at, but he wants me to ask it.

Where do I even begin with this topic? "Are you strictly into women? I mean, is Connor more than a platonic—"

"Only women." There's no waiver in his voice. "Dick doesn't do it for me. Pussy does."

I inhale sharply, the sound of that single word on Ronan's lips stirring something deep inside. "But Connor and you have been with women together."

"He's been involved from time to time, yeah."

"Just Connor? I mean, you haven't tag-teamed with other men?"

He hesitates. "Once, with a couple. Why all the questions about men and Connor? Is this something you've wanted to try?"

"No."

"Because Connor would be game—"

"*No.*" Oh my God, just the thought has my cheeks burning.

A slight frown furrows his brow. "So what are you concerned about, then?"

"I'm not concerned. I'm just pointing out how different we are."

"Right, the whole vanilla thing." He snorts, echoing my words from yesterday. "Tash and I would have been labeled that, and I never had any complaints, if that's what you're getting at."

Tash. She's the one who was texting him on the cruise.

"Do you still talk to her?" I ask as nonchalantly as possible, holding my breath as I wait for him to lie.

"I didn't until recently, but we've reconnected as friends. She's coming to the hotel this weekend with a bachelorette party. Look, I don't care who you've been with or not been with." He pushes a strand of clinging hair off my forehead with gentle fingers. "And I'm not really interested in running through our score cards. Are you?"

"No, I don't think I am," I admit. Maybe it's better I don't know how many women Ronan has slept with. That way, I can deceive myself into feeling like I'm enough for him. On a positive note, he didn't lie to me about his ex. That's something. "So, you went to Alaska and then what?"

Something flickers in his eyes that I can't read. "Then I went back to Miami. I still wasn't anywhere near ready for a relationship. About a year ago, I decided to turn over a new leaf. No more meaningless hookups and friends with benefits. Then I came to Mermaid Beach, and I met you." He steps in closer, until our chests graze each other, and stares down at me with an intensity I wasn't expecting.

What is he telling me—that he's looking to settle down?

Another wave of nerves hits me with the stark reality that I am pregnant with this man's baby.

Is it wrong to continue this charade? To hold this enormous, life-altering secret from him? Maybe not, but I haven't digested it myself. I'm not about to ruin the illusion of whatever this is between us yet.

But the weight of this is almost too much to bear, and suddenly, all I want to do is use his strength. On impulse, I lean in and rest my cheek on Ronan's chest.

He stiffens for a split second, but then his body relaxes, and his muscular arms fold around me.

If Ronan is all wrong for me, then why does this feel so right? Why do I suddenly wish I could live in these arms all night, every night? Drag him into my bedroom and forget all my worries.

I know where that would lead, though. Not that I'd complain.

A loud rooster caw sounds, followed by another. It's Ralph's signature call. "Frank's home."

Ronan groans. "His timing is impeccable."

I try to pull away, but Ronan's grip only tightens.

"Are we going to get in trouble, being in here together?"

"*I*'ll be fine," I joke, though I'm not so sure. What's Frank going to say when he finds out my big news? There's not much I can keep from that guy for long. And if Ronan does what I expect him to when he finds out—ghost me—then God help him if he crosses Frank's path in this town.

"I should get home now anyway." He says this, and yet he holds me for another one ... two ... three long seconds before pulling away. "I have to memorize facts about Phyllis's cats and Layla's life-altering trek up Kilimanjaro. Don't ask," he mutters when he sees my face pinch with confusion. "I can't wait until this week is over."

"Me too." Though it won't change anything. "The sooner I get used to having that stupid hotel beside me, the better."

With another strange, hard look flickering across his face, he reaches around me to turn off the tap. Collecting my towel, he drapes it over my shoulders to cover my upper body. The simple move is gentle and kind.

I tug at his soaked shirtsleeve. "This wasn't smart."

"No, but it was safe. If I'd undressed, you would have taken advantage of me."

"Shut up." I slap his chest playfully.

He gathers my hand before I have a chance to pull away, weaving his fingers through mine. His other hand curls around my nape, pulling me toward him until our bodies are flush again. A grazing thumb strokes my skin, back and forth, teasing and comforting me at the same time.

I tip my face up to meet his penetrating gaze. "Ronan." His name is barely a whisper. *There's something I need to tell you.*

But no, not yet. Not now.

Without any hesitation, he leans in to meet my lips with his in a fervent, frantic kiss, as if he wants to squeeze as much intensity into this moment as possible before we're forced apart. And maybe we will be—not by Frank or any other outside forces, but by the reality that we can't seem to be this close without losing control. Even now, with my hand fisting his shirt, wishing for it to vanish, for *all his clothes* to vanish, I sense our good intentions for an honest conversation about to go awry. My body certainly isn't helping matters, as it slides against his, reveling in the hard length pressed against my stomach.

All I would take is a quick unfastening of his belt and fly, a tug on my bikini bottom string, and I could have Ronan exactly where I like him—inside me.

As if sensing my thoughts, and perhaps sharing them, Ronan's lips suddenly break free of mine. "I really need to go," he whispers, the muscle in his jaw taut.

My breathing is ragged. "Phyllis's cats."

"Something like that." He releases me and backs up, collecting first his pocket's contents from the shelf, then his shoes. The prominent bulge in his clinging pants is unmistakable.

My pulse races as I chastise myself for staring. That's how I got into this mess in the first place.

"I have a dinner thing tomorrow night," Ronan blurts suddenly.

"A dinner thing?" I echo. "Okay ..."

"Come with me."

"To your dinner thing?" Is Ronan asking me out on a date?

"Yeah." His smile is wry. "It's at the hotel."

Caution creeps in. "Who's going to—"

"Henry Wolf."

My mouth gapes. "Are you crazy? You want me to have dinner with Satan himself?" The man would probably instruct the chef to poison my food.

"Listen ..." Ronan purses his lips as he seems to choose his words. "I think it would be good for both of you to get to know each other."

"Why? Do you think I'm going to be charmed by Henry Wolf, and everything he put me through in the last five years will suddenly be okay?" Does Ronan think I'm a fool?

"No, he's a fucking prick. You won't like him."

"So then why would I go there to meet him?" I'm baffled. "And, also, I thought he told you to stay away from me."

"Yeah. He did."

"So then ..." A thought strikes me. "Henry Wolf doesn't know you're inviting me, does he?"

"He doesn't need to know. And I don't care about him. It's Abbi that I want you to meet."

Satan's wife? "Why?"

He bites his bottom lip. "Because she's one of my best friends, and it would be good if she met you."

Why do I feel like there's more to his reasoning? Either way ... "I can't sit across from a table and play nice with that asshole. I won't be able to control myself. I'll throw my butter knife at him, and then I'll go to jail for assault." I'll be forced to have a baby in prison!

Ronan chuckles. "There'll be a bunch of people. You won't have to sit across from him. I promise."

I'm shaking my head when he pushes, "Just think about it, okay? I'll come by tomorrow at around six, and if you're ready to go, great. If not ..." His eyes rake over my towel-wrapped body, lingering on my bare thighs. "I'll convince you to come."

"Good luck with that." My stomach clenches, though. Something tells me Ronan could convince me to do just about anything.

Another door slams shut, signaling more arrivals.

"Six o'clock. Wear something nice." He strolls away, his bare feet leaving wet prints on the stone.

5. Ronan

This is either my smartest idea or one of the dumbest things I'll ever do. Only time will tell.

The plan began to percolate in my brain somewhere between the moment I laid eyes on Sloane and when she sank into my arms, her body taut with stress, but it didn't truly formulate until I pulled away and admitted to myself that I'll do anything to keep this woman in my life.

Anything means sabotaging Henry's big plans for Mermaid Beach.

I can't sit back and watch as he blows up her entire life, and if there's any hope in hell of convincing him not to, it's going to be through Abbi. There's no one else on this planet Henry cares about pleasing but her. If I can get Abbi in my corner, I might have sway, and the only way to get Abbi in my corner is for Sloane and her to become friends.

So, tomorrow night it is. I'll throw Sloane over my shoulder and carry her out if I have to.

As long as King Kong isn't standing in the driveway, on guard.

"Hey, Frank." I stroll past him toward my car, pretending the sharp points of the gravel aren't cutting into my bare feet.

He grunts in answer, his heavy brow furrowed at my dripping clothes. Getting into that shower fully dressed also probably wasn't a smart idea, but with Sloane in that bikini, it was the only way things wouldn't go too far, too fast.

On the plus side, the sight of him has killed my erection.

Skye and the other coffee shop girl with the short dark hair loiter behind him, their eyebrows crawling halfway up their forehead.

"Hello, ladies."

"Hello," they echo, synchronized, giant smiles splashing across their face.

A guy sits on the porch of the blue trailer, cigarette in hand, watching quietly. One of her staffers I haven't met. I wonder if he was one of the guys I axed from Wolf's hire list.

I wait until my back is to them before I allow a wince. Why didn't I at least slide on my shoes? This is going to be the most uncomfortable drive home ever.

And I'll be doing it with a sizeable pile of rooster shit on my hood.

Again.

———

Connor's bare ass is the first thing I see when I step into the kitchen. "Come on, at least put some briefs on. Your sister is here." Not that Ryan hasn't had the misfortune of seeing her half brother's junk once or twice.

He finishes chugging orange juice from the carton and then wipes his mouth with the back of his hand. "She's not getting up for another hour or two." He eyeballs my golf shirt and dress pants. "Why are *you* ready for work?"

I grab a coffee pod and travel mug and set the machine to brew. I wish I had time to stop at Sea Witch for a real coffee and a chance to see Sloane. Better yet, I'd rather just wake up next to her. "Golf pro session starts in twenty minutes." Archie wasn't kidding when he said he'd drag the guy out of bed if he had to. The sun just crested a few minutes ago. Official tee-off times aren't until 7:00 a.m.

Connor's grin is iconic. "Wow, you really want to impress Wolf, huh?"

"More like I'm trying to not embarrass myself." I survey the kitchen. "Did the cleaners come?" A perk that comes with the house that we only discovered one morning when we rolled out of our beds to find strangers inside. They come once a week but never this early. When I crashed last night, there were dishes in the sink and tequila spilled on the counter.

"You're kidding, right?"

"Right, I forgot." Ryan's eyelids are incapable of shutting until the kitchen is spotless. "You coming in later?"

"Yeah, I think so." He bends his injured knee. "The icing helped."

So did a day having his dick polished by Katie and Rachel, I'll bet. "Dorian will be pleased. He was seconds from weeping yesterday."

"Are you surprised I'm his favorite?"

"Nope." And I don't know how Connor does it because he is always the most annoying person in the room.

But there's something more important we need to discuss. "Look, Britt and her friend are staying here this weekend, so don't be inviting anyone else, okay?"

"Shut the fuck up." Connor slams the fridge door and turns around to give me a full-frontal view. "I'm going to meet Little Lyle?"

"Not like *that*, you aren't." I jut my chin at his flaccid penis. "And she's off-limits, so don't even think about it."

"*Dude*." His laughter is way too raucous for this time of day. "You, of all people, don't get to lecture me about staying away from sisters—"

"You didn't even know Ryan until a few years ago." It's a weak excuse, I know, but I'll use everything in my arsenal where Britt's concerned. "I swear, you lay so much as a hairy little pinkie toe on her and our friendship is fucking over." I deliver that with my index finger in the air and the hardest look I can muster at this hour. "She's my baby sister, and unless you can commit to never looking at, talking to, or so much as breathing in any other woman's direction for the rest of your goddamn life—"

"Okay, okay, I got it." Connor's hands are in the air in surrender. "Is her friend hot?"

"Yeah, and also off-limits." Dani's been Britt's best friend since they were five years old. I taught that kid how to ride a bike and picked her sobbing little body up when she fell off said bike. She's as close to a sister to me as anyone can be without being Britt. The last thing I want is for either of them to end up with a guy like Connor. Or one like me, for that matter.

Connor's face twists with displeasure. "Fuck, man, you're killing the weekend party vibe, and it's only Tuesday."

"There is no vibe here this weekend. No parties, no strip Marco Polo, and no walking around naked." Shit, I almost forgot. "Tash might be staying here too."

That earns a raised eyebrow. "The ex is coming to Mermaid Beach?"

"Yeah." I give the thirty-second rundown about the Golden tickets and Belinda's instructions.

By the time I'm done, Connor is shaking his head and laughing. "And she rides at dawn, you sucker."

"Not happening. Not on me, anyway. I'll barely be here. My schedule is jam-packed. I don't have time to think, let alone anything else." I fell asleep reading about the Axis Core CEO's rare mineral collection.

"Really ..." A pensive frown touches Connor's face, so contrary to the comical cowlick sticking straight up in the air. "So you don't mind if I show her around."

"Around town or your dick?"

He shrugs noncommittally.

I think on that for a solid five seconds. Does the idea of Connor and Tasha hooking up elicit any sort of reaction—a tight chest, a burn of jealousy, the urge to punch him in the face, like I felt yesterday when Sloane was asking questions about our sordid past and I thought she might be interested in hooking up with us both?

No, it doesn't.

Not even a little bit.

That reality makes me smile. "Have fun playing tour guide." I head for the stairs.

———

"Olivia McEowan," Archie prompts, his short legs working double time to keep up with the pace of my long ones down the hall.

"McEowan," I echo, digging through my memory to find relevant facts. "CEO of Black Titan, a multinational oil and gas company with operations in Texas and Alberta, Canada. Olivia took over for her father ten years ago, after he died in a skydiving accident that investigators deemed suspicious but could never prove foul play. News flash: someone definitely fucked with his parachute," I ad-lib. "Olivia owns a horse ranch and likes to bathe in her billions after Sunday church." That last part is also in interpretation but likely accurate.

Archie snorts.

"Her close friends call her Ollie, but she doesn't allow anyone else to. Husband left her for the nanny. Three children, all girls, all compete in equestrian sports. The youngest shows Olympic promise in ..." I struggle for the specific one.

"Show jumping—"

"Show jumping. Honestly, man, equestrian sports

and competitive duck herding? This is what I have to work with?" I toss an annoyed glance his way. "What is the point of meeting with these people anyway?"

"To get them to book their events here." He says it like I should know this. "You've got a meeting with Belinda about it this afternoon. It's in your calendar. She wants to go over special events targets for the next two years."

"*Two years?*"

"Oh yeah! These companies book years out, and the contracts are huge. We're talking millions."

I whistle. This is the first I'm hearing of this.

"And corporate has big prizes for the people who bring in the biggest contracts."

"What kind of prizes are we talking about?"

"Oh boy, I don't know. Cars, vacations, that sort of thing."

We round the corner and push through the doors of Opal Reef. Chester is waiting for us.

"What's the verdict?" I ask by way of greeting.

His hollowed cheeks blow out with a deep exhale. "So, the good news is I got someone in late last night to assess the system."

"And?"

"And it's what Ray thought it might be—a faulty part that is about to kick it."

I curse. "Do they have the part?"

"In Switzerland, so I made him sit in that chair—" He points to one of the dining tables in the corner. "—until after midnight when he could call his head office in

Zurich. They put the part on a FedEx plane. It should be here by 4:00 p.m., and then he'll come and install it ..."

Chester's words drift as a form appears in my line of sight, her long, fiery red hair gleaming in the midmorning sun.

Abbi approaches, her pastel pink dress hugging her round belly. It's only been a few weeks, and yet she's grown noticeably. She's still all baby, though. Baby and tits. There's a radiant glow about her. I've always heard that about pregnant women, but I've never actually seen it until now.

God, she is *so* happy to be carrying Henry's child.

And I'm genuinely happy for her, even if he is a prick.

"Ronan?"

"Huh?" Chester's gruff voice breaks into my reverie.

"I was just saying that if all goes as planned, it'll be good as new tonight."

"Perfect. Thanks for being on top of this." I drop a pat on his shoulder. "If there are any delays at all, let me know immediately." With that, I move to close the distance to Abbi, embracing her in a hug. "I was hoping I'd run into you." I inhale deeply. She smells like her strawberry body cream but also, fuck, like Henry's cologne. I know that scent. He must have rubbed himself all over her before they parted ways, like an animal marking their territory.

"Same." She pulls away, regarding the dress shirt I swapped this morning's golf shirt for, the top buttons undone. "I heard you're still resisting the tie."

"You mean the noose?"

"Is that what you wore to my wedding? A noose?"

"That was an exception." And it sure fucking felt like I was dying that day. "Seems I don't have a lot of say in what I wear, but I draw the line at ties." They remind me of church picnics and Sunday dinners at my great-aunt Edna's, who smelled of mothballs and baby powder and forced me to eat liver.

"Someone has to make sure you don't show up to important meetings in rock band T-shirts and jeans," she teases, reaching up to adjust my collar.

"Who's been tattling on me?" Belinda, obviously.

"More like looking out for you." Abbi's hand drifts, patting my chest on its way back down to her side. "So? How are things? Really?"

"Is this for an official report to His Highness?"

"No, it's between you and me. I promise." Her expression is earnest.

God, it's been years since Abbi and I traded secrets. She was always so easy to talk to. The overwhelming urge to dump everything out into the open hits me. But where do I even begin? Definitely not standing here, in Opal Reef, with people lingering nearby. I check my watch. It's 10:00 a.m. "You've probably had breakfast."

"My first, yes." She rubs her belly, her eyes twinkling with mischief. "But I heard the pastry chef is doing a trial run and needs volunteer samplers."

I chuckle at her appetite and holler over my shoulder, "Archie, reschedule my next hour for me, 'kay?"

"But you have—"

"I don't care. Tell them Mrs. Wolf is hungry." I drape

an arm around her shoulder, a friendly gesture that would piss off Henry to no end. "Lead the way, Red."

———

SHE MOANS through a bite as I watch her devour a freshly baked *pain au chocolat*. Fiona Crumb, pastry chef extraordinaire according to the hotel's website and aptly named, was only too happy to send a platter of various treats to Seraphina's for Henry Wolf's wife.

We've since abandoned our table and found a cabana to stretch out in—aka hide—while admiring the expanse of gulf water and white sand. It truly is an idyllic spot, despite the oppressive heat that the ceiling fan does little to combat.

Everything will change tomorrow, when the wave of media open attendees rolls in and the hotel is buzzing with activity, but for today, it's just Abbi and me and a few staff prepping for the onslaught of activity.

I ordered them to leave us alone.

"You have a little bit of ..." I gesture at the corner of my bottom lip to mimic where a glob of chocolate smears hers.

She attempts to lick it off before reaching for a napkin. "These things are always so messy. Sorry."

"No need to apologize. I don't mind watching you lick chocolate sauce off yourself, Red."

"Ronan!" Her cheeks pink.

This has always been our usual MO when we meet up: I drop flirtatious innuendo that makes Abbi blush furiously while dirty memories cycle through my mind. I end up leaving with a raging hard-on and overwhelming jealousy aimed at Henry.

This time, however, I'm not overwhelmed by lust—even though we're lying next to each other and a sheen of sweat coats her skin—because I'm too focused on all I need to get off my chest.

"So? Tell me, what's going on?" she prods, rolling onto her side to face me.

"I need your help."

A frown of consternation furrows her pretty face. "With?"

Fuck it. I may as well lay it all out on the … well, cabana bed. "With stopping your husband from blowing up someone's life."

———

"WHEN DID he tell you all this?"

"About the eminent domain stuff? Yesterday morning, while we were touring the course. You didn't know anything about it?"

"He never mentioned it, but Henry always has a dozen projects on the go, with a hundred fires to fight. I don't know how he keeps up with all of it." She's quiet for a moment, likely digesting what I've detailed—which is everything since the moment I stepped into the Sea Witch—while she scoops out jam from a pastry's center with her index finger.

The longer I watch her do it, the more my base needs return to the forefront. "Seriously, can you eat that like a normal human being?"

Her finger pauses midway to her mouth to lick the jam off. "What do you mean?"

"I mean, you're killing me." I may be laser focused on Sloane, but I'm, well, *me*, and I've imagined Abbi's mouth doing that exact thing to my dick on more than one occasion. It's a little distracting, to say the least.

Her eyes widen with understanding as they shift from her finger to me, down to the growing bulge in my pants. "Seriously? I'm a sweaty beached whale right now."

"Shut up." I chuckle.

Thankfully, she abandons the treat on the plate between us. "So, Henry actually banned you from this woman."

"Basically, yes. And Belinda threw in her own threats."

"And then you slept with her anyway."

I open my mouth to argue in my defense, but she holds her sticky hand up.

"I'm not saying they had any right to make demands like that."

I heave a sigh, relieved she's not automatically taking Henry's side.

"But this is a mess, Ronan. You know how Henry gets when it comes to business decisions and especially when someone's trying to stop him."

"Can you blame her for fighting it? That's been her home all her life! Imagine if some massive company decided to open up next door to your parents' place." I've never been to the farm in Pennsylvania, but even Henry has admitted it's beautiful countryside. "Or if Henry lost

Wolf Cove for whatever reason. That place means more to him than anywhere else. Especially his grandparents' cabin."

"That would devastate him, and he would fight it, tooth and nail," she agrees. "But I don't see how this will end well for Sloane."

"I guarantee you all this eminent domain bullshit wouldn't be a topic of conversation if he hadn't lobbied for it." Henry himself said the local government will do anything to please him. If he told them he doesn't want an access road next door to the hotel, I'd bet they'd listen. "There's got to be a way to change his mind."

The pained look on Abbi's face isn't hopeful.

"I need your help. Sloane already wrote me off in the beginning because I worked here. I think she's coming around, but she won't want me within a hundred miles of her when she finds out about this, and I can't lose her." Not that I have her yet. But I'm fucking determined.

A soft smile curves her lips. "You really like this one, huh?"

"I can't stop thinking about her," I admit. "And when I'm with her, it's like ..." I struggle to find the right description. "Time stops, and I don't give a shit about anything else. Does that make sense?"

"You're such a romantic," she teases.

"I don't know what I am, but I haven't felt like this about anyone since ..." My voice fades

"Since Tasha," she finishes, incorrectly.

I avert my gaze as I mumble, "Right." Abbi never did seem to pick up on how I truly felt about her. Sure, at first, I was still hung up on my ex, but those feelings quickly faded as she took on a prominent place in my life that summer. I didn't let on, though. I knew she was in love with Henry. Once they reconciled, all I cared about was keeping her in my life.

"Okay." She reaches out to collect my hand in hers. "I don't know how I can help, but I'll try. I'll do whatever I can."

I hold on tight so she can't pull away. "You've got to keep this between us for now."

"Of course."

"Henry figured out that I hooked up with her, but he thinks it's the usual. He can't know I have feelings for her. Not yet anyway." All he cares about is his precious fucking business plans, and he'll see this as an obstacle he has to crush. "I mean it, Abbi." I never use her real name.

She nods emphatically.

"And I want you to meet her."

"Really?" Excitement glints in her eye. "Okay. When?"

"I'm working on that." Sloane never agreed to tonight, but she also didn't say no. What am I going to find when I show up at her place? Her in a dress or a bikini? Or her not there at all. "Just know that when it happens, I'll need you as backup to deal with Henry so he doesn't fire my ass." He's not the type to keep giving people chances. I'm surprised he's given me more than one, but I have a feeling my luck card's about to max out.

"So you want to use me?"

"More like hide behind you, if I'm being honest."

She giggles. "That's okay. I understand. Okay, I'll be

your shield against my husband, but I cannot promise anything."

"He won't be happy with me." Again, I question my sanity.

"When is Henry ever really happy?" she mock whispers.

"When he's with you." I give her hand a final squeeze before letting go.

"Okay, so that's one big piece of news. What about Mermaid Beach? Are you liking it here?"

"Loving it. I mean, how can you not?" I gesture out at the gulf. "Nothing beats this."

"And the job? How's that going?"

"Let's see." I stretch out onto my back. "I hate golf, and yet I spent two hours with our pro at the ass crack of dawn today, learning how to swing a club so I don't look like an idiot tomorrow." Marcus, the pro, said I was surprisingly good for a beginner, but he was likely blowing smoke up my ass.

"So, is this job something you can see yourself doing long term?"

"You know, I think I'm starting to. I'm still lost and relying on everyone else to figure out what the hell I'm supposed to do, but I don't feel as dumb as I did a few weeks ago."

"That's promising."

"It is." I pause. "I know you had a lot to do with it, so thank you."

She shrugs. "Honestly, it didn't take more than a casual mention once to Henry. After that, it was all him, and you impressed him, Ronan. You earned the chance."

Her smile is encouraging. "How is working with Belinda?"

"How is working with Belinda." I echo her question while choosing my words carefully. "She's been great, actually. Training me. We've spent a lot of time together. There's a chance she may want to fuck me again, but other than that ..."

Abbi's eyebrow arches. "A chance."

"More like a definite."

"Ronan—"

"I'm not going to. I swear. Even if Sloane wasn't in the picture, I wouldn't ..." I let that denial trail off because it's probably a lie.

We share a look and then burst out with laughter.

And that's how Henry Wolf finds us.

"When I asked where my wife was and they told me she was meeting privately with my director, I wasn't expecting this." He sizes up our intimate and horizontal position. "How *cute*." Nothing in his tone matches that word.

"Hey, honey." Abbi rolls onto her back to peer up at Henry, one hand smoothing over her belly. "We were just taste-testing your chef's menu. This one is my favorite. It's called a beignet, and it has rose petal jam. Here, try it." She reaches the donut-looking thing and holds it up to him.

"I had one not long ago." Henry studies it, then her and me. "That's what you were doing in here?"

"Well, yes. And catching up. Why?" There's the slightest edge to Abbi's voice, the same edge that always appears whenever Henry's tone hints at suspicion.

I stifle the urge to smile. How that jealous, controlling prick ever allowed that night in Wolf Cove to happen is beyond me, but I'll be forever thankful for his momentary lapse in lucidity.

"Because I've seen how you eat those, Abbi," he retorts smoothly, "and I doubt Ronan heard a single word you said."

"I have no idea what you mean." A devilish glint flickers in her expression as she collects a dollop of jam spilling out of the treat. This time when her finger reaches her mouth, she takes her time, sucking it off.

His jaw clenches.

This is one of the things I've always loved about Abbi—she's all sweet and innocent ... until she's not.

But I don't need to stay here and picture them fucking, which is what they'll be doing in T-minus-five minutes or however long it takes him to drag her to their suite. "He's not wrong, Red. Consider me suitably tortured for the day." I slide out of the cabana.

"Text me later about that thing," Abbi calls out.

"Will do."

"What thing?" I hear Henry ask as I walk away, his voice softer now that they're alone.

"None of your business. Put your hand here. She's kicking. I think she likes sweets."

I smile as I take the stone path back toward the hotel. Whatever else Henry is, he's a doting husband to her. Maybe that's why I'm not leaving here with that same burning envy I normally feel that Henry has what I want.

Does that mean I'm finally moving on?

Or, more than likely, it's because I think I've found a woman who can make me as happy as Abbi would have.

As happy as Tasha did.

Or, dare I hope, happier?

There's only one way to know for sure. I dig out my phone.

> Don't flake out on me, Sea Witch. 6pm sharp.

6. Sloane

"A baby, Sloane?" Gigi's hand abandons her knitting to clamp over mine.

"Looks like it." I decided that confessing my sins while I braided her hair was the best approach.

I knew she would never admonish me. But when she turns in her seat to peer up at me, her wrinkled face is brimming with excitement.

"This isn't good news, Gigi. I'm terrified and feeling incredibly stupid." Compound that with Ronan's visit yesterday, and I can add confusion to the mix of emotions that grips me with unrelenting fervor. I thought I had him all figured out. Now, I don't know ...

Dare I hope that he's a decent guy?

"Oh, honey, that's normal." She squeezes my hand before releasing it. "I remember when I was pregnant, I had never even changed a real baby's diaper before."

"Neither have I," I admit, tying off her braid. Sure, I've held a baby here or there, but as soon as they started to fuss, I've happily handed them back. "And this was totally avoidable."

"That doesn't mean it's wrong." Gigi pats the chair next to her, silently instructing me to sit. Her brow furrows with thought. "You know, your mother said almost the same thing when she came home after her fling with that fool." She has always refused to call him my father. As far as she's concerned, he doesn't deserve the title. "It was unplanned too, and she was petrified. Didn't know what to do. Thought her life was over. But she managed just fine."

"She was nineteen, Gigi." When I was that age, all I cared about was making money during the day and having fun with my friends at night. "Plus, she had you to help her." I might not have had a father in my life, but I had two strong women who supplied me with a fierce amount of affection and care.

"And you're thirty-one, which is a far cry from nineteen. You have a house and a thriving business."

As long as Cody's tongue-wagging doesn't lose me my staff.

"*And* you still have me. Don't dig my grave yet," Gigi chides with a soft laugh. "Plus, you have Frank."

I chuckle. "He's not exactly a wet nurse."

"No, but he will always be there for you. That man is more loyal than a honeybee to his queen." She peers at me. "Did you tell him yet—"

"No." I can't imagine he'll be *more* pleased with Ronan when he finds out. Skye and Rebel said they thought they'd have to form a barrier when Ronan strolled past them yesterday, his clothing sopping wet. And the look Frank gave me after was priceless—half amusement, half disappointment. I'm not ready to be judged by him, or anyone, yet. "You're the only person I've told. Ronan doesn't even know yet."

"That hotel director. He's the father?"

"Yes. It's his." Saying it out loud feels wrong. I shouldn't be telling others when he doesn't even know. But this is Gigi. She trumps all.

"When are you going to tell him?"

"I don't know if I will. We don't really have that kind of relationship."

"Ah ... I see." Her eyes twinkle with amusement. Gigi was a heartbreaker in her day. There was never any shortage of admirers, her spunkiness drawing them in like cats to a sun spot, but she was never willing to settle down. She pauses. "Do you *want* that kind of relationship with him?"

I'm shaking my head, but the denial is stuck in my throat. I don't know the answer anymore. I'm still sure he's all wrong for me, but what if he's not? If what he said was true, he can handle a relationship. He's looking for one. "I really don't know, Gigi. I don't know anything anymore."

"Well, like I always say, a good, hard test will let you know quickly if you should waste your time with this hotel man."

"You mean like an accidental pregnancy?" I chuckle. "He's going to run for the hills."

"Then he can stay up there with the rest of the chickens. You'll do just fine without him." She waves her hand dismissively.

She always makes things sound easier than they are. Then again, at her age, she's seen and done a lot, and lived through a lot, always coming out on the other side.

"There's also the thing about Mom. Her cancer? She was thirty-one when she died."

"No need to remind me, dear." A dark cloud passes across her face before it's gone in the next instant.

Gigi was stoic about Mom's passing. *We can't control these things. It was just her time,* she'd tell me. But sometimes, late at night, I'd hear her crying.

"What if it's hereditary?" My checkups have always come back clear, but that doesn't mean the next one will. My doctor suggested genetic testing and to not wait too long to have children, in case the worst case happens and I'm facing treatments and surgeries. "What if *this* is my shot?"

"It's fair of you to consider that. It's a worry." She nods in agreement. "But I don't recommend making big decisions based on what-ifs. Better to have solid footing."

The last thing I have is solid footing. "Please don't say anything. I'm not ready for people to know. Not until I've figured out what I'm doing about this giant mistake."

"It's no one's business until you're ready to make it theirs." She reaches out to squeeze my knee. "And it may be a mistake, but that doesn't mean it won't also lead into a wonderful thing. My marriage was a colossal disaster, but I got your mother out of it. She fell for an idiot, but we all got you out of it." Her face lights up. "For what it's worth, you'll make a wonderful mother, Sloane."

Her validation brings me a wave of comfort I didn't know I needed. "You really think so?"

"Of course I do. I've always thought so. And, self-ishly, I hope I get to see it happen. But *only* if you're ready. The good thing is you have some time to get ready if that's the path you decide to take."

I let out a huge sigh of relief. My problem isn't solved, but Gigi always knows just what to say to lift the weight off my chest, even if only temporarily. "Ronan invited me to dinner tonight."

"Well, that's a good start."

I give her a knowing look. "At the hotel, with his boss, who doesn't know Ronan is inviting me."

"You mean, Henry Wolf?" She hoots. "This Ronan fellow may be handsome, but he doesn't seem too bright."

"Yeah, I don't know what he's thinking, honestly. But it gets better, Gigi. Henry warned him to stay away from me because of all the problems I caused. And now Ronan wants to bring me there, even though Henry Wolf will probably fire him for cavorting with the enemy."

"Let's pray the child gets your brains." She breaks off a chunk of her macadamia scone. "Did Ronan say why he wants to bring you into the lion's den, so to speak?"

"Just that he wants them to get to know me. He doesn't seem to like Henry, but he's good friends with Abbi Wolf, Henry's wife. It's her he wants me to meet."

"Introducing you to his friends. That says something."

"I guess." You don't introduce the new woman to your close female friends if she's just a casual fuck. Is this Ronan's way of proving he has feelings for me?

But what will Abbi Wolf think about the crazy rooster commune lady who plastered all sorts of unsavory posters, including headlines that dragged her? Does she know about those? Which reminds me ... Talk of Abbi Wolf and Alaska last night has stirred up dust in the far recesses of my memory. I can't quite remember why it all sounds so familiar, and the only thing I can think of is that I likely read something in an article. I need to go mining for information again.

Gigi watches me quietly as she nibbles away.

"So, what do I do about dinner?"

"Do you want to go?"

"No."

She arches a wrinkled eyebrow.

I could never get a lie past Gigi. "I mean, I want to know Ronan better, especially given our situation."

"That he has no clue about," she chips in.

"Right." In a public setting where our clothes have to stay on. Then again, Starfish Island is pretty public, and that didn't stop us. "But it's the hotel. Aren't I being a giant hypocrite by showing up there now, after everything?"

"Why? You were invited."

"Not by Henry Wolf. He doesn't know what Ronan's planning."

"Maybe he'll have no idea who you are."

"I guess there is that possibility." I've never met the man; he never involved himself in any of the council meetings. Unless Ronan makes a point of introducing me as the crazy rooster commune lady, I could be completely incognito, just arm candy. "I could pretend

I'm someone else." Am I that good of an actress, though? Likely not.

Gigi hums. "I imagine it'll be a nice meal."

"I would hope so. And it's not just him and his wife. There will be a bunch of people there. Ronan said it's a casual, friendly thing."

"Aren't you just a little curious to meet this billionaire man and see what all the fuss is about?"

"Maybe," I admit with reluctance. "At least so I can say, yes, I've met him and can confirm once and for all that he is, indeed, the douchebag we all think he is."

She tsks. "Neither the hotel nor the man is going anywhere, whether you like it or not, so you may as well make peace with it."

"You're beginning to sound like Frank."

"Frank's a wise man. Why do you think I kept him around all those years? You should listen to him!"

"But can you imagine how awkward a dinner with Henry Wolf would be?"

"For you or him? I say put on a dress and let the man feed you. Be sweet as peach pie. That's what I'd do."

"I'm not good at that."

"Fine, then spit in his face and call him a filthy ghoul while you get your fill of caviar." She cackles. "Oh, to be a fly on that wall."

A knock sounds.

Like a child about to get caught doing something naughty, Gigi stuffs the last piece of her scone into her mouth and, crumpling the packaging, drops it into the nearby trash.

I shake my head but grin as I call out, "Come in."

Frieda pushes through the door, a tray of medications in one hand and a blood pressure machine in the other. She's one of the daytime nurses and probably my favorite. "Good morning, ladies. How are we feeling today?"

"Pretty well," I offer as Gigi chews and swallows the evidence. "I just braided her hair, and we were catching up on things. I've got to head out now. Lots to do." A blood test or two, for starters.

Rita sets the tray down and begins opening caps. "How'd you sleep last night, Gigi?"

"The usual. Had that strange dream with those monkeys again."

"Oh yeah? What were those little rascals up to this time?"

"Can't remember. But they were definitely there."

Frieda hums. "Must be all those sweet treats you've been sneakin'."

"I don't know what you're talking about. You have me confused with someone else."

My phone chirps then with an incoming text, and I choose to answer it rather than get dragged into Gigi's lie.

RONAN:

Don't flake out on me, Sea Witch. 6pm sharp.

My stomach flutters with nerves. He's not going to let up. This is beginning to feel like a chase. I'll admit, I like it.

"What's that about?" Gigi asks. "Is that your baby daddy?"

"Haha, funny." With Frieda's back to us, I shoot Gigi

a glare in warning. What the hell? She used to be a vault for unmentionables. If this is her idea of keeping a secret, half of Mermaid Beach is going to know within the week.

"Oh, silly me, I'm getting my slang mixed up. Too old to keep up, I guess." She flashes wide "oops" eyes at me.

Good recovery attempt. I hope it's enough.

"Okay, Ms. Parker, let's check that ticker of yours." Frieda mouths "congratulations" as she passes.

Nope, not good enough.

With a heavy sigh, I bend over to kiss Gigi's forehead. "I'll talk to you soon."

She seizes my cheeks and holds my face close to hers. "You're never alone, remember that. The Sea Witch is your family. Your village."

I smile to mask my apprehension. I wish that were true, but the deeply rooted community Gigi fostered over the decades feels like it's slipping away. How long before everyone is gone?

She releases me. "Oh, to be young and wild again. Such exciting times."

"Glad I'm able to entertain you."

"You kidding? This is better than those daytime soaps in the rec center. Have fun tonight."

"You're so convinced I'm going."

"Of course you are. You can't help yourself."

She's likely right.

"Into the belly of the beast!" Gigi shakes her fist in the air before stretching it out for Frieda. "Wear that peach number."

"I forgot about that dress." It was a splurge for a friend's wedding. Cody got drunk and spilled an entire beer on me. I was so angry. But the dry cleaners worked their magic. I haven't worn it since. I haven't had any reason to.

"It's stunning on you. Oh, and the perfume." She winks. "You know the one."

———

I squeeze the Cherokee into a parking spot outside my doctor's office, but I don't rush for my appointment just yet. There's something—or someone—I need to speak to first.

Digging out the scrap of paper I jotted Ryan's number down on, I punch the digits into my phone and hit Call.

And wait as it rings. Maybe I should have called from the main line. She's likely screening random numbers. I don't blame her; I do the same. I'll just leave a message—

"Hello?" The feminine voice in my ear is wary.

"Hi, Ryan? It's Sloane from the Sea Witch."

"Sloane! *Hey*! How are you?"

"I'm great," I lie, staring out at the medical center sign. "Listen, I wanted to check in to see how Katie's doing." Another lie. Ronan has already filled me in on their friend's injury, and while I may have a valid reason to call on behalf of my business, why I'm really calling has nothing to do with Katie and everything to do with learning whatever I can about Ronan.

"Better! The swelling has gone down, but her foot is basically purple, and she can't walk on it. We hung out around the house for most of yesterday, which I don't mind because this place is incredible, and I am so jealous," she rambles. "Kyle went out and got her crutches, so that should help with the flight home."

Her boyfriend seems like a great guy. "When are you leaving?"

"Later this afternoon. Kyle and I are enjoying a few hours on the beach." Sounds of a child's squeals and a man's shout of greeting punctuate her claim.

"Great. Well, I hope you guys had a decent time on the cruise, even though it didn't end well."

"Oh my gosh, we had *the best time*."

"Even when you puked?" a deep male voice chimes in the background. I assume that's Kyle.

"Right. Other than the epic hangover. I may have been a little bit drunk."

"Really? Couldn't tell."

"You're lying, but thank you for that."

I smile, even though she can't see it. I like Ryan. I'm struggling to picture her with Ronan, though.

"I'm actually glad you called. I'm a little fuzzy about parts of the afternoon, but I'm pretty sure I said a few things I shouldn't have."

Normally I would shrug it off with a "we've all been there" excuse, but that won't get me the answers I need. That's why I don't waste any time when I say, "You mean about Ronan and your brother going home to screw Katie and Rachel?"

"Yeah, that." Her nervous laughter betrays her awkwardness. "Listen, I don't know what's going on with you and Ronan, and it is none of my business, but for what it's worth, he's a really decent guy. It might not be obvious in the beginning, but trust me, he is. He's super loyal and a good friend, and if he says he'll do something, he'll do it. Or he won't do it. Do you get what I'm saying?"

"I think I do." She said the same thing on Sunday, though she's trying to be more discreet now, given her current boyfriend is next to her and probably doesn't want to hear about how wonderful her fuck buddy was.

"Honestly, Ronan's biggest fault is that he's best friends with my brother, who is an ignorant meatball with only one thing on his mind. I think he might actually die if he goes too long without getting laid."

I chuckle. "Yeah, Connor seems like he'd be a lot sometimes."

"Try all the time. Don't get me wrong, I love him to death, but sometimes I want to put a pillow over his face while he's sleeping and hold it there until he—"

"Babe," Kyle chides softly.

"Right. I would never do it. I just want to sometimes. Anyway, Ronan was kind of lost for a while there, after his breakup with his ex."

"Tasha," I offer.

"Yeah, I think that's her name. I'm surprised he mentioned her. He doesn't talk about her much. He's not one to divulge personal things, as I'm sure you've noticed."

I hum in agreement. But Ryan seems to chatter plenty, which is to my benefit. "So, he's not lost anymore?"

"You mean because of her? Oh, that's long over for him, ever since he came back from Alaska."

"What about anyone else? Has he been seeing a lot of other women?" It's probably wrong to pump the girl for information, but it's the best way to validate what Ronan told me last night.

"I don't think so. I mean, I don't live with them anymore, but I know he's settled down some. Connor's been calling him a monk for months. He talked about running an intervention."

That guy really is something.

Kyle laughs.

"Obviously, I said no. There's nothing wrong with him. I just think he's tired of living that life. Anyway, I'm glad you called. I hope I didn't ruin things for him with you."

"No, it's okay. We aren't serious." What an ironic claim, given where I'm heading now, which is as serious as it gets. "Listen, I hope you guys come back to Mermaid Beach again, and when you do, we'll make up for the lost hour next time."

"Oh, we will definitely be back, and absolutely! I was actually going to leave a review for your company. I'm gonna go do that now."

Mention of a review brings back my conversation with Ronan on the cruise. My cheeks flush. "Okay, well ... until next time!"

We end the call, and I take a few moments to digest everything Ryan said. Sure, she and Ronan are friends, but I'd like to think she wouldn't steer me toward him if he were like, say, Connor—whom she seems openly willing to drive a bus over at the first opportunity. Girl code still exists, doesn't it? I don't know many who would lie about their manwhore friend when it comes to dating them. My gut says Ryan wouldn't.

Which means Ronan was telling me the truth. He's looking for a relationship.

I peer up at the doctor's office as a burst of nervousness explodes in my stomach.

I doubt he's looking for this.

7. Ronan

"These numbers aren't accurate."

"I pulled them from the booking system—"

"Which does not include the contract with Gray-Stone that Mr. Wolf's assistant confirmed an hour ago," Belinda says crisply. "Please send updated figures to everyone in this room immediately."

Minnie's head bobs in obedience.

There's a long pause, and then Belinda's eyebrows arch. "Immediately means now, so that this meeting isn't a waste of time."

"Oh. Right. Okay. Give me five minutes!" Minnie dashes out, her tablet pressed to her chest.

Poor girl. I can't imagine what being Belinda's assistant is like. It might be worse than working under Henry. Every time I've seen Miles, he's either running or bugging out on caffeine.

"Will one contract make that much of a difference for our purposes today?" Lena asks, voicing a question on the tip of my tongue.

Belinda's heels click at a leisurely rhythm as she rounds the desk. "That one contract is an eight-figure commitment from a major company. It is one of the largest ever booked with Wolf Hotels, that Henry himself wrangled, and it will all but cement Mermaid Beach's record-breaking first year results, which is Henry's stretch goal. So, yes, I'd like you to see this contract and understand what is expected of you."

Lena and I share a high-browed glance as Belinda does her lap, her short skirt hugging her curves.

Meanwhile, a brunette I haven't met yet sits across from us, her oversized rectangular-frame glasses magnifying large eyes on a small face. She hasn't uttered a single word, and Belinda hasn't introduced her, but that hasn't stopped the woman from staring at me like an owl sitting on a branch.

Not many people can make me uncomfortable. This one? I'm resisting the urge to squirm.

"As one of you is well aware, and one of you is painfully oblivious about"—Belinda cuts a glance at me—"in addition to your roles running departments at this hotel, you are expected to network and sell Mermaid Beach as a prime location for multiday large-scale events. These events are critical to our success. The meeting room bookings and catering tabs that come with events are substantial, as you can see." She gestures at our open tablets in front of us.

I scan the file that lists our various rates and whistle. "Twenty-five grand for a coffee station? Jesus, what are we serving? Do animals shit out these beans?" I watched a documentary on kopi luwak. No, thank you.

Owl Girl's jaw drops.

"Eloquent as always, Ronan," Belinda murmurs. "Beverage stations are just the tip of the iceberg. The more we bill, the more profit we make, and Henry has set steep targets for us. Some say too steep," she adds under her breath, and I hazard that *some* is her. "But regardless, we are expected to aim for it. All this is to say that the Events department is an invaluable partner for us, which is why Eleanor here"—she gestures to the stranger in the room—"reports both directly to me as well as into head office. She is our boots on the ground to ensure every event operates without a hitch. She has her own team of coordinators. Eleanor, you know Lena. This is Ronan."

Right, Eleanor from Events. I remember seeing that name in the org charts now, as well as a few emails about the first golf tournament. I smile at her.

She averts her soul-searing gaze.

"Eleanor and her team have been working very closely with me for the media open, but they are neck-deep in planning events. Expect to receive weekly updates and regular meeting requests from her going forward."

Can't wait.

"Now, before Eleanor begins highlighting our upcoming events, I want to talk about the President's Club. Again, this is more for you, Ronan." She strolls by, enjoying every moment of my ignorance and her ability to remind me of it in front of others. "Each year, total profit dollars earned from contracts are tallied, and the general manager with the highest numbers wins." Her hands curl around the headrest of a leather chair as she turns to face us. "I expect to win."

"And what do you win?" I ask.

"Cash bonuses, jewelry, an exotic trip. One time was a two-week stay in Bali and this." She taps the face of her diamond-encrusted watch. "Another time, it was a luxury cruise."

It's clear Belinda is a frequent flyer of this President's Club. Not surprising, given how much Henry relies on her. "So, let me get this straight. Lena and I bust our asses to sign these contracts, and you reap the rewards?"

"What can I say, perks of being the general manager." Belinda studies her nails. "Directors are also suitably rewarded."

"With what?"

"Hotel vouchers and bonuses." She shrugs. "That sort of thing."

I was already in a bad mood coming into this meeting, but now I'm annoyed. No one told me I'd have to be a salesman to line Henry's gold pockets. "Well, it sounds like this GrayStone contract has guaranteed your club seat." I lean back in my chair, making a point of stretching out my thighs. "I'd prefer the cash bonus, thanks. How about you, Lena?"

"Always a fan of cash." She's enjoying watching me hang myself with our boss.

Belinda sneers at my leisurely position. "These meetings you have lined up over the next few days? All this prep work you've been doing to ingratiate yourself with our special guests? I expect results."

"Kissing ass is not one of my strong suits, if you

haven't noticed yet." Now I'm just poking the bear. But, fuck it, Henry's going to fire me anyway once I walk into dinner with Sloane tonight.

Our tablets chirp with an incoming email from Mindy.

Belinda stares at me for a lengthy moment before peeling away. "You may begin, Eleanor."

At the sound of her name, the owlish events manager begins rhyming off events and projections like a programmed computer.

All the while, Belinda's eyes bore into me.

———

"Stay back a moment, please, Ronan," Belinda beckons in a clipped tone.

I sink back into my chair as the ladies leave. I should have known I wouldn't get away that easily after being a dick.

Belinda saunters over to shut the door behind them. "Okay, what the fuck has gotten into you today?"

It's more about what I've gotten into. Or who I've gotten into.

"I had a shitty sleep," I say instead. "I was up early."

"Yes, I heard you dragged our pro out on the course."

I sigh. "Okay, give me whatever lecture you're dying to give."

"Who says I'm going to lecture you?"

"Because I recognize that tone, I've heard it so many times before. You want to make me feel like a complete idiot, so go ahead. Let's have it."

Instead of retaking her chair, she settles onto the boardroom table, her ankle brushing my knee as she crosses her legs. That skirt of hers is climbing dangerously high. This undoubtedly breaks an HR rule or five.

Then again, we broke all those rules and then some in Wolf Cove two years ago.

"I haven't spent hours training you only for you to fall apart during one of the most important weeks of the year," she says calmly.

"You haven't trained me to be a fucking salesperson."

"Is that why you're in such a little snit?" She studies my face. "You have exceeded my expectations up until now. The sky is the limit for you at Wolf if you apply yourself."

"You mean, if I earn you diamonds and vacations."

"And cash bonuses, don't forget those," she quips, sliding her glasses off to set them on the table beside her. It's a rare sight when she doesn't wear those.

Guilt tickles my conscience. I'm giving her a hard time, and there's no good reason. With a sigh, I point at my tablet, abandoned on the table. "Do I have to memorize all those price lists and shit before tomorrow too?"

She laughs. "No. That's nitty-gritty stuff. That's for Eleanor and her team to iron out. We focus on impressing upon these people the benefits of hosting their events at Wolf Hotels. You are selling a partnership. A relationship."

"And these meetings I have over the next few days are all with women because you expect me to do *what* as part of selling this relationship?"

"I know what you're insinuating, and don't be silly.

That is definitely not part of your job description." She rolls her eyes. "You're meeting with Olivia McEowan from Black Titan."

"Oil and gas."

"Yes. She has been a white whale for Wolf Hotels. When her father was alive, the company's corporate events were held at Wolf. Since she's taken over, she's axed the budgets by more than half. Wolf hasn't hosted them at any of our locations in nine years. We used to make almost as much with them as we've secured with GrayStone."

I whistle. "That must hurt."

"It does. Convince her to choose us again."

"How am I supposed to do that?"

"Be yourself. But with your pants on."

I arch an eyebrow.

"Come on. If you can convince Jacob Farnsworth to suck Will Darling's dick, you can do anything you set your mind to."

The reference to that night in Alaska is so unexpected I burst out laughing. "Hey, I didn't convince anyone to do anything. And that match-up was Connor's idea."

"Funny, I recall your little fuck club being a joint effort," she counters smoothly.

I shrug. Everyone who stepped into the pitch-black cabin knew there was a chance they could be partnered with a member of the same team. No one forced them. Obviously, they had questions, and our twisted little game was a safe way to get their answers. "For what it's worth, Farnsworth discovered something important about himself that night. Last I heard, he was living with a guy in New York." Which is a far cry from his days growing up Mormon in Utah.

"I'm not surprised. He seemed to be enjoying himself *immensely* that night, from the eyeful I caught."

I chuckle. What a night for the security team and Belinda to bust up our after-hours entertainment.

"I have to say, this is a far better version of you than the one in the meeting."

"Sorry," I mumble. "I was being a dick."

She studies her painted nails for a beat. "What were you and Henry arguing about yesterday morning?"

"Nothing."

She cocks her head. "You expect me to believe that?"

"Why? What'd he tell you?"

"Absolutely nothing."

"Like I said, then." Belinda's going to find out soon enough, and when she does, she's going to want to skin me alive. Is that what all this building tension in my shoulders is about? Me knowing I'm likely about to fuck everything up in my life over a woman, and yet I'm diving headfirst into shallow waters? "Just under a lot of pressure these days to do the right thing." In so many ways. Like, the right thing to do is warn Sloane about what's coming, but I'm a coward. It's not even the confidentiality agreement I signed that I care about. It's Sloane punishing me for my association.

"Yes, I can sympathize. Hotel openings are always very stressful, even if you're not new." She pauses. "There are ways to help manage that stress, though."

"Like what?"

She makes a point of slowly uncrossing and recrossing her legs, but not before giving me a clear view up her skirt and the lack of panties.

My chest rises with my deep inhale. Her meaning could not be clearer, and this is crossing into very dangerous territory. How the fuck do I get out of it? "This might be against the rules." It's *definitely* against the rules, not that I've ever cared.

"And when have you ever been concerned about that?" she says, echoing my thoughts. "You certainly didn't that day at the old Wolf cabin."

I didn't care about a lot of things during my time in Wolf Cove, and that day will go down in history as one of the most unexpected fucks of my life. "I know who will care. Your boss."

"Right." She leans back, holding herself up with outstretched arms. "Should we ask him for his blessing? Sure, maybe after he's done fucking his former assistant who's now his wife."

Touché. Though Henry is a fan of playing the "do as I say, not as I do" card.

"Didn't you say this would never happen again?" I'm grasping for straws, but reminding her of her deep regrets the last time her hormones got past her level head seems like a good idea.

"I didn't think it would either, and yet here we are." Something soft flickers across Belinda's normally stony face. "In case you haven't noticed, I work a lot. I don't have time for relationships. But I do have needs. And so do you." Steady eyes bore into mine. "So why don't we just fuck and get it out of our system."

Hell, she's throwing back my words from yesterday.

Belinda uncrosses her legs again, this time leaving them parted.

Fuck me. How do I find myself in these situations? Honestly, this is probably karma coming around to bite me in the ass for all the women I haven't called back, even though I was always clear that I wouldn't.

If I were the old Ronan, I'd already have my fly undone and Belinda's skirt hiked up around her waist. But I'm not that guy. I don't want meaningless. Not anymore. There is only one woman I want.

And it's not the one laid out like a buffet treat in front of me now.

Acknowledging that nearly brings a smile to my face —I've evolved!—but I stifle it because that reaction at this particular moment might get my balls ripped off.

I need to get out of here, pronto. "Belinda, don't get me wrong, I think you are smoking hot." I settle my hands on her bare knees and gently pull her legs together. "But we should keep this professional." I stand as a wave of déjà vu hits me. I said the same thing to Sloane weeks ago.

That was a lie then.

But it's not now.

A stunned look passes across Belinda's face—has she ever been turned down before?—before she seems to snap out of it. "Yes, of course. I don't know what I was thinking. This was completely out of line. I understand if you'd like to report me to HR for—"

"Shut up." I can't help but laugh. "I'm not reporting anyone for anything." I'd have to pull out my own laundry list of scandalous behavior. It's a mile long and would get me fired a hundred times over.

She clears her throat as she quickly retrieves her glasses. "Okay, then."

I try to soften the blow to her ego. "If this were any other time in my life, I would be all in. Again." Hell, if this were even a few weeks ago, before I met Sloane. I'd regret it after, but I know I wouldn't turn her down. I'm not Superman.

She purses her lips, her eyes flittering up to meet mine. "Let me know if you change your mind."

"I will." But I won't. Not while Sloane's in the picture.

"I'll see you at dinner tonight." Clearing her throat, she hops off the table and struts away at a clipped speed, unlocking the door on her way out.

And I breathe a shaky sigh of relief.

———

"You said no?" Connor stares at me like I just admitted to ripping up a winning lottery ticket.

"Dude." I push my office door shut. "She Basic Instincted me."

His jaw drops. "No fucking way."

"*Way*. Like, fully."

"What does that mean?" a voice chirps out of nowhere.

I spin around to find Archie sitting in one of my chairs. "Where the fuck were you hiding!"

"I wasn't ... I was right here, waiting. For our meeting," he stammers.

I hadn't noticed him. I left the meeting and saw Connor standing at my door, so I yanked him in and downloaded on him in a hurry, and fuck, I didn't notice Archie there.

I know how gossip works around here. This would be terrible for Belinda if it got out.

"Listen to me carefully." I aim an index finger at his face. "You never repeat a single thing you just heard in here. Not to anyone. Not even to Gizmo, do you understand?" There's only one picture on Archie's desk, and it's of a cat whose hair is as orange as his owner's.

"I didn't hear anything." He shakes his head furiously.

"Good."

"Wait, but how does Gingersnap not know what getting Basic Instincted means? How old are you?" Connor waves his hand. "Actually, never mind. I don't care if you came out of the fucking womb two weeks ago, everyone should understand what that means. Sharon Stone is a rite of passage. In fact, you're gonna watch that movie tonight. I expect a full report by tomorrow at 9:00 a.m.!"

"Okay, settle down, Professor." I take a deep, calming breath. "Archie, give me five before our meeting. Do me a favor and go find Eleanor from Events. Tell her I'm bringing two people with me to dinner so she can plan accordingly."

"Got it." With a cagey look at Connor—who is easily

twice his size—Archie scurries out, shutting the door behind him.

"What dinner?" Connor asks the moment he's gone.

"The one you're coming to with me. It's here, tonight."

"Seriously? Why didn't you tell me?"

"I did. You forgot," I lie. If I counted on my hands the number of times he's left me in the dark about plans he's made for us, I'd run out of fingers, several times over. Payback's a bitch. "Wear something nice. Abbi'll be there."

That distracts him. "I haven't seen her in forever. How's the, uh—" He holds his hands out in front of his belly.

"Growing."

"Damn." He smiles wistfully, and I know he's thinking about that day in the truck. "Who else are you bringing?"

"Sloane." *I hope.*

"Neighbor girl?" He frowns. "She and Henry good now?"

"Nope. He doesn't know I'm bringing her."

"But he's gonna be there."

"Yup."

His frown deepens. "What the fuck are you up to, Lyle?"

"Honestly, I'm not sure. It's a long story that I don't have the time to get into, but I'm bringing Sloane, and they're going to meet her, and Abbi's gonna love her." *I hope.*

And then I'm going to ride in like a white knight and

derail Henry's capitalistic dreams, even though the woman still has no clue about any of it.

"So ... I should pack my bags and get ready to head back to Miami, then?" Connor muses wryly.

"Maybe, but not yet."

"For the record, you're fucking nuts."

"I probably am," I agree.

"And have you thought about what Belinda is gonna do?"

"She'll defer to Henry, and I have Abbi to help me with him." Belinda's devoted to a fault. If Henry maintains his cool over Sloane, she won't attack.

"Dude, forget about that. What about what just happened over there?" He tosses an aimless thumb toward the hall beyond my door.

"Belinda's not looking for a relationship. She has an itch she needs scratching, and I was an easy option." At least, she thought I was, and probably for good reason—because I usually am.

Connor looks at me like I'm about to jump into alligator-infested waters. "You rejected *Belinda*, and now you're about to stroll in with another woman. A *younger* woman."

"Who she despises. Shit." I'm beginning to see where Connor is going with this, and he's right—Belinda will have the nuclear codes at the ready and aimed at me. Or worse, Sloane. "Okay, I need you to do something for me."

"What?"

"Belinda."

He barks with laughter. "Yeah, right. Funny guy."

When he notices I'm not laughing along, his mirth fades. "Oh, you're serious."

"Yeah."

"You want *me* to scratch Belinda's itch?"

"I want you to see if she's willing to let you scratch it." There were three of us in that cabin room that day, and she didn't seem to have a preference. "But do it discreetly."

He groans. "Fine, but if I get fired for this, you better fix it."

"Fine." If I'm not already fired for showing up with Sloane. But I'm banking on Abbi not allowing that to happen. "Just be you. If she hasn't sacked you for that yet, she won't."

He drops a meaty hand on my shoulder. "The things I do for our friendship."

"Yeah, you're really hard done by."

"I really am. And, you know, I was thinking earlier about what Mermaid Beach is missing. Something that would solve problems like this."

"This oughta be good," I mutter.

"The first rule of fuck club is ..."

Despite everything, I laugh. "You idiot."

———

I weave my sleek black car up the pothole-riddled driveway. It's five minutes to six, and my palms are sweating. I haven't been nervous to meet a girl since ... I can't remember when. But Sloane never responded to my text, and I have no idea what's waiting for me here. I don't know if she's playing hard to get or avoiding me. I pray it's the former. I'm up for a good chase.

Her Cherokee is here. That's a good sign.

So is Frank's pickup.

I park next to it and climb out, adjusting the collar of a clean dress shirt. I go through at least two a day in this heat.

The hens are busy grazing on feed in their coop, but Ralph wanders nearby, watching with those beady little bird eyes.

"Not today, motherfucker." I pull out the carrot I sent Archie to grab from the hotel kitchen, snapping it up into bits and tossing them toward the trailers—and away from my freshly washed hood.

He scuttles after the bright orange chunks.

The sound of a door creaking draws my attention to the house and the figure standing on the porch.

Damn. All I can do is stare.

For too long, I guess, because Sloane starts to fidget.

"Does this work for your dinner thing?" Her toned arm stretches as she pinches the skirt, drawing the gauzy pink material away from her body.

I can't decide where to look first—on the slit that shows off her shapely legs, the plunging neckline that hints at those perky breasts, her delicate shoulders, the tendrils of ash-blond hair that cascade down her back in loose curls.

Finally, I land on her mesmerizing face. "You match the hotel color scheme." The fuck if I know if that's the right shade of pink, and that was probably a stupid thing to say.

She falters. "That wasn't my goal."

Yup. Stupid. "You're perfect." She's more than perfect. She's a vision.

Her eyes drift over my midnight-blue shirt and gray pants—tailored to my body as everything in my closet is quickly becoming—but she doesn't say anything.

"If I step away from my car, will he shit on it?" He's halfway through his treats.

"Fifty-fifty chance."

"I guess I'll risk it." I close the distance to the porch as Sloane slides her purse strap over her shoulder and takes the steep set of stairs down in delicate gold sandals that show off dainty feet. Even her feet are sexy. Her back is bare save for two thin dress straps that crisscross down. There's so much exposed skin, and my fingers itch to touch every square inch of it. "Where is everyone?"

"Frank's out for a swim. No one else is home yet."

I'm two feet away when I catch the first waft of her perfume. I inhale deeply. "God, you smell good." I step in closer and inhale again. "What is that?" It's like salty ocean air mixed with a spicy floral. It's intoxicating, but everything about Sloane makes my blood roil.

"Just a perfume from Gigi." She lifts her chin in defiance. "So we're clear, we're not having sex tonight."

I school my expression. "Okay."

"I mean it, Ronan."

"So do I. And honestly, it's probably the best thing I've heard all day." Between Abbi and her pastries and Belinda ambushing me, eliminating sex from the equation is smart. If I have to deal with my frustrations in the shower later, so be it.

Sloane's curious frown has me chuckling.

"Long story, and you don't want to hear the details. I'm just happy you showed up. I expected to find you in a bikini again."

"I was considering it."

"And I was getting ready to beg."

"Wait. You said 'convince' yesterday. But if watching you beg is an option, I'll be back in a sec. I just need to change ..." She takes a step back, up one stair, putting her at eye level with me.

I slide my hand around her nape, keeping her in place. Silky strands of hair tickle my fingers. "We don't have time for games now, but I'll be happy to play later." Though I'll be the one helping her get this dress off.

Soulful jade eyes peer into mine. A heavy, worried look clung to them yesterday. Now ... I'm not sure what I'm seeing there.

"Better day today?" I whisper.

"I'm not sure yet. I'll let you know." Her gaze drops downward, to my mouth.

I can't hold back any longer. I lean in and kiss her, first tentatively, my lips grazing hers, the tip of my tongue tracing the seam of her mouth, tasting a hint of cherry from her lip gloss. But the second she responds, I deepen it, sliding my tongue against hers in a slow-moving, intimate dance. Screw Henry's dinner party and my obligations; I could stand here all night, doing *this*.

A dull thud sounds, breaking us apart.

Her throat bobs with a hard swallow. "That was my purse."

"I'll get it." I stoop down to collect the woven box

before she can flinch a muscle, stalling on a sublime view of the sexy slit in her dress. It's high—higher than I realized, reaching almost to her hip. It would take no effort to lean in and bury my face between her thighs right here.

Fuck me. I've changed, but not that much. This is going to be too tempting to ignore.

Her breathing is a touch ragged when I get to my feet and slide the purse strap over her shoulder.

"I really like this dress."

"Good." She clears her throat. "It's staying on me tonight."

"As it should." I can easily work my way under it.

Her eyes narrow a touch, like she doesn't believe me. "Right. Well ... we better go. Ralph's almost out of carrots."

"I have more if needed." I slip my arm around her back as we walk to the car.

This feels right.

This feels good.

Henry Wolf is not fucking this up for me.

8. Sloane

Ronan pulls his sleek car into a spot in the shade outside the hotel. "You good?"

"Debatable." I'm about to lose the battle I've been fighting with my nerves all afternoon since I retrieved this dress from its garment bag. "How is this going to play out? What name are we going with? Ann or Sarah, or ..."

He cuts the engine. "You're into role-playing? Is that your bag?"

"No, but it's probably better if you don't introduce me as, you know, the 'crazy rooster commune lady.'" I air quote that ridiculous nickname. "Sloane is unique, but there are a million Sarahs. Or Avas. I've always loved that name. Or ..."

He slides out of the driver's seat without answering.

I'm careful with the hem of my dress as I climb out of my side, ever aware of the revealing slit that Ronan's focus snagged on earlier. I could feel his hot breath on my skin as he was crouching to collect my purse. It was nearly my undoing, and less than minute after I declared a no-sex night.

I am doomed with this man—absolutely zero control—a reality I am aware of but continue to deny like a fool.

A row of luxury cars lines up next to us. A Porsche 911, a Viper, another Porsche, a Jag. "Seriously, what kind of dinner is this?" I ask.

Ronan rounds his bumper. "Mostly friends. It's supposed to be casual. Whatever that means with these people."

"*These people?*" I guess they're not Ronan's people. Where did he come from, besides Indianapolis?

"Yeah, rich-from-birth elite, trust fund brats. Except for Abbi. And as far as introducing you as anyone other than who you are, there's no point. Henry will recognize you."

I frown. "How? We've never met."

He shakes his head, his laugh derisive. "Never assume he doesn't know everything about everyone in the room."

"That's creepy."

"It sounded worse than it is. I just mean he has an investigator on retainer."

"An investigator? Henry Wolf had me investigated?" I don't know why that's shocking.

Ronan exhales heavily. "This is not going well."

"No, it's really not."

"Listen." He steps forward and settles his hands on my biceps, his thumbs gently stroking my skin. It's a gesture that's likely meant to soothe but instead stirs my pulse. "He had his people do some digging, given your, how should I call it—" His plump lips twist with a hint of amusement. "—passionate opposition to the hotel. He knows what you look like, which is why he didn't want me anywhere near you." His eyes scan my face. "He knew I wouldn't be able to resist you."

"What does it matter, though, if we're together? The hotel is built. The damage is done." Why did it matter in the first place?

"It doesn't. If he doesn't like it, fuck him. Anyway, I told Abbi about us, and she really wants to meet you."

Hearing Ronan say the word *us* makes a flutter stir in my chest and pushes aside any little red flags that I sense waving in my subconscious.

But I still have doubts. "So, you're not worried about Henry firing you anymore."

"Nah, he's all talk. And if I'm wrong, oh well. It's just a job. I can find another one."

"Another one like *this* one?" I have no idea what he did to get his position here, but it can't be a dime-a-dozen role. He's staying in a beach mansion, dressed in pricey clothes, and driving a sports car. If he isn't one of "these people," it means this job is spoiling him. "Are you always this reckless about important things in your life?"

Ronan collects my chin between his thumb and his index finger. "No, I just have my priorities straight and will never choose a fucking hotel—or *any* job—over important people." His gaze is penetrating as he leans in to kiss me softly on the lips. "Ready?" he whispers when he pulls away.

I nod, because I can't seem to find words.

I am pregnant with this man's baby. This irresponsible, possibly brainless, most likely soon-to-be unemployed manwhore.

And I think I'm swooning.

"There's one familiar face for you." Ronan juts his chin toward the concierge desk, where a broad-shouldered blond man leans over the counter, chatting with the woman standing behind it.

"Huh. I barely recognize him without his board shorts." Connor is transformed by upscale dress clothes that hug his muscular body in all the right places. He looks good. If I didn't know what a buffoon he is, he'd earn more than a second's glance from me.

"Yeah, he's a brute, but he can clean up. Con!" he calls out.

Connor peers over his shoulder at us, his blue eyes snagging on my plunging neckline for a few beats. With a pat against the desk and a wink for the woman, he strolls toward us, a slight limp to his step. "Ahoy, Captain," Connor says by way of greeting.

I'm about to respond with a simple hello, but then he envelops me in his beefy arms until I'm smothered against his chest with my arms pinned between us and inhaling a potent citrus-and-leather cologne.

This is a completely inappropriate and ridiculous greeting—I barely know the guy, and he's acting like we're long-lost pals—and yet I find myself laughing as I endure.

"Fuck, you smell good, Cap." Connor inhales.

"Okay. You can let her breathe now," Ronan chides.

I press my hand against his hard middle, and he eases up on his death grip, allowing me to break free. "How's the knee?"

"A little sore after being on it all day." He bends his leg as if in proof. "Nothing like poor Katie, though. She's gonna be on crutches for a bit. They should be landing in Miami right about now," he adds, checking his watch. "Good thing Kyle's with them to help with the luggage. Why she packed all that shit for three days is beyond me. She was in a bikini the entire time anyway."

Connor might be an ignorant meatball, as Ryan put it, but he's a meatball who cares for his friends. "Yeah, I heard. I called Ryan earlier to check in."

"You did?" Ronan's eyebrows arch with surprise.

"Of course. It was the right thing to do." Even if Katie wasn't the reason I did it.

"And what'd she tell you?"

"Basically what Connor just said. Plus, that she's writing the Sea Witch a glowing review."

The corner of Ronan's mouth twitches. "Anything else?"

"Why? What else could she have told me?" There's a playful challenge in my voice.

He shrugs. "Who knows? She's related to this bigmouth." He jerks his chin toward Connor. "I never know what's going to come out of his trap. Was she sober?"

I chuckle. "I don't think she'll be drinking again for a while."

"Oh, yeah." Connor grimaces as if remembering the

unfortunate turn of events on Sunday. "I made her clean that bathroom."

"She probably cleaned the whole house before they left anyway," Ronan throws in.

"I hope she folded those towels I left on the couch." Connor rubs a palm over his jaw. "Damn, I miss living with her."

I shake my head. "You guys live like frat boys, don't you?"

"Why don't you come over tonight and see for yourself?" Connor's gaze shines with a mixture of curiosity and something I can't identify.

I'd assume it was an innocent invitation if I didn't know what these two have gotten into in the past. Is he hoping Ronan will share me?

Would Ronan share me with his friend?

My stomach tightens with unease at that thought. "Maybe another time."

"Come on, you gotta. Wolf set us up with a killer pad. Four-story house right on the beach. Pool, rooftop patio. It's mint."

"He set *me* up," Ronan corrects. "You are a squatter."

"And I shall reap the benefits. Opal Reef?" Connor asks, backing away.

"Seraphina's first. Cocktails for sunset."

"Okay, then let's roll. I'm fucking famished." Connor pats his stomach and the washboard abs I know are hiding under there.

"You're always famished," Ronan says.

"You should be happy I'm so predictable." He aims for a lengthy hallway.

I smile at their easy banter. Maybe Connor's invitation was innocent and I'm imagining things. I shouldn't assume he's attracted to me, even though he's an incessant flirt and as smooth as butter on a hot day.

Cody joked a few times about inviting Rebel or Skye into our bed. I should have caught the red flags, but that's beside the point. My answer was always an abrupt no, followed by a fight. No, I wasn't willing to share him.

He never suggested bringing another man in—to share me. I can't even wrap my head around that.

How many of the women Ronan and Connor end up with have never considered the possibility until they find themselves facing these two? They're charming and easygoing, the vibe around them warm and inviting. Add in a few drinks, and how many would decline?

Would I, honestly?

A mental picture hits me then as my imagination takes off in sordid directions of where this night could end, and a furious flush heats my cheeks.

"You good?" Ronan settles a hand at the small of my bare back, the heat of his touch sending a warm shiver along my spine.

"Yeah. Great." Though I'm beginning to wish I were completely clueless about these two and their extracurricular activities.

We fall into step with Connor, me sandwiched between the two tall pillars of easy confidence as we stroll. I take in the arched ceilings with tropical plant leaves painted in murals over them, and the marble floors, and the stone water fountain that spouts water from a mermaid's mouth. The décor is rich and lush; every detail appears painstakingly considered. Even the air smells expensive—of Japanese cherry blossoms.

"Not bad, right?" Ronan asks as if reading my mind.

I shrug it off with an "It's all right." No way will I be caught dead admiring this place. I will admit to myself, though, I may have cursed every day of this build and prayed for spontaneous fires, termites, even a hurricane to tear it down, but as I walk along the corridor, it would be a luxurious hotel to stay in.

Up ahead, two female staff members tend to a lush living wall. When they note us coming, they pause their task to watch us approach with rapt interest. Or rather, watch the two men who bank my sides. I can't fault them for that. Ronan and Connor were both granted divine gifts in the physical department. They could grace magazines. Hell, Ronan basically did for the Wolf wedding.

Clearly, they appeal to the staff of the hotel. But do people around here know exactly how good of friends these two are?

"Hey, Con," the dirty blond calls out, pulling off her gloves to smooth a crease in her botanical green uniform.

"Lily." Connor flashes a million-watt smile in greeting as his pace slows a touch.

"You having people over this weekend?" she asks, toying with her ponytail.

The brunette pretends to be focused on a succulent while stealing frequent glances at Ronan.

It sounds like these girls have been to their house. They're both young and attractive. Did they all hook up? Am I going to be looking at *every* woman and wondering this?

"Nope. Sorry, got out-of-town guests," Ronan answers for him.

"Next week, for sure," Connor promises.

"We'll see." Ronan spears him with a warning glare.

Lily shrugs. "Okay, sounds good."

I get a cursory glance from both women then, just enough for them to assess my dress, my face, perhaps Ronan's outstretched arm and their level of competition, before they offer a chorus of "laters".

"Stop inviting women that work in my department home, man," Ronan scolds as soon as they're out of earshot. "You're gonna get me into shit with HR."

"Why? *You're* not fucking them."

But by his tone, it's clear that Connor is.

"I can't remember the brunette's name," he continues. "Mary? Marie? No ..." He pauses, scratching his chin in thought, before he suddenly snaps his fingers. "Marni. That's it. Damn, she was something. She does this thing with her tongue—"

"*Dude.*"

"What, I can't even talk about it now?" Connor scoffs. "Just 'cause you're the big kahuna around here, the top dog, the grand pooh-bah—"

"Shut up," Ronan mutters.

Connor leans in to mock whisper, "He used to be *way* more fun."

"I can only imagine." But the ill feeling that started to build in my stomach has vanished instantly.

"You know, he got kicked out of a bar in Miami once for getting a blow job in the middle of—oof!" His words cut off as Ronan's hand leaves my back to reach around and shove him.

My mouth gapes.

That seems to egg Connor on. "And you wouldn't believe what he ordered me to do tonight. His boss, Belinda, needs—"

"I swear to *fucking God*, Con," Ronan warns with a growl.

They exchange looks, and a silent conversation seems to pass over my head—literally and figuratively.

With a devilish grin, Connor finally quiets.

"So, what's on the menu for tonight?" I ask, steering the conversation away from Connor's needling and stories of Ronan's past sexcapades.

"No clue. I was told I have to be here, so I'm here. I'm sure it'll be good, though." Ronan's fingers trace a circle on my back before his palm settles there again.

I stifle my sigh of contentment.

"Fuck, I hope it's not like that weird shit they had at the wedding," Connor complains. "What was it called again? Those flying fish eggs."

Ronan chuckles. "Tobiko."

"They had that weird crunchy popping texture." Connor's face morphs with disgust. "I'll try anything once, but, man, I'd rather drink a glass full of cum than ever put those in my mouth again."

I grimace.

"Yeah, see?" He points at my face. "That's me, but with tobiko."

"Did I say he cleans up well?" Ronan shakes his head at his friend as we swing right and out of a set of doors

"Wow." It slips out from my lips unbidden.

"Right?" Ronan nods in agreement as we take in the hotel's outdoor bar that overlooks the beach and the gulf waters. I've seen it from the other side, while walking along the shoreline, but the vista from this angle is decadent.

The color scheme is sand and gold, which only amplifies the idyllic view of the fiery sunset descending into the water horizon. Palm trees sway above while an expanse of stonework allows for various levels, maximizing the opportunity for a good view. Front and center is a square bar with a roof above and seating all around to accommodate at least two dozen patrons.

Twenty or so well-dressed people mill around, chattering in small groups, while a server in a blush-colored uniform weaves around with a platter. I see what Ronan means now, about my dress matching the hotel's color scheme. Not quite, but close.

"Sliders. Now, that's what I'm talking about." Connor charges away, leaving Ronan and me alone.

"He seems very food motivated," I note as we watch him carve a path through people.

"Yeah, I had a golden retriever just like him when I was a kid. His name was Pickles. You couldn't trust him with food on the counter, and he humped a lot of legs." Ronan shifts his stance to face me. "You seem on edge tonight."

"Do I?" I shouldn't be surprised. I have a lot going on —this surprise pregnancy, crashing my archenemy's dinner party, dating a guy who enjoys casual threesomes with his best friend. "Wouldn't you be if you were about to meet Henry Wolf for the first time?"

He studies me for a few beats. "You sure that's all it is?" Ronan is too perceptive, far more than I expected. But I should have. I've had him pegged all wrong since the moment he stepped into the Sea Witch.

I decide to flip it around. "Why? What do you think I'm on edge about?"

He steps in closer, his fingertips toying with the gauzy material in my dress. "Does Connor make you uncomfortable?"

"No." The truth is he doesn't, despite his boisterous personality and invasion of personal space. There is something oddly comfortable about being around them.

"Is it because of what I told you about Connor yesterday?"

"You mean your penchant for threesomes?" No point being vague.

A hint of a smile curves his lips. "I don't know if I'd call it a penchant."

"What would you call it, then?"

"More like a drunken 'sure, fuck it, why not' situation."

"Funny, my drunken 'sure, fuck it, why not' situations usually involve ordering extra meat on my pizza."

"Doesn't sound too different." Ronan smirks.

"Oh my God." My face flushes as we both share a laugh at the double entendre I didn't intend.

But I can't let it go yet. "And how often do you find yourself in that sort of situation?" Because I need to know what I'm getting myself into, if I'm setting myself up for a guy who's not ready to give up that lifestyle.

His humor slides off as a somberness takes over. "Over a year now. Since Abbi and Henry's wedding."

"At a *wedding*? I mean, how'd it happen?" How do these two friends end up in these compromising positions?

"You want details?" he asks skeptically.

"I don't know," I giggle nervously. "Maybe?" Is it curiosity about this man or a need to prepare for pitfalls, because I'm quickly seeing how a few drinks around them could lead to all kinds of unexpected things.

Ronan falters. "I don't share specifics. It feels wrong."

"Oh, right. Of course." Ryan did warn that Ronan doesn't kiss and tell. Still, an unexpected wave of disappointment washes over me that he won't be open with me.

Ronan cocks his head as he studies me for a few beats. "But you're the type that needs to know, aren't you?"

I swallow. "Yeah, I think I am."

He pauses, his lips pursed. "It wasn't a—"

"Hello, hello! Fancy meeting you here," a familiar voice cuts in.

I spin on my heels and find Jeremy in a peach-colored button-down and beige dress pants, holding a tray of champagne flutes.

"Hey!" My smile is genuine, even if his timing is lousy.

Jeremy nods at Ronan. "Sir, good to see you again."

"Oh fuck, don't 'sir' me, man. Seriously."

Jeremy chuckles. "Okay, got it."

"You're working here tonight?" I ask. Obviously, but it's a Tuesday. The deal Ronan negotiated was weekends only.

Jeremy shrugs. "They needed an extra body last-minute, and I was finished my cruise shift. Missed you out on the water again today."

"Yeah, I had some appointments and other things. I'll be back tomorrow."

"Good. Don't expect a great review for *Tiki One* today." Jeremy widens his eyes with meaning. "I thought Frank was going to toss one of the guys over the rail."

I groan. "Can't wait to hear that story." Though as bad as it is for business, it's always entertaining hearing Frank's version of events.

Jeremy holds out his tray. "I know this isn't Sapporo, but—"

"Yes, please." I don't let him finish before I snatch a glass and take a sizeable gulp.

Only when my mouth is full of champagne do I remember that I can't drink it. At least, not until I make a decision.

Panic erupts inside me, and I do the only thing I can think of—I spit the champagne back into my glass.

Jeremy and Ronan wear matching frowns.

"It's gone bad," I croak, the only excuse I can come up with for my unladylike action, and a terrible one at that.

"Really?" Jeremy lifts a glass, sniffs it, then samples it. "Tastes good to me. More than good. It's Cristal."

"Uh, yeah, I guess I'm not a champagne kind of girl," I lie, setting my glass down on a nearby table. Dammit, when will I ever get a chance to drink Cristal again? And how am I going to get through tonight, let alone the next nine months, without a single drink?

"No worries, I'll get you your beer," Jeremy says.

"No!"

"Uh ... okay?" His gaze narrows with an unspoken question

I adjust my tone. "A tall glass of water for now would be great. My head's been hurting on and off all day."

"You got it. Comin' right up." Jeremy strolls away, pausing to hand out champagne to a couple in his path.

If Ronan thinks anything of my odd behavior, he doesn't let on, too busy surveying the crowd.

"He's not here, is he?" I looked for Henry Wolf but couldn't spot him. I've seen a thousand pictures of the man's face, but maybe he's photoshopped and less handsome in real life.

"Not yet. Come on, let's do the rounds." His hand slides into mine as if that's where it belongs, as if that's where it's always been, and he guides me to where Connor is, chatting up two men who look familiar.

"Brisket and cantaloupe," Connor says by way of greeting, holding up a half-eaten slider. In his other hand is a tall pint of beer. "Who woulda thought."

"Strange combo," Ronan agrees.

"Whatever. Like I said, I'll try anything once." Connor winks at me, his words laced with innuendo. "Guys, this is Sloane, but we call her Cap. Sloane, this is Merrick and Preston."

"They were groomsmen at Henry's wedding," Ronan elaborates, shaking each one's hand in greeting.

The wedding. Of course. It's hard to forget faces like these. It makes sense that they'd be Henry Wolf's friends. They're dripping money.

"So, 'Cap.' That's got to be a story," the raven-haired man on the left says, his British accent posh-sounding.

"Not really. I run a small tiki cruise company, and I sometimes play captain."

"Captain of a tiki cruise." A condescending glint sparkles in his eye as he says the words *tiki cruise*. "I think the term *skipper* would be more appropriate?"

"I don't give a fuck what you stuffy bastards think. She's 'Cap' to me, and that was one fun ride." Connor gives my bare shoulder a friendly squeeze before he's distracted by a passing platter of mushroom tartlets, and he's gone chasing food again.

"It was a great day." Ronan's warm palm caresses my back again.

"You guys are certainly selling it." Preston notes the affectionate move. "Maybe I'll charter one of these cruises while I'm here." His hazel eyes drift over my dress, stalling on my neckline before lifting again. "Get the full tour."

Surprise, surprise. I don't think I like Henry Wolf's friend Preston much at all. And he clearly knows Ronan and Connor well enough to assume this "fun ride" comes with more than just a trip to Starfish Island.

I plaster on a wide, fake smile. "Just let me know and I'll make sure Frank treats you right."

Beside me, Ronan chuckles.

"I think she just called you a pompous prick." The guy with cropped, dark ash-blond hair on the right—Merrick—murmurs.

"Well, it wouldn't be the first time a woman has called me that." Preston sips an amber-colored drink, seemingly unbothered as he scans the white walls and balconies behind us. "The bastard really outdid himself with this one."

"Makes me wish I could move the Empire near the ocean," Merrick agrees. His words are wistful, and yet his features are stony, unyielding.

"The Empire?" I ask curiously.

Crystal blue eyes slide back to me. There's something heavy and dark in them. "My hotel in Vegas." He says it so nonchalantly.

"Right. Of course. And where is *your* hotel?" I ask Preston.

He grins. "I don't own hotels. I just make people enough money so they can fund them."

"Don't let their soft, manicured hands fool you. These two have worked hard for everything they have," Ronan quips, his tone laced with sarcasm.

"We can't all curry favor with Wolf's wife for our good fortunes." Preston smirks, the twinkle in his eye a challenge, like he has a secret he's not sharing.

Ronan sips his champagne. If the taunt bothers him, he's good at hiding it.

"Are you local to Mermaid Beach, Sloane?" Merrick asks as Ronan draws circles over my back with a teasing fingertip. His hands aren't soft or manicured. They're toughened by calluses, the scratchiness delicious against my skin. I hadn't really noticed when they were all over me before, but I'm acutely aware now.

I clear my throat, temporarily distracted. "Born and raised." No need to mention where, in case they've heard about the crazy neighbor.

"And what do you think of this new hotel?"

"It's ..." I search for a word that doesn't force me to lie and settle on "something."

Merrick's stony face cracks then, revealing a beautiful smile. "You're not a fan."

"She hates it." Preston laughs through another sip before waving down a waiter to get a refill. "Do me a favor and allow us to be there when you share your opinions with Wolf. We like watching his enormously inflated ego get knocked down a peg or four."

Ronan snorts

Clearly, they haven't connected the dots.

"I wonder what he would say if we told him that he's missed the mark on this one," Preston continues.

"You're angling for a throat punch tonight?" Merrick asks. "Because he thinks this is the pinnacle. More than Alaska."

"Nothing is more precious to him than Alaska," Preston counters.

While they argue about which luxury hotel is Henry Wolf's favorite, my attention wanders, first to Ronan to gauge his opinion as he watches their chatter—does he like these guys?—then around Seraphina's.

A blond woman with sharp features and red lipstick

stands in a small group ten feet away, staring at me, her face hard with displeasure.

Who could that be? It's not Abbi, I know that much.

"Oh, hey, here you go." Jeremy swoops in then with a tall, stemmed glass filled with ice and strawberry slices floating in a pink-tinged concoction. A pale pink rose floats on top.

"What is this?" I ask warily.

"Just something I whipped up that I thought you'd like." He leans in to whisper, "No booze, I promise. I'll keep 'em coming all night." With a wink, he peels away and continues on with his tray of drinks.

My stomach drops as his meaning sinks in. Shit. Jeremy figured out that I'm pregnant. How the hell did he put two and two together so quickly? I knew he was smart, but he's a guy.

"That looks good," Ronan says.

I hum through a sip, stealing a glance to see him watching my mouth with interest. Nothing about his demeanor says he has any clue what's really going on here. Thank God. I'm not ready to ruin this thing between us yet. "Is it just me, or is that blond woman at my two o'clock trying to murder me with her eyes?"

With a casual sip of his drink, Ronan follows my direction. The quiet "fuck" that slips from his lips is delayed, but it's clear. "It's not you she has it out for. Not yet, anyway."

Connor swings back around then, carrying a crostini in his hand. "Here, try this, Cap," he says through a mouthful.

"I'm not really hung—" My words are cut off as he thrusts the appetizer into my mouth.

"What the fuck?" Ronan scowls at him as I struggle to chew, my taste buds identifying the potent flavors. Peach, ricotta cheese, lemon, and ... balsamic vinegar?

"But it's delicious!" Connor argues.

"I don't care. Don't shove shit into her face!" Ronan adjusts his stance as he squares off against his best friend.

"Relax, man." Connor wears a *what the fuck is wrong with you?* expression.

Preston tsks as the tension mounts. "Huh. Well, isn't this cute? Someone finally doesn't want to share—"

"Shut the fuck up," Ronan warns without peeling his eyes from his best friend. "I think Belinda's looking for you."

Connor gives his friend another long, hard look before nodding. "Yeah, boss. On it." And he's gone again.

Ronan watches me wash down the appetizer with a gulp of my drink. "Sorry, he shouldn't have done that."

"It's fine." It didn't upset me as much as it obviously did Ronan. "And he wasn't wrong. It was delicious," I admit.

"Yeah?" He reaches up to slide the soft pad of his thumb over the corner of my bottom lip. When he pulls away, I see the smear of white cheese I missed. "You want more?"

"No." If not for the anticipation of meeting Henry Wolf and the intimidating woman sizing me up, I'd hunt down the platter myself.

Ronan does another skim around the patio before

downing his champagne in one gulp. "Let's get out of here."

"But we just got here."

"We'll be back in time for dinner. Come on." He slips his hand through mine and nods toward the beach.

I hold up the glass in my other hand. "What about—"

"Bring it." He leads me away, Preston and Merrick chuckling.

9. Ronan

I didn't realize how much tension I've been carrying around until now, but the farther we get from the hotel and all those people, the better I feel.

Fuck, why did I blow up on Connor like that? He was just being himself.

Sloane walks quietly beside me, picking out the strawberry slices from the fancy water Jeremy made her and slipping them into her mouth. He couldn't just fill a glass with ice. He had to make it a fucking art piece. Clearly, he's in love with her. I'll bet all her staff is. Probably Frank too.

Shit, I'm jealous. That's what this is. The only other time I've experienced this is with Henry, because he has what I want. What I want*ed*.

But now, it's Sloane, and I'm in competition with every other male out there. I'm not used to this—to feeling like the woman I'm with is undecided about whether she even likes me as a person. And then I had to go and lose it on my best friend like a douchebag.

On impulse, I reach out to graze her fingertips with mine.

I get a coy smile in return.

Okay, that's a good sign. I entwine my hand in hers.

"So ... Preston and Merrick." Her bare feet sink into the soft white sand. We kicked off our shoes and left them next to the stairs from the hotel to walk along the beach.

"What about them?" What does she think about guys like that? Because all I ever see are women throwing themselves at these rich bastards.

"They're Henry Wolf's friends, but not yours."

"No. I mean, I got to know them because of the wedding, and I get along fine with them, but those guys are from a different planet."

"Yeah, I got that vibe."

"They grew up with summer houses and unlimited credit cards in their wallets. I grew up in a three-bedroom back split with a teacher and an electrician who didn't believe in paying an allowance for chores because I needed to be a contributing member of the family. I went to the community pool and mowed the neighbors' lawns for cash. I don't have their kind of money, and I never will."

Sloane's face softens. "I prefer that."

"Yeah? Why?"

Her pretty lips twist as she considers her answer, and all I want to do is kiss them. "Because you know what it's like to work for what you have."

I chuckle at the irony. "Honestly? I don't feel like I've earned anything that I have right now. I mean, that beach house? The car? These clothes?" I gesture at myself and then give her a meaningful look. "A month ago, I was picking up trash and popping beach umbrellas in Miami. I was a low-level grounds crew sort-of supervisor."

Her eyebrows arch with surprise.

"Exactly."

"Well ... You must have done something right to impress Henry Wolf. I don't know him, but he doesn't seem like the type to hire people who can't do their jobs."

Yeah, I went into a collapsed mine shaft to save his ass, and I've kept a lot of secrets. Hardly résumé builders for this role.

"Not growing up in their world is a positive. You understand the other side of life too. The everyday people side. There's value in that."

"I guess."

She's quiet for a moment, and I take that opportunity to stroke the meaty part of her thumb with the soft pad of mine.

"Are you parents still alive?" she asks suddenly.

"My parents? Yeah. They're getting ready to retire. My sister still lives with them, but she'll probably be moving out soon." Which reminds me, I need to get her exact flight details so I can pick her up from the airport on Thursday.

From the corner of my eye, I sense Sloane studying me as we walk. What I would do to be able to read her mind right now.

Up ahead, the beach veers, and the jetty forms the harbor. The harbor that Henry wants to destroy. "I've never seen a beach like this anywhere else in the world."

"Have you traveled to a lot of places?" she asks.

"A few. But I want to see more. You?"

She shakes her head. "I don't even have a passport."

"It's not hard to get one."

"Yeah, I know. I'm just …" She shrugs. "I don't know. Gigi was always happiest around here, and I guess I'm like her. I can't imagine a place I'd rather be in than the one I have."

Her words are a gut punch. Guilt about what I know —about what's about to happen to her paradise—coils around my neck like a noose.

Do I ruin the night and tell her?

"I'm supposed to go to Hawaii one of these years. Frank goes back to Oahu every now and then to visit his mother, Anela. That's how we know him. Anela used to babysit my mother when they lived there. She and Gigi kept in touch. A few years after my mom died, Frank showed up. He said he was tired of island life, but Gigi knew it was because Anela sent him here to help us. And he hasn't left since." She smiles wistfully.

"He sounds like someone you can count on." Who's probably in love with her.

"He is." She bites her bottom lip as her forehead wrinkles.

"You're doing it again."

"Hmm?"

"When you get that worried look and your forehead scrunches up." It's cute and sexy, but it's obvious she's not telling me something important, and I don't like that. Then again, who am I to complain, given I'm keeping life-altering details from her. "What's going on, Sloane?"

"Nothing." She smooths her expression. "You don't even know me well enough to know when I'm worried."

She's not wrong. Except … "I know certain things about you very well." Like the feel of her soft lips against mine and the way her entire body quivers when she orgasms.

Her cheeks flush. She peers over her shoulder at the hotel in the distance now. "We're almost at the harbor. Should we turn back?"

I check my watch and then the sun. It's descending, but we still have about forty minutes before we're expected in Opal Reef for dinner, if the schedule Eleanor sent out is accurate. "No, not yet." I'm beginning to worry that I didn't think this through. What if Henry drops the bomb on her tonight as a fuck-you to me for bringing her? He's a vindictive bastard, and I'm not ready for this thing between us to end.

She tucks a strand of hair behind her ear. "Okay. Well … what do you want to do?"

That's a loaded question. *You, Sloane. I want to do you, in every way imaginable.*

"I want you to myself for a little while longer," I say instead.

Her throat bobs with a hard swallow. "We have water in the hut. You thirsty? Because I could really use something cold."

I admire the sheen that coats her skin. It's still hot out. "Yes." Perfect. Let's go to the hut.

10. Sloane

"This might not have been the smartest plan." Ronan winces as he steps on the loose gravel. The parking lot is empty, blocked by the thick rope across the entrance to keep people from using us as a free lot after hours.

"Ow!" I hiss in pain as an especially sharp stone digs into my heel. Ronan said he wanted to be alone with me, and this place was the first thought I had, but I realized my error after we climbed the steps and remembered our shoeless feet. "Why don't we turn back? I can live without water for—ah!" I squeal as Ronan scoops me up into his arms and carries me toward the little teal-and-yellow Sea Witch hut.

"No, we both could use a cool-off." His assessing gaze drags over my exposed leg where my dress has fallen back at the slit, and that muscle in his jaw flexes. "Your Gigi built this herself?"

"Yeah. She did everything on her own that she could. Loves working with her hands." She was never afraid to bust out a saw or a hammer. Now, she occupies those same hands with knitting needles and paintbrushes. "She's pretty incredible."

"Sounds like it." He sets me down gently.

I punch in the code and push through, leading Ronan inside.

"Holy hell." He tugs at his collar as if to emphasize the heat. "You said we could *cool down* in here?"

"I probably should have warned you." I set the empty glass from the hotel on the counter and reach into the mini fridge to grab two waters.

"How do you not die in here?" He cracks his and chugs.

I roll the bottle across my neck as I admire the way his throat pulses with each swallow. "It's not so bad when the ticket window is open. Plus, these help." I turn on the oscillating fan, and it kicks on at the highest speed, fluttering loose pages lying on the desk where Skye left them. Next, I slap the switch on the wall, and the white AC box above comes to life with a death rattle and hum. In moments, a blast of cold air shoots out, hitting my shoulders. "Shut the door?"

Ronan does as instructed, sealing us into this cramped space under the dim single naked bulb above. "Some days, it works better than others, but if you sit up here—" I demonstrate by shimmying my butt onto the bar fridge. "—you get the air blowing right down on you." I lean back against the wall with a sigh.

He finishes his water and tosses the empty into the trash can. "You're hogging it."

"I am." And secretly praying he'll use the excuse to get close to me.

My wish is granted in the next moment as Ronan eases forward, his strong hands settling on my knees to part my thighs and fit his body close. My heart races in anticipation of those skilled fingers scaling my legs upward, under my dress and my panties.

But he doesn't make a move on me, closing his eyes and tilting his head.

God, is Ronan ever beautiful. I could watch him all day and night and never tire. The more time I spend with him, the more time I *want* to spend with him. That probably doesn't bode well for me. Jeremy took no time at all to deduce my secret, and Ronan's not a stupid guy. When he finally clues in …

Maybe he'll be okay with it.

I nearly laugh at myself. The guy is twenty-six and virtually a stranger. He may say he's looking for a relationship, but I highly doubt he's looking to skip a few steps and go right into swollen ankles and dirty diapers. I need to be realistic. All this excitement, anticipation, hope that I feel in this moment will likely evaporate in an instant.

But right now, in this moment, I beg for time to stand still. "So, you were about to tell me about your threesome on Henry and Abbi Wolf's wedding night before Jeremy interrupted."

Eyes still closed, he smirks. "Was I?"

"Yes. Now that we're alone, you may continue." Because I'm genuinely curious about how one finds themselves in bed with not only Ronan but Connor.

Well, I think I can figure out *how* one might end up with Connor. All a woman has to do is look at him and be breathing, and the invitation will appear.

"Here you are, talking about sex again. Don't you have anything else on your mind?" he teases.

"Honestly? When you're around, I'm not sure anymore." Is it because I've been starved for affection since Cody? Or is it just Ronan's appeal? I'm pretty sure it's the latter.

His eyelids crack open. "It wasn't technically a three-some because there were four of us."

My mouth makes an O-shape.

"Two hotel servers who were working the reception dinner that night. They brought us back to their cabin, and things just happened."

"How do you just sleep with two women in one night?"

"Well, let's see." His index finger skims my inner thigh, teasing me with soft back-and-forth strokes. "They were attractive, and they took off their clothes. I think you can piece the rest together."

I swallow against the odd sensation building deep inside me. We're talking about Ronan fucking random women while my body aches for him to touch me intimately. I'm equal parts fascinated and resentful. "So then you and Connor stripped and just dove in?"

He chuckles darkly. "Odd choice of words, but ... yeah. I guess."

My next question stalls on my tongue as Ronan's hand skates under the slit in my dress, his fingers brushing my lace panties, dangerously close to my center but not hitting the mark yet.

The AC's rattle drowns out my ragged breathing as we stare each other down, as if each is trying to read the other, to gauge the reaction to the line of questioning.

"So, did you and Connor, like, *swap* halfway through?" I swallow against my racing pulse.

"Something like that." Ronan's index finger slides under the seam to tease my sensitive flesh. His chest rises on a sharp inhale.

"How many times have you done something like that?" My voice trembles as I do my best to play nonchalant. Meanwhile, heat is rushing to my lower belly in spellbound expectation.

He opens his mouth but stalls on his answer. "Enough times that I know it's not what I want anymore."

"And what do you want now?" I think I know what he's implying but need to hear him say it.

"You. All day, every day." He leans in to capture my lips with his at the same time that his finger sinks deep inside me.

I moan as I seize his nape with one hand, the other settling on his jaw as my body bows into his intimate touch. Everything else around us—the hot, sweaty little box of a hut, the noisy AC, the tension from the hotel, the pregnancy—all falls away into oblivion as his tongue invades my mouth, sliding across mine in a dance that I never want to end. I'm truly addicted to this man, to every inch of him.

"Seriously, what is that scent?" He breaks free and

dips his head to press his face against my neck, inhaling dramatically. "Fuck, I can't get enough of it."

I tip my head back, giving him better access. "I don't know what it's called, but it was Gigi's. She swears it lures men in and casts a spell on them."

"I believe it." His thumb joins in below, drawing slow circles over my clit as he strokes in a skilled, unhurried rhythm.

If he keeps this up, I'll be sitting in wet lace all night long. "Wait." I wriggle my hips, working my panties down.

He frowns curiously. "You said no sex, right?"

"A girl can change her mind." Or rather, my body has changed it for me.

Heat blazes in his eyes as I hike my gauzy skirt up around my waist until the cool metal of the fridge presses against my bare skin and my lower half is exposed. "Don't get my dress dirty." It's already going to be creased.

"I'll try." He steps back and guides my panties the rest of the way off, setting them on the desk. But instead of unbuckling his pants, he drags the chair over and settles into it.

His intentions are clear the moment he guides my legs over his shoulders. "You know how long I've been thinking about making you come on my tongue?" His hot breath skates across my bare flesh, his gravelly voice stirring a hum deep inside me.

"Get on with it, then," I rasp, my body trembling as my nerves erupt over how exposed I am, even in the dim light.

Ronan leans forward.

I cry out at the first swipe against my core and spend the next few moments trying to process the reality that I'm sitting on the minifridge in the Sea Witch hut with Ronan's face buried between my thighs, the fine stubble from his jaw scratching against my sensitive flesh. It normally takes me months to trust any man before I can allow him here. But with Ronan, things are different. I feel safe.

"Do you enjoy doing that?" I ask after a moment.

He pauses and pulls away to look up at me with hooded eyes. "Do I enjoy eating your pussy?"

I swallow, his dirty words spiking my pulse. "Yes."

Holding my gaze, he seizes the backs of my thighs with strong hands, hiking my legs up until they're completely folded at the knees and spread wide. A billow of gauzy pink fabric bunches around me.

I grip the corners of the fridge beneath me to keep from sliding off—not that Ronan would ever allow me to fall.

"It's the best thing I've ever tasted in my entire life." He leans in and pushes his tongue into my center.

A breathless "oh my God" escapes me. I gasp as I feel it slide deep inside, and then he's devouring me, his lips and tongue teasing and swirling and stroking, while the firm grip on my thighs never relents. The fleeting thought of fingerprint bruises skitters through my mind but vanishes in the next moment when he releases one leg, freeing up his hand to thrust two fingers inside me.

"Watch," he demands softly.

A guttural moan crawls out of my lungs as I do as told, as he pumps mercilessly and my body responds shamelessly, his fingers slipping in and out without resistance. Have I ever been this wet for a man before? It won't take long for me to orgasm. In fact, it'll be a record. I can feel it building along my spine.

As enthralled as I am by this erotic spectacle, I struggle to keep focus, my head falling back as all my senses are consumed by Ronan. It's almost too much. He's almost too much.

I'm caught off guard a moment later when Ronan's slippery fingers slide out of me and glide farther back. "One day, when we have the time, I'm going to lick every fucking inch of this gorgeous, tight body," he promises, stalling at the puckered skin. "There won't be a part of you that I can't perfectly see every time I close my eyes. That I won't know how it feels." He gently prods, his meaning clear. "But right now, I need you to come. Can you do that for me?"

"Yes?" It comes out like a breathless question. Ronan sounds like he's in pain.

"Good girl." His mouth on me again, this time sucking on my clit while his fingers thrust at a new, punishing beat meant for one reason and one reason only.

I reach down, collecting a fistful of his hair as I roll my hips in tune with the rhythm, my body coiling tighter and tighter as I watch, vaguely aware of the pinkie finger that prods, invading a part of me that has never been touched by a man before. Cody tried, but I refused. With Ronan, though, it doesn't faze me. All I want to do is come for him.

And a moment later, I do.

In a wave of shudders and cries, my orgasm explodes

in the tiny Sea Witch hut, every muscle in my body tightening as he drags the euphoria out of me. My hips grind against his face without concern for anyone but myself and chasing this high for as long as I can.

When the moment finally fades and my body is nothing but a quivering, boneless rag, Ronan jumps to his feet. His fingers quickly work over the buttons of his dress shirt, stripping it off and tossing it to the desk in record time.

I watch with eagerness as he unfastens his pants, pushing them and his briefs down in a rush, and suddenly, his perfect, taut body is in front of me, his hard length looking ready to explode. He takes a step closer, stroking it once ... twice... before angling the swollen head toward my center.

"Fuck me," he mutters, stalling.

"I'd really like to."

He chuckles as he fumbles for his pants pockets, pulling out his wallet. "I almost forgot. Again. Give me a sec."

A condom. That's what he's going for. "What's the point?" I say the thought out loud carelessly.

His hand pauses, a tiny frown flickering across his brow. "What do you mean?"

Shit. My panic stirs. "We've already done it without."

"Right." He studies the condom in his palm and then me, sprawled out, waiting for him.

I swallow. "You haven't been with anyone since, have you?"

"No. You?"

I laugh at the idea as I reach out with my leg, hooking his hip with my heel to pull him into me.

But Ronan has other plans. With strong hands seizing under my thighs, he lifts me off the minifridge and switches spots, seating himself on top of the cool metal and pulling me onto his lap until I'm straddling him. "That's more like it." He leans back against the wall as the cold air washes over him, hardening his nipples and sparking gooseflesh.

"So you want me to do all the work, is that it?" I tease.

"There's no work, babe." His fingers work the small zipper at my back down. With a delicate, unhurried touch, he guides my dress up. I lift my arms up over my head to help, and in moments, it's lying neatly on the desk beside us.

His eyes are molten as they drag over my body, naked save for the gold chain adorning my neck. "There's no work, babe. Only fun."

I lift my body up, positioning myself. Our moans fill the cruise shack as I settle down, my body stretching deliciously as he sinks into me, inch by inch.

This isn't anything like last time, when we crashed into each other like two cars colliding. Now, our bodies rock against each other, slowly, rhythmically, like waves lapping at the shoreline, our gazes molten as they remain locked, my arms draped over his powerful shoulders, his hands resting at my waist.

"See? Does that feel like work?" he whispers when he's fully inside, his thumbs stroking my ribs.

"No." This feels like heaven, like I've died in this shack, as icy air skates across our bare flesh. I'll gladly never leave here, leave this moment between us. When it's only us and nothing else matters.

Ronan breaks our staring contest first, his gaze averting downward, over my naked body. His mouth follows as he pulls me closer, until his outstretched tongue can reach a pebbled nipple.

I sigh with delight as he begins teasing and sucking. "God, that mouth of yours."

"What about it?"

Wrapping my arms around his head, I pull him in closer. "I want it everywhere." Honestly, it could be on any—*any*—part of me, and I know I'll enjoy it.

He drags his teeth over my breast, sending shivers through my body as he releases it with a wet, popping sound. "And it will be, I promise." He moves to the other nipple.

I watch as his tongue laps at it, our bodies still moving in tandem, the hints of another orgasm beginning to taunt my core.

Molten eyes peer up to meet mine. "You are so fucking beautiful," he whispers.

I push a few wayward strands of hair off his forehead and then lean in to scrape my teeth across his earlobe and whisper, "You make me feel that way."

With a groan, he claims my lips with his, kissing me intently as his hips start moving with a faster, jerky rhythm. His grip on my nape tightens as he thrusts upward, his other hand nestling in between us to stroke and squeeze the bundle of nerves that'll make my body sing again.

I do my best to match his pace and effort, my arms

curled around his head, until my thighs burn and sweat coats my back. In a rush, my inner muscles clamp down on Ronan's cock with another orgasm.

"*Fuck*," he groans in a deep, raspy voice. His hands are like vise grips as he throbs inside me, unloading streams of his seed in pulsating waves that seem to go on forever.

At least he can't get me pregnant twice, I muse, as I remain draped over his firm, hard body, the air thick with the scent of sex.

"That was—" His breaths are ragged. "Incredible."

I hum in agreement, teasing his neck with the tip of my nose. Whatever concoction of scents makes up Ronan —mint, soap, clean masculinity—I wish I could bottle the scent, bring it home with me, pour it all over my sheets. Better yet, I should just bring Ronan home and make him roll around naked in my bed—

A phone cuts into the moment, the ringtone of dueling banjos.

Tension instantly cords in Ronan's limbs. "Shit. What time is it?"

11. Ronan

The sun has sunk into the gulf by the time Sloane and I are sliding on our shoes and climbing the steps at Seraphina's. Most everyone has gone inside, leaving only the staff and Connor, hunched over the bar with a pint of beer, in conversation with Jeremy, who laughs as he loads dirty glasses into a dish rack.

"Hey, man." I drop a hand on his shoulder, both in greeting and as a wordless apology for earlier. "Thanks for the call. We lost track of time."

"Yeah. No problem." He peers over his shoulder, first at me, then at Sloane, at her tousled hair that screams just fucked.

We might not be the only ones, given the smear of red lipstick on Connor's shirt collar. I do believe that is Belinda's shade. "Hey, Jer. Can I get a drink?" Sloane asks, setting her empty glass on the counter. She refused to leave it behind, joking that Henry Wolf would find a way to charge her with theft if he found out.

"Yeah, I got you. I'll come up with something good." Jeremy winks and abandons his cleaning task.

Her fingertips graze my forearm. "Where's the restroom? I'd like to freshen up?"

"Inside those doors and to the left." I nod toward the building. "I'll grab your drink and meet you there in a few."

With a secretive smile, she takes the steps up, her dress billowing with a slight breeze.

"You fucking owe me," Connor says into his glass.

"I don't know. Looks like you might owe me." I flick his stained collar. Connor's been itching to hook up with Belinda again forever. He talked about that day for months after.

"You kidding me?" The usual dumb grin on his face is absent. And does he have a fat lip?

My concern swells. "What happened?"

He chugs the rest of his beer. "She chose violence."

"Wait. So you two *didn't* fuck?"

"Oh, we did." He winces as he stands. "I wouldn't use your desk again without giving it a good wipe down."

I cringe. "What the—"

"For the lady." Jeremy slides a glass filled with a purple-tinged water and lavender sprigs poking out.

"Thanks, man." I collect the glass, and we peel away from the bar. "You used *my* office?"

"She insisted. I wasn't gonna say no."

If that isn't Belinda sending a message ...

"Is there any blood through my shirt?" He gives his back to me.

"*Blood*? No."

"I'm surprised." Connor limps as he climbs the stairs, and I can't tell if it's because of his knee or some new injury he earned doing my bidding. The idea of the latter leaves me feeling guilty. I snapped at the dude and then fed him to a lioness.

"She also grilled me about Sloane. Wanted to know her name, where you two met, if we've fucked her together. All the good stuff."

That much, I expected. I guess Henry didn't share his PI's pictures with her. "What'd you tell her?"

"I played dumb. Said I didn't know where you guys hooked up, and I just met her tonight. Threw out a bunch of names that start with S. Susy, Sally, Sandra ..."

His forgetfulness wouldn't be hard to buy. It's Connor, after all. He struggles to remember the names of women he's balls-deep in. "And then?"

"And then she broke my dick, man!" he whines. "Seriously, I don't know if it'll ever work right again."

I chuckle. "I'm sure it's gonna work fine. Test it out on someone else if you're really worried."

"I saw Margo come in."

"There you go. Tell her you have a problem you need her to fix." That woman is *always* game, and she has the hands of a master masseuse specializing in the male anatomy.

The corner of his mouth twitches, and then, finally, his broad grin returns.

That's more like it. "Sorry about earlier."

"No worries. I heard you loud and clear. This one's different, huh?"

"Yeah. She is." I don't know if that worries or excites me more. Now I have something to lose.

"Worth getting canned for?" He points toward Opal Reef's propped-open doors and the dozens of people in tailored, expensive clothing milling about. Some I recognize, like a svelte, willowy Margo in crimson red, her black hair longer than when I last saw her, reaching her shoulders in a shiny curtain. Her photographer boyfriend stands next to her as they laugh with Preston and his "date" for the evening—a brunette with filled lips and a blank, unimpressed expression. A stony-faced Merrick stands next to her and listens quietly, unamused.

Many others, I've never met, but I can guess they're either rich or influential or both. And looming at the center of it all, with his back to us, is the great and powerful Henry Wolf himself.

Is it worth losing this job for a chance at waking up next to someone I care about? "If it comes to that, absolutely."

Connor regards me intently for a moment. "Well, giddyup, then. This is going to be entertaining to watch."

The ladies' room door swings open, and Sloane strolls out, her flyaway hair tamed, her dress smoothed out as best she can. "Better?"

"Sure." I rake my gaze over her chest, searching for a glimpse of those perfect nipples I know are hiding beneath. "Though I liked you in the hut too." When she was naked and riding my dick.

Heat sparks in Sloane's eyes. She may call herself a vanilla lover, but I'll bet she's more risqué than she thinks, and I can't wait to test that theory out.

"The sex hair was hot. See you two on the other side." Connor hobbles away.

Sloane watches him with concern. "His limp is getting worse. Is he okay?"

"He will be." And I'm sure his encounter with Belinda will become another one of his legendary stories. I hand Sloane the lavender drink. "What is it, anyway?" Something on our menu, I guess? Though it doesn't look familiar.

"No idea." She sniffs it before taking a sip. "But it's what I needed."

"Our little walk was what *I* needed, so thank you."

"Yeah?" Reaching up, she finger-combs a few strands of my hair into place. "There. That's better."

"I can still taste you on my tongue."

A slight flush pinks her cheeks as if she's remembering the moment her fists clenched and her pelvis rolled against it. "That's what the beer is for."

"Nah. I like it. Repeat, later?"

Her mouth parts, and excitement sparks in her eyes. "Let's get through dinner first, okay?"

"Fair enough. Ready to meet your favorite guy?" All I want to do is take her back to her place and keep her there forever. Ideally, naked.

Her chest rises with a deep inhale. Hard to believe I had her trembling beneath me only twenty minutes ago for an entirely different reason. Now, she's full of trepidation. But she rolls her shoulder, and the simple act seems to steel her nerve. "Let's do this."

I slip an arm around her back to hook her waist—in

case there's any mistake that she's here with me—and lead her in.

Eleanor and her team have spared no effort in organizing tonight's "casual" dinner, rearranging candle-clad tables into two lengthy, wide rows, giving everyone a seat with a view of the aquatic tank. A woman plays the white grand piano in the corner, the soft, classical music serving as quiet background noise against the bursts of laughter and chatter.

My goal to find Abbi is momentarily forgotten as a mermaid glides effortlessly through the water, her pink-and-cream iridescent costume shimmering under the lights.

"They *do* actually look like mermaids." Sloane pauses to watch the performer with awe. "Honestly, I was thinking it'd be tacky, but her costume is art."

The costume might border on obscene for the prudish, hugging the performer's body like a second skin, leaving little to the imagination in some areas. "For what it cost, I should hope so." When I saw the byline in Lena's budget, I nearly choked.

"It's not just what she's wearing. The way she moves and the tail and ... *everything*."

The performer spins and twirls, a small line of bubbles escaping her nose as she moves gracefully.

"Where do they learn to swim like this?" Sloane asks.

"I told you. Mermaid school." I give the same answer as before, because I still don't fucking know.

"Oh, right, yes, *that* place." She cuts me a dry look, but it slips off just as fast. "You know, they have these kinds of aquatic shows in other places too. Did you hear about that one where a performer was attacked by a fish?"

"Uh, *no*, I did not hear about that."

"Yeah. Same idea as this. It was a few months ago. I can't remember where it was."

I eye the marine life with renewed wariness. "What kind of fish?"

"A big one? I hope that doesn't happen here."

"If it does, that's Lena's department." Add it to the list after chefs who maim themselves and housekeeping staff who fuck in the guest rooms.

Sloane takes in the room. "This is different than I expected."

"And what did you expect?"

"With some of the crazy headlines I've seen about him and his friends? I don't know. Strobe lights and EDM? Whips and chains? A sex den?"

"That's not until later," I deadpan.

She falters. "You're joking, right?"

Not as much as you might think. And that's not a question I can answer without divulging secrets better taken to my grave.

A cobalt-blue dress catches my notice followed quickly by lengthy red hair. Abbi's in deep conversation with a server carrying a silver platter. Bonus, Henry is nowhere nearby.

"Come on." I lead Sloane over by the hand.

"... sushi's a big no-no." Abbi's hand smooths over her belly.

"Of course, that makes sense," the pretty blond server

with corkscrew curls says. "Let me ask the chef to put together a plate for you."

"Oh, no, you don't have to do that." Abbi waves her off.

"I insist, Mrs. Wolf. I'll be back in less than a minute." She ducks away, her mission imperative.

"Hey, Red," I call out.

Abbi spins around, her eyes flashing wide on Sloane before darting back to me. "Ronan! I was looking for you. I heard you took off."

"Just for a walk on the beach." I lean in to kiss her cheek, catching a whiff of her shampoo. It used to be my favorite scent, but Sloane's spell-casting perfume has officially assumed top spot. "This is her," I whisper.

"You were supposed to give me some warning," she hisses back in my ear.

By the time I've pulled away, Abbi has her smile firmly affixed. "*Hi*. You must be Sloane."

Beside me, Sloane stands frozen for a few beats before seeming to snap out of it. "Yes. Hi. It's nice to meet you." She hesitates, her gaze dropping to Abbi's belly. "I didn't realize you were expecting."

"Oh, yes." Abbi beams. "A few more months. I can't wait to meet her, but also to have my body back."

An unreadable look passes over Sloane's face. "Wow, that's ... congratulations."

"Thank you." Abbi's eyes flitter to me before she continues. "I've heard a lot about you."

Sloane winces. "Yeah ..."

"I mean, from Ronan," Abbi clarifies with a laugh. "I don't get involved in Henry's business stuff."

"Here you go, Ms. Wolf." The server is back as fast as promised, handing Abbi a small plate with delicacies from one hand before offering the platter balanced in her other hand to us. "Seared scallops?" A stack of napkins miraculously appears. The woman's an octopus.

"Is that tobiko?" I ask, eyeing the little orange balls.

"It is!"

I collect one. "Make sure you head over there to that blond guy." I point to where Connor is, next to Margo. "He *loves* tobiko."

Sloane presses her lips together as if to keep from laughing.

"Absolutely." With a beaming smile up at me, the server strolls away.

"The service here is unreal." Abbi sizes up the choices on her plate with delight.

"Have you been to the spa yet?" I ask before stuffing the scallop into my mouth. It's the first thing I've eaten since Abbi and I sprawled out in the cabana this morning, and I'm famished.

"Yes! They have a great prenatal massage and ..." Abbi's words trail a moment before my name is called by a deep, male voice.

12. Sloane

How did I forget that Abbi Wolf is pregnant? Now that I'm looking at her swollen belly, I do recall seeing a headline or two somewhere announcing the news, but it obviously slipped my mind. Now, it's thrown me off-balance from the word *hi*.

Henry Wolf spawning hasn't softened my hate-filled feelings toward him, but I feel an odd kinship to this woman as I eye her specially selected plate of food and wonder if I've eaten anything harmful tonight. Maybe I should have spent the day reading up on dos and don'ts of pregnancy instead of styling my hair and steaming my dress.

"Ronan." The cool, overly calm voice comes just as Ronan is stuffing a scallop into his mouth.

Somehow, I know who it belongs to.

My pulse thumps in my throat as we turn to face the imposing figure behind us.

Okay, so the magazine photos have not been airbrushed. Henry Wolf is as handsome and tall and commanding as he appears in print, and then some, as he looms over our huddled group like a brewing storm.

Ronan can't answer. His mouth is full, and he's chewing slowly. But he meets Henry Wolf's hard gaze with one of his own, and a wordless exchange seems to happen in that lengthy stare.

"They brought me a plate of food. All safe for the baby," Abbi interrupts the nonverbal showdown. "The service is fantastic. You should tell whoever's running this night."

Henry Wolf finally relents. "I'm glad to hear that." He's wearing a simple black dress shirt and tailored pants, and yet he somehow looks more elegant than the men in full suits.

"Have you met Sloane yet? Ronan's ... uh ... girlfriend?"

Dissecting, cold blue eyes land on me, and I fight the urge to shrink. There is no doubt he recognizes me from his PI's exposé. "Sloane Parker. Our renowned neighbor. No, I haven't had the pleasure." Grim humor dances across his face.

So this is what it feels like to stand face-to-face with the billionaire who has ruined my last five years of sleep.

Okay, let's dance. I steel my spine. "So great to *finally* meet you, Henry."

"I'll bet." He turns his attention back to Ronan. "I knew you had a set on you, but I didn't think they were this big."

Ronan smirks, squaring his shoulders as if preparing for a physical confrontation. "Guess you needed a different angle to see them." There's an edge to his voice as he delivers what seems like a taunt.

Henry's jaw clenches.

Meanwhile, next to me, Abbi's face flushes a bright red.

What on earth are they talking about?

"So, Sloane, what do you think of my new hotel?" Henry asks suddenly.

I hesitate, replaying my conversation with Gigi from earlier today. Peach pie or spittle, which do I choose? For Ronan's sake, I go with the former, because something tells me spitting in Henry Wolf's face during cocktail hour isn't how I want to be remembered.

But I will not lie, and I sure as shit am not kissing anyone's ass. "It's everything I imagined it would be." Right down to the arrogant owner.

Henry's hard expression cracks as he bursts out with laughter that sounds genuine.

Abbi and Ronan share a wary look. This must not be the expected reaction.

Even I can't keep confusion from skittering across my face.

Henry's mirth ends on a heavy sigh, just as clicking heels approach from behind.

"You seem to be enjoying yourselves." The blond who was staring me down earlier joins our little group, her voice a seductive purr. "Dinner is about to begin."

"Belinda, have you met Ronan's girlfriend?" Henry's smile is smug and loaded.

I resist the urge to deny the label. Belinda. This is the

general manager, Ronan's immediate boss, who was also not a fan of my art project or of me.

"I have not yet, no," she answers in a clipped tone, her eyes dragging over my dress in an assessing manner. "Ronan never mentioned a girlfriend, though Eleanor told me that he added an extra person last-minute."

"This is Sloane Parker. She lives next door to the hotel." Each word is enunciated in a calm, even tone.

"*Next door.*" She glares at Ronan. "Is this a joke?"

"No. I'm sure I mentioned her at our afternoon meeting today. You remember the one, right?" Ronan meets Belinda's gaze unflinchingly.

Clearly, something happened in this meeting because she looks like a keg of gunpowder about to erupt.

"*I* insisted that Ronan bring Sloane tonight so we could meet her," Abbi says in a rushed tone, reaching out to grab my free hand. "I can't wait to get to know someone so important to one of my closest friends. Right, hon?" She peers up at her husband with an innocent smile.

How does she fake that so well?

"Oh, yeah. I've been dying for this moment." There's the perfect blend of dryness and mocking in Henry's tone. "In fact, Belinda, can you please make sure Sloane and Ronan are seated next to me and Abbi?"

I stifle my groan.

Belinda's painted red lips purse. "But we've put—"

"Move them." The two words are delivered sharply and leave no opportunity for rebuttal.

She stiffens. "I'll see to it right now." With one last scathing glare for Ronan, Belinda storms away.

The pianist has wrapped up her performance, and servers in pressed uniforms are forming a line by the kitchen doors, signaling dinner. Guests take the hint, moving in to read the seating cards as ambient music comes to life over the restaurant speakers.

"After you, Abigail." Henry steps back and gestures toward the head of one table before leading his wife away.

"I guess that could have been worse," Ronan murmurs as soon as they're out of earshot.

"You were right. This dinner is going to be *so* much fun," I mock.

Ronan smooths his calloused hand over my bare shoulder. "Should we make a run for it?"

"No, it's too late. You made your bed, and now you're gonna lie in it."

"As long as you're there with me."

"Well, good news, then, because ..." I cast a hand dramatically toward the table, where Belinda is shuffling seating arrangement cards with a scowl.

Ronan steps closer, his hand cupping my nape. "The sooner Henry realizes you are in my life, the better." My breath hitches as he leans down to kiss me tenderly.

"Now, do I need to confiscate your butter knife or will you behave?" he whispers against my lips.

I'm caught in a haze, this growing pull toward him—both physical and emotional—beginning to overshadow everything else. "I make no promises."

His deep, dark chuckle invades my body. "That's my girl."

"WE HAVE PAIRED wines with each course this evening, as you can see on the menu cards set in front of you," the server who brought Abbi her plate earlier announces to our end of the table. "Each course has three options to choose from, and we will tailor your pour, unless you vehemently oppose."

Six more servers are spread out in sections to cater to smaller groups, and a small army waits behind us, each carrying wine bottles at the ready. In total, there must be close to forty people here for dinner tonight and almost as many staff.

"What is your name?" Henry asks calmly as he studies the card, never looking up.

"Umm ... Jacqueline. Or Jacquie's fine."

"When was the red snapper brought in?"

"This afternoon at about 3:00 p.m. Caught an hour before by Captain Dave," she answers without missing a beat.

Dave Rogers is known around here for guaranteeing the freshest day's catch and gets paid well for it.

"And the king crab?"

"Our shipment arrived early this morning." She holds her breath as she waits for his response. I imagine serving the owner of Wolf Hotels is nerve-racking at all times, but especially so when he's grilling you.

"My wife claims she had impeccable service from you earlier." Finally, Henry acknowledges the server with a glance. "Keep it up, Jacqueline." He uses her full name, just as he called Abbi by hers earlier.

Jacquie's eyes flitter to Abbi, who smiles up at her with encouragement. "If there's nothing else, I'll give you a few minutes to decide on your meals."

He waves a hand in a *that'll be all* gesture, and Jacquie scurries off.

Ronan and I exchange glances from across the double-wide table, an array of candles and florals a formidable barrier. Belinda separated us, seating Abbi and Henry at the very end as table heads—the king and queen. At least I'm closest to Abbi and not him. Ronan gets that honor.

On my other side is a man with a smooth Parisian accent who said a polite hello but has otherwise been caught up in conversation with Margo Lauren, the raven-haired supermodel seated next to Ronan. She's even more striking in person than the magazine covers she graces, if that's possible.

It would have been much kinder of Belinda to seat me and Ronan next to each other and pair these two up, but I don't think showing kindness was a part of the equation where she's concerned.

"How long do they swim for?" Abbi admires the aquatic tank, where a new mermaid skims through the water, this one in lavender-and-cream scales.

Henry abandons his menu card and leans back with his drink—scotch, if I had to guess. "I believe they change every twenty minutes. Is that accurate, Ronan?"

"My realm is the tank itself, not who or what swims in it," Ronan answers wryly. "Lena will have to answer that."

Henry briefly scans faces as if looking for this woman

named Lena before dismissing the topic. "Sloane, how is your grandmother doing?"

"She's good," I answer warily.

He takes a sip. "Ruby, right?"

"Yes."

"And it's been what, now? Two years since you put her in an assisted-living center and claimed her properties?"

My mouth gapes for a moment. "I didn't put her *anywhere* or claim *anything*." There's more bite in my tone than I intended, but he blindsided me with that jab. Plus, he's tossing around Gigi's name as if he personally knows her, as if he gives a shit what happens to her. I take a calming breath. "She registered herself at Palm Oaks, and she loves it there."

He hums. "I've never understood how anyone can enjoy living in one of those places."

I can't help myself. "It's quieter than the last few years at her home. No constant hammering and saws and drills all day long. But I'll be sure to let her know you asked about her." I mock frown. "Wait, did you two ever actually meet or are you just regurgitating what your creepy PI told you?"

Henry studies me a moment. "No, I don't believe we did, officially."

From my peripheral, I note Abbi chugging her water.

Jacquie returns then, ending a chance for me to toss another barb. "Okay, folks, have we decided?" She peers down at Abbi, prompting her to begin.

I steal a glance across the table at Ronan to find him studying me, the corner of his mouth curved upward. At least he's not annoyed by me antagonizing his boss.

"Well, I can't have the wagyu tartare or the smoked salmon. What about the blue cheese in the pear appetizer?" Abbi holds up the menu, pointing at the line. "Is that unpasteurized?"

"Very likely, yes, but we have an excellent vegan substitute that the chef has confirmed is safe for you."

Abbi's face lights up. "Yes, perfect. And then the salad, but can you substitute the goat cheese? Again, the unpasteurized thing." Her face squishes up like she's afraid to impose on people. As if her husband doesn't own this hotel and can literally demand everyone walk on their hands and sing for their suppers. "And the chicken in puff pastry and risotto is fine."

Jacqueline nods, mentally cataloguing everything like only the most exceptional fine-dining servers can manage. The next test is not mixing things up.

"And for you?" Jacqueline waits for me expectantly.

Fuck. How am I supposed to know about unpasteurized cheeses and smoked salmon. What the fuck even is wagyu tartare? How am I thirty-one years old and not aware of any of this? I guess because I've never been pregnant before. I still don't even know if I'm keeping it— a decision I have to make *very* soon.

"Oh, um, you know what? Everything Abbi ordered sounds great, so I'll just do the exact same." At least that way, I'll know I'm not eating something I shouldn't.

"The vegan substitute as well?"

"Yes. I try to avoid dairy as much as possible. Dietary

thing," I lie, thinking about the wheel of camembert waiting for me at home.

"Perfect." Jacqueline moves on to Henry and Ronan.

"That entree is going to be so good." Abbi adjusts her napkin on her lap. "The pastry chef here is incredible."

"Good because I'm hungry."

"Ronan and I ate a plate full of her pastries this morning, and they were to die for. Well, actually, *I* ate them." She giggles. "Ronan had maybe one bite."

Abbi Wolf is nothing like I imagined her to be. Sure, she looks like the photographs—polished and gorgeous, her hair a fiery red that you can pick out from across the room. But I expected a snooty, greater-than-thou woman, and she's warm and friendly and unpretentious, and she is putting in a genuine effort to tame her husband for me. Or perhaps it's for Ronan. That's more likely the case.

Either way, I hate to admit it, but I like her, despite her choice in husbands. I suppose I can't blame her. She married a disgustingly handsome billionaire who seems to dote on her.

The man to my left leans over then, throwing an arm across the back of my chair and invading my personal space as he says, "Abigail, I brought my camera. When will we take your photos?"

"Oh!" She bites her bottom lip in thought. "Maybe tomorrow morning if you have time? Henry will be golfing."

"No, Henry must be present," Henry says, referring to himself in third person.

Abbi scowls at him. "Relax. They're maternity pictures. With my giant belly hanging out."

"Joel, what will Abigail wear for this photo shoot?" he asks calmly.

"Uh, how do we say ... less is more?" Joel says with a grin. He's classically handsome, though there's a devilish gleam in his eye that I don't trust.

"Less is more." Henry's smile is superior as he regards his wife. "I'll be there for this photo shoot."

She opens her mouth to answer—or argue.

"This is not a negotiation."

With a heavy sigh laced with irritation, she asks, "And what time can you work me into your schedule?"

"Talk to Miles, but we will make something work." Henry leans in to whisper, but I'm within earshot to catch, "You are not taking off your clothes for another man unless I am there. You know the rules."

I immerse myself in my lavender water while pretending I didn't hear that last part. The rules? What does that mean? If Henry is there, his wife can strip for other men?

"Joel, have you met Sloane?" Abbi asks, gesturing to me. "She came with Ronan."

"Just a quick hello when we sat down. It is a pleasure to meet you, Sloane." My name in his accent is enchanting.

"Joel was our photographer at our wedding," Abbi explains. "And the pictures he took are out of this world. I still look at them all the time."

"I've seen them. I mean—" I stumble over my words, not wanting to come off sounding like a stalker. "—they were all over the internet."

"Ugh." Abbi rolls her eyes. "Yeah, the media would

not leave us alone for a while there. It's gotten better, though. They've moved on to their next target."

I know. I had endless material to pull from with those headlines while the paparazzi were in a feeding frenzy. And now I realize who I'm sitting next to—Joel the photographer, aka the pervert who takes intimate pictures of women mid-orgasm. My cheeks flush as I make the connection. Okay, maybe it's not so odd or controlling that Henry isn't keen on leaving his pregnant wife alone with *this guy*.

"It seems I have time in the morning for a shoot," Joel purrs in my ear. "What do you say?"

"Me?" I squeak.

"Oui. I am always looking for a model and this face ... This body..." His gaze dips down into my cleavage.

"Uh ... I don't know how to pose." That's the truth. I see all these girls in their bikinis at Starfish Beach, arching their backs, sucking in their cheeks, and all I can think of is how ridiculous they all look.

"It is no effort at all. Well, no effort for you. I do all the work." He winks.

Oh my God. Is he hitting on me?

I try to catch Ronan's attention, but he and Margo are deep in conversation. I wish I could hear what they're discussing, but the buzz of voices is too loud.

"Sorry, I'm working tomorrow. Maybe another time." As in never o'clock.

"For your first course." A male server appears over my shoulder, holding a bottle of white. Thankfully, it forces Joel out of my personal space. "A Chenin Blanc, its blend of fruit and nuttiness a perfect complement to the blue cheese and pear."

Before I can deny the offer, he's filling my wineglass.

"None for me, obviously." Abbi holds her manicured hand over the glass. Something I should have done.

"That's okay, we have a lovely nonalcoholic for you." Another server appears to fill her glass, smiling at her as he pours.

"Abigail, you will be coming to the grand opening of the chateau, oui?" Margo asks as a third server comes around to pour red wine into her glass, as well as Henry's and Ronan's.

"Probably not. The baby will only be a few months old." Abbi rests a hand on her belly. She touches it a lot, I've noticed. I guess that's a normal thing that all pregnant women do? Will I end up doing that?

"You must! It is my crowning achievement!" Margo drapes her arm over the back of Ronan's chair as she leans in. It's very intimate and personal. "Henry, I insist that Abigail comes. How can we open the Wolf Chateau without you both there?"

"We'll see how things go." Henry swirls the freshly poured red wine around in his glass. "But I promise I'll be there."

Her bottom lip curves downward in a pout.

"Margo and Henry are opening a boutique Wolf hotel in Margo's family castle in France," Abbi explains without me needing to ask. "The first of its kind for the hotel chain."

"That sounds exciting." Another friend of his opening a hotel.

The supermodel pauses to assess me. "You should visit too."

"Your boutique Wolf hotel in France." I can't help but laugh. These rich people have no concept of budgets and responsibilities. "Yeah. Maybe one day."

"Sloane isn't impressed by my luxury hotel chain," Henry says smoothly. "She much prefers the comfort of her colorful little mobile homes."

I grind my molars as I try to decipher what he means. Is that his sophisticated way of calling me trailer trash?

Abbi's frown his way says she's wondering the same.

Margo says something in French that I obviously don't understand, but it doesn't take a genius to understand it's about me, her eyes grazing over me while she speaks.

Henry's jaw clenches through a sip of his wine, and then he confidentially rattles something back, his French almost as smooth as hers.

They toss words back and forth.

"I hate it when they do this," Abbi mutters through a sip of her fake wine.

"Do they do this a lot?" It's beyond rude.

"Every time they're together."

I reach for my glass and then remember that I can't have any, so I veer for the last of my lavender water. If there was ever a night to inhale booze, tonight would have been it.

Margo asks another question in her native tongue.

"No," Ronan answers before Henry can and then flips into French, his tone calm but his face stony.

I blink in surprise. So Ronan speaks French. Another

thing I didn't know about the guy. There are *so many* things I don't know about him.

Margo reaches up to toy with the ends of Ronan's hair at his nape while she answers him. It's an intimate move.

My jealousy burns. Is she hitting on him, right in front of me? Or is this how they always are?

A darker thought enters my mind almost immediately.

Have Ronan and Margo slept together?

"Joel and Margo have been dating for years," Abbi says, as if reading my mind and gifting reassurances. It does little to ease my concern, though.

Ronan takes a lengthy sip of his wine, and then he says something back to her. After a beat, Margo slides her hand away from him. "It would please me greatly to see you at my chateau one day. Both of you." She caps that off with a coy smile for me, one that holds many secrets.

I think I hate Margo Lauren.

I *definitely* want her far away from Ronan.

The waitstaff files out of the kitchen then, their arms laden with the first course.

"I suppose now is as good a time as any." Henry taps his wineglass with his fork, the telltale dinging sounds drawing a hush as he stands. "Good evening, everyone. Abigail and I would like to thank you all for coming tonight to celebrate the new Mermaid Beach location. After five *very* long years with more than one hiccup along the way"—his gaze darts to me so quickly I doubt anyone notices—"we finally open the doors to patrons this weekend—"

"What are we if not patrons? The pig's arse?" Preston hollers, earning a round of laughs.

"If we don't have your credit card on file, you don't count," Henry throws back smoothly.

"But they *do* have yours, so cheers to that." The obnoxious Brit lifts his glass in a toast, and several others follow suit.

Henry smirks. "On that note, let's raise a glass to William Wolf."

Everyone reaches for their glass, forcing me to do the same or become the petty asshole refusing to toast a dead guy.

"He was the true visionary behind this place. He purchased this land decades ago with nothing more than anticipation. The only mistake he made was not getting his hands on more of it, back when it was easier to do so."

I roll my eyes—and hope Henry catches it—as I meet Ronan's stare.

He mouths "*What a prick.*"

"Now, everyone, eat, drink, and enjoy yourselves tonight on me because the next time you come, you'll be paying heavily."

A hum of laughter and voices fills the space, though I doubt he's joking.

I pretend to take a sip before setting the full glass down, just as a plate appears before me.

Oh well, like Gigi said, at least I'm getting a fancy meal out of this, at Henry Wolf's expense.

13. Ronan

Connor plows through the door into the restroom just as I'm buckling my belt. "Fuck, man, that meal was up there with their wedding." He's not limping as much, at least, but his bottom lip has turned a darker shade of purple.

"What'd you have?"

"King crab, baby." He unzips his pants in front of the urinal and unloads what must be several pints into the drain. "How's dinner with the big boss going?"

"Probably as good as dinner sitting across from our general manager." Given their earlier hookup, I would have expected Belinda to move Connor as far away from her as possible.

He tips his head back with a groan. "Dude, I didn't think it was possible for her to hate me more, but I'm pretty sure she does. If she could reach me under the table, I think she would have speared my nuts with those fucking heels of hers by now."

I chuckle as I wash my hands. "Nah, you're still useful to her."

"You mean my dick is." Connor finishes up and joins me at the sink. "So, how many times has Wolf fired you so far?"

"Hasn't yet, but I'm waiting for it." The guy likes to bide his time, feel in control. He's said almost nothing directly to me through dinner, though I'm sure the snide comments to Sloane were meant to antagonize me. It worked. I nearly snapped more than once.

But Sloane beat me to the punch every time, tossing back words coated in animosity but decorated with a smile. She does not shrink around Henry Wolf like everyone else seems to, and that is sexy as hell.

"And what's Margo up to?" Connor asks.

"Being Margo." I replay her lewd proposal at the dinner table, delivered in French so neither Sloane nor Abbi understood a word. "Let's just say she was really hoping we might join them later in their room. She wants to get to know Sloane better." She already knows me well enough after a night of debauchery for Abbi's birthday last year.

Connor's eyebrow arches. "And you said no?"

"That's not Sloane's thing." And having Joel—or any guy—around her is turning out to be not *my* thing. I joked about taking her butter knife away, but I nearly threw mine at that French fucker's forehead earlier when I caught his eyes down her dress.

Damn it, Belinda. She could have seated us together, but she had to be a bitch. That can be remedied, though. I'm going to go out there and swap seats for dessert. I should have done it three courses ago. I'm the idiot for that.

"Well, I'm definitely not saying no." Connor checks his hair in the mirror. The guy has had a perpetual hard-on for Margo for years. His dick stands up when he even hears her name, I swear to God.

"That's fine. Just don't be surprised when you look down and it's not Margo's lips around your cock." From what Abbi's hinted at, Joel might be a big fan of pussy, but he likes to get in on the action wherever he can.

"Huh? What do you mean—"

The door swings open then, and Henry walks in.

"And on that note, don't wait up for me." Connor strolls out, tossing a "great dinner" on his way past.

There's no need for me to linger either. I make my move for the door.

"Have you told her about my plans for Mermaid Beach yet?" Henry calls out.

His question stalls my feet. "If I had, do you think she would have sat through dinner?"

He unfastens his zipper. The sound of streaming urine fills the otherwise empty restroom. "Why not?"

"Because you told me not to."

"As if you give a shit what I want. I also told you to stay away from her, and you brought her here tonight, introducing her as your girlfriend."

"That was Abbi, not me." Not that I'm complaining. It has a nice ring to it.

"So why haven't you told her yet?" he presses.

I sigh heavily. "Because she'll be devastated. You're taking away her home, her business. Her life. And she'll probably end things with me because of my ties to this hotel."

"Yeah, you're right. She probably will. She seems like a spiteful person." He finishes up and moves to the sink to wash his hands. "So, what, tonight's just a 'fuck you' to me? To show me how much you don't care about my opinion?"

I chuckle, but there's no mirth in the sound. "Contrary to what you think, everything is not about you."

"For that woman out there, it is all about me. Everything to do with Mermaid Beach is about me." He lathers soap over his palms as he checks his reflection in the mirror. "You don't fight a dying battle for five years without some level of obsession."

He's not wrong. Sloane has been fueled by rage and hatred for far too long. I saw it in the beginning, when she found out I worked here and dismissed me in her next breath. "What's your point?"

"My point is you're an idiot for getting involved with her because it won't end well for you, but you knew that, didn't you? That's why you conned my wife into sitting in your corner for tonight. Don't worry, she didn't admit to anything, but I can see what's going on, what your cute little cabana time earlier was really about."

"You sound jealous."

"Of you? What would I have to be jealous of?" Henry dries his hands with one of the high-end paper towels. "Abigail is my wife, and regardless of whatever twisted little bond you two forged, she'll always choose me over you. You've known that, right from the start."

"No one's arguing that." It used to burn, that knowledge, the wish that it could be different.

"So then what's the point of all this? You brought Sloane here. What do you think's gonna happen next? That I'll abandon a multimillion-dollar plan to revitalize this area? For her? For you?"

That's the problem with Henry; he's too goddamn smart. One of *many* problems I have with him. "Mermaid Beach doesn't need revitalizing. It's perfect as it is."

"That's where you and I differ in our opinion. I see great potential, and given I'm the one with the fucking global hotel chain, I think I know what I'm talking about." His polished dress shoes scrape across the marble floor as he saunters toward me. "It's just business. It's not personal." A slow smile curves his lips. "Well, maybe a little personal."

Who's the spiteful one now?

"She's gonna fight this in court, and she'll drag it out for years. I'll make sure of it." I charge out, my body vibrating with rage.

He's right on my heels, his hand like a vise on my forearm to stall me. "And what do you think fighting again will do to her?"

"Nothing worse than what you're planning on doing to her life," I spit back, yanking my arm from his grip. "Imagine if some rich cocksucker showed up and forced you out of Wolf Cove."

He smirks. "That's impossible. I'm always the richest cocksucker around."

"Yeah, with the least amount of empathy, you callous prick."

His smugness evaporates as his teeth clench. He opens his mouth to respond, but a bald man strolls past, on his way to the bathroom. Lena's accountant husband, based on where he was seated during dinner.

It gives us a moment to calm down before we start shouting and cause a scene.

"My, they're getting along well," Henry murmurs.

Abbi and Sloane are huddled over their desserts, locked in a deep conversation, Abbi's hand clamped over Sloane's. While I've been assaulted by Margo's incessant sexual innuendos and Henry's silent glowers, those two have been chattering nonstop, Sloane peppering Abbi with questions about her pregnancy, Abbi getting all of Sloane's family history here in Mermaid Beach.

"Good." It's what I wanted to happen. Part of it, anyway.

Henry harrumphs, watching them. "She may have been a royal pain in my ass, but she is beautiful. I can work with that."

I frown. "What is that supposed to mean?"

He shrugs nonchalantly. "There's more than one way to get a woman to bend to your will, right? Maybe I should fuck the resistance out of her."

A flare of anger unfurls in my stomach, igniting the blood in my veins. Did I just hear that correctly? "You're toying with the idea of cheating on your pregnant wife, on *Abbi*, and fucking my woman?" Because with every passing minute I spend with Sloane, I'm more and more determined to make her mine.

"Cheating? No." Henry snorts. "Abbi would be there and participating. You know how she is."

"No." Those days are done and have been since the wedding. Abbi told me herself.

"You can be there too. It wouldn't be the first time you watched, right? Actually, if I recall, you owe me. How about this time, *I'll* come from behind—"

My knuckles make a sick cracking sound as my fist collides with his face.

14. Sloane

"What kind of vitamins do you take?" I ask casually as Jacquie sets our desserts in front of us. The dinner was hands down the best meal I've ever eaten, I hate to admit. I'm beyond stuffed, but I couldn't say no to the lemon tart.

"Oh, gosh, I can't remember the brand. They're basic prenatal vitamins. You can get them anywhere. Miles got them for me. That's Henry's assistant." Abbi leans back in her chair. "I didn't even have the blood work results back yet, and Henry sent him out to stock our cupboards with those and decaf coffee. That one, I nearly killed him for."

"You're not supposed to have coffee," I say out loud. That one, I knew, but I had forgotten.

"My doctor said one cup a day would be fine."

Shit. I drink three to four. I guess I need to stop doing that too.

"My husband can be so controlling sometimes, but he means well."

Until he's trying to buy you out of your home because he wants your land.

I steal a glance toward the restroom doors, where Henry just disappeared. Connor is strolling across the room, but Ronan is nowhere to be seen. "How much grief is Henry going to give Ronan for bringing me here tonight?"

"Probably a lot, but don't worry about it. Ronan has no trouble standing up to my husband. He's one of the few people who gets away with it."

"Why is that?"

"Because Ronan saved Henry's life, for one. There was this collapsed mine shaft in Alaska that Henry went into." She shudders.

"Oh, I read about that." It was all over the news. "That was Ronan who went in to get him?"

"And Connor. They found some other way. They were so crazy for doing it, but I can never thank them enough. Henry might not be here if they hadn't." Her lips purse. "They're close friends of mine, and Henry respects that."

"Fresh one for ya." Jeremy appears then with another rose-and-strawberry mocktail, along with a second that he sets in front of Abbi. "And I thought you might like one too."

"Oh, thank you." Abbi hesitates, frowning at the glass. "What is it?"

"Don't worry, Mrs. Wolf. No alcohol in that." He flashes a megawatt smile.

"This is Jeremy," I introduce. "He's one of my sea captains at the Sea Witch, who works here part-time now too. Actually, he's my only sea captain at the moment, unless I count Frank."

"Do not count Frank. We need to keep him far away from the tiki cruises. How are you feeling? Are you good? Do you need anything?" He peers down at me in earnest.

"All good."

"I got you, boss." With a squeeze against my shoulder and a wink, Jeremy swiftly disappears as quickly as he came.

Abbi is still frowning at our drinks.

"There's definitely no alcohol in them."

"Oh my God," she mumbles, and when she looks at me, there's awareness there. "You're pregnant, aren't you?"

"What?" It comes out in a squeak. She caught me off guard.

"You didn't drink any wine. Not even a sip during the toast. You brought it to your lips, but you didn't drink."

I falter on my excuse. "I'm not a wine drinker." She noticed that?

"And you ordered everything I've ordered, exactly how I've ordered it. And all these questions you've been asking, about what I can't eat, and vitamins, and doctor appointments."

"I was just making conversation." But even I hear how weak that sounds. My shoulders slump in defeat. "It was not planned. I found out yesterday, and I don't know what I'm doing yet."

"Does Ronan know?" Her eyes widen. "Wait, it *is* Ronan's, right?"

"Yes, of course!" A nervous laugh escapes me and,

with it, a bubble of tension. There's relief in not holding this secret so tightly. Except ... "He doesn't know yet. You can't tell him. *Please.*"

Abbi leans in, placing her hand over mine. "I won't say a word."

For some reason, I believe her, even if she doesn't owe me anything.

But given how quickly she and Jeremy figured it out, how long before Ronan does? Maybe that'd be a blessing. He'll stop calling and showing up and making me fall harder for him.

I sigh heavily. "What do you think he's going to say?"

"Honestly? I have no idea. This is huge."

"Life-altering."

"Yes." She nods in agreement. "And Ronan hasn't given off family man vibes. He certainly hasn't lived a life my mama would approve of. Then again, neither have I, by her standards," she mutters dryly.

"I have a good idea about Ronan's lifestyle. I mean, there's Connor." I give her a knowing look. "And I met Katie and Rachel on the weekend."

"Oh, yeah. Their history with Ronan is something. I've seen it up close and personal once. Unintentionally." She holds her hands up in surrender. "But from what I know, a lot of the things he and Connor used to get up to aren't happening anymore. Not with Ronan, anyway. He's looking for something more serious." She hesitates before smiling. "I know he's crazy about you. He told me this morning."

My chest swells with warmth. It's followed quickly

by panic. "Will he still feel that way after he finds out?" My voice is thick with doubt.

She pauses to consider that question. "The one thing I learned about Ronan is that people are always underestimating him. I used to too. Now? I consider him one of my very best, most loyal friends. If there's someone I can count on, besides my husband, of course, it's him. Every time, without fail."

"But if I decide to have it, I don't want him to feel trapped or forced. I want him to be in my life because he wants to be."

"Tell him that." She nods with encouragement.

I'm about to ask her how she thinks I should break the news when a commotion rises near the restrooms, where Henry holds a hand over his left eye.

Meanwhile, Ronan marches toward our table, fury etched in his stony face.

"I'm ready to go. You ready?" He rounds the table, ignoring the countless shocked looks from both guests and staff. Even the mermaid has paused her swim and floats mid-tank, watching.

"I guess?" I swap glances with Abbi, who looks as confused as I feel, her brow furrowed with worry as she watches her husband, who squints as he tests the corner of his eye with his finger.

Holy hell, Ronan punched Henry Wolf in the face.

"It was nice to meet you." I shoot one last pleading look for Abbi's silence before climbing out of my seat, my cheeks flushing from the gawkers.

Ronan leans in to press a kiss against Abbi's forehead. "Sorry, Red, but he deserved that one, I promise." His attention snags on the plate in front of me that I haven't touched. Grabbing it in one hand, he leads me past Henry, toward Opal Reef's doors.

Ronan slows long enough to toss a "Fuck you, Wolf" before he shoves the door open, grabbing and holding it so it doesn't swing back on me.

We're halfway down the hall before I say, "So you really like lemon tarts."

"What? Oh." He looks at the plate, then at me. "It's for you. I didn't want you to miss out."

"Right." I wait another beat and then dare ask, "What happened?"

But Ronan shakes his head, holding his right hand out in front of him to inspect his reddened knuckles.

"You hit him hard."

"I did."

"And he *really* deserved it?"

Ronan's teeth clench. "He *really* did."

"So ... I take it you're no longer a director for the Wolf?"

"The fuck if I know. Yeah, probably. Assaulting the boss is definitely grounds. Whatever. It's for the best. I wasn't cut out for this." But I sense no relief in his voice when he admits that. I think he liked his role, even if he claims he has no idea how to do it.

What does that mean, though, for Ronan staying in Mermaid Beach? Will he go back to Miami? To Indianapolis?

He can't leave.

Just the idea of Ronan gone ignites panic in me.

"I have an opening," I blurt, thinking out loud. "For a

tiki captain. Or, as Douchebag Preston insists, a skipper. I mean, it's nothing like your job now." Or his job up until five minutes ago.

Ronan's hard mask finally cracks. "I might have to take you up on that. I've got a lot to figure out. I'll need to return my car and find a new place to live." He reaches up to pinch the bridge of his nose. "Connor'll probably have to move out too. Fuck, he's gonna kill me."

"I have an empty trailer you guys could stay in." The one Dave and Ted were supposed to be in.

"A trailer next to the hotel." He chuckles. "Man, this is getting better by the minute."

"What? It's comfortable! I'm mildly offended."

"No, I'm sure it is. I didn't mean it like that, I swear." He leads me down a narrow hallway. It's a different direction than we came in, but it lets us out in the parking lot and to his car quickly.

Holding my door open for me to climb in, Ronan sets the dessert plate on my lap.

I admire his body as he rounds the car, his stride even and calm, despite his heavy mood.

The drive to my house is short but quiet, Ronan swerving to avoid an especially deep pothole.

"I need to get that filled." Frank raked the ground twice this year, but we need more gravel.

"Don't bother," Ronan mutters.

"What?" I frown. "Why not?"

He hesitates. "No reason. I don't know why I said that. My head's just not here."

The parking area is jammed tonight, with cars in

front of each trailer, plus Mick's pickup next to my Cherokee.

Ronan pulls up in the only spot on the other side. "What's going on here?"

"Just staff out by the fire pit. We do it every night." And it looks like everyone's here. "We can sit out there, if you want?"

He smooths his palms over the steering wheel. "I think I'm peopled out tonight."

Ronan might be peopled out, but I'm not ready to say good night to him yet. "We should get some ice on that." I nod toward the angry bruise on his knuckle.

He tests his hand by opening and closing it. "It'll be fine. I've had worse."

"You punch a lot of people?"

His mouth kicks up at the corner. "Only when they deserve it."

What could Henry possibly have said or done to earn Ronan's fist? Something tells me it has to do with me.

Shaking my head, I unfasten my belt. "Fine. Would you rather go and sulk at home alone or come inside and watch me eat this?"

His gaze shifts from my mouth to the tart and back to my mouth. With a crooked smirk, he opens his door and climbs out.

"Yeah, thought so." I slide out, wondering what dirty thoughts might have just flittered through his mind. That's fine. I can work with that.

I meet him at my porch steps as the faint notes of a twangy instrument carry in the quiet night.

"Is someone playing a ukulele?" he asks.

"Yeah. Frank."

Ronan's eyes pop. "King Kong plays the ukulele?"

I bark with laughter. "Yeah, he does. You want to go see?"

He pauses to consider that. "Maybe another time."

"No more peopling."

"Exactly."

I lead Ronan into my house, acutely aware of the tension still radiating from his rigid body. Faint music drifts out of the speakers. Skye or Rebel must have had it on while they were making dinner. Thankfully, the kitchen is spotless. They've already cleaned up.

Ronan wanders to the patio doors. "They do this *every* night?"

"During high season. Unless it's raining." I set the white china plate on the island, where Ronan and I sat that day, reviewing his hire list. It feels like so long ago now. "It's a tradition Gigi started decades ago and one of the best parts of the summer. When we're fully staffed and everyone's here, it's a real party." I fish a fork out of the drawer. On my way past the freezer, I grab a bag of peas. "Come here."

Ronan abandons his spying perch and joins me.

"Here. Hold this against your knuckles." I slap the frozen peas into his good hand and then, collecting his injured hand gently, guide them together.

Just as quickly, he sets the bag down to free his hands. Seizing me by the waist, he hoists me onto the counter, pushing my thighs apart so he fits in between them. "You promised me a show."

"A pastry show?"

He hums as he slides the plate closer and collects the fork, handing it to me.

"Ice it, now." I tap the peas.

With an eye roll, he rests the back of his hand against the bag while watching me intently.

I dig into the tart with my fork, breaking off and spearing a chunk on the tines before lifting it to my mouth to slip in, acutely aware of Ronan watching. The flaky, buttery texture begins melting against my tongue almost instantly. "Oh my God," I moan around the mouthful, forgetting my manners. "Abbi wasn't lying. This pastry chef is good." The shell for the chicken was decadent, but this is out of this world.

"Her name is Fiona Crumb."

"*Crumb?* You're messing with me."

He chuckles. "I wish I was."

I sever another forkful, this one with lemon curd on it, and slide it into my mouth. Another moan escapes me as the tart flavor explodes on my tongue.

Ronan watches with a private smile.

"Is this some sort of weird fetish of yours?"

"What? Watching you eat like a ravenous cavewoman?"

"Shut up! Here." I fill a fork and shove it into his mouth, earning his mumbled "fuck" as he chews.

"See? I can't help it. Thank you for stealing this." I shovel in another mouthful. Okay, maybe I *am* a bit ravenous.

Ronan abandons the bag of peas, his hands settling on my hips as he pulls me to the edge of the counter until his body is flush with mine, the split in my dress revealing my entire leg. I can feel his hard length pressed against me. Bad mood or not, Ronan would rather be here with me. That's something.

I load the last piece. "Want it?"

"Yes." He opens his mouth, and I move the fork for it.

Only to swerve back and pop it into mine with a wink. "Sorry, can't help myself. Ravenous cavewoman, remember?"

I've barely swallowed when his mouth is on mine with a punishing kiss, his lips moving frantically as his arms tighten around my body.

The patio door creaks open, breaking us apart just as quickly.

I clear my throat and manage to croak out a "Hey, Frank."

Frank grunts in response as he ambles toward the dishwasher with an empty dinner plate, a tiny ukulele slung over his shoulder. It's almost comical.

Ronan steps back, pushing my thighs together and discreetly adjusting himself in one smooth move. "Good to see you again."

"What's with the peas?" Frank asks in response.

"Oh. You'll love this." I pause for effect. "Ronan punched Henry Wolf in the face tonight."

It's rare to get a reaction out of the big guy, but now, he arches his bushy brow. "Henry Wolf. Your boss."

Ronan's chest heaves with a sigh. "He had it coming."

"Don't doubt it." Frank scratches his chin, his assessing gaze drifting over Ronan as if re-evaluating an old, scrappy car that he's previously deemed unfixable. "So what now? You fired?"

"Probably. But it's okay. I'm gonna be a tiki captain and live in one of the trailers." Ronan winks at me.

Frank's eyes light up. "Does that mean *I* don't have to do it anymore?"

I chuckle. "Don't worry, I'm back on tomorrow afternoon."

"Good, 'cause I can't stand those people."

"You mean the tourists who support the Sea Witch?"

"Yeah, them. You know what the idiot did today? Tried to take the wheel from me. Said I wasn't goin' fast enough."

Ronan whistles. "Ballsy."

"Right?" Frank snorts. "Take over from *me*."

"And so what did you do? Told him politely that it's against protocol, right?" I ask.

"Yeah, that's *exactly* what I did. Talked to him nicely. If he says I threatened to dangle him over the water, he's lying."

I frown at Frank's back as he washes his hands in the sink.

Ronan's shoulders shake with silent laughter as he mouths "*King Kong*."

"Oh, by the way, a woman dropped off a résumé this afternoon to apply for the job."

"Is she hirable?"

"I only skimmed it. She has boating experience. Didn't see chronic pot smoker listed, but I'll let you come to your own conclusions."

I hope this one works out. "I'd love another female captain."

"Figured. I told her you'd call her first thing in the morning."

"Thanks, Frank."

"Uh-huh. Night." He nods to Ronan and then strolls away. A moment later, the front door clicks.

"Well, he didn't threaten to rip my arms off and beat me with them," Ronan murmurs.

"No, that's special for Cody. But I think Frank's warming up to you," I say through a yawn. The excitement from the day must be catching up to me because I'm suddenly exhausted.

Ronan reclaims his position between my legs, only long enough to lift me off the counter by the back of my thighs. His lips are on mine again, this time in a gentler manner, almost reverent.

I rope my arms around Ronan's neck as he carries me down the hall.

"Which room?"

There are only two. "Left."

He pushes the door open blindly, using the hallway light to find a path to my bed, setting me down on the edge of the mattress.

My hands instantly go for his belt buckle, unfastening it with fumbling fingers that move on to his zipper. I have it halfway down when a deep male voice calling out "who's your daddy" suddenly fills my bedroom.

"Is that your phone?" I ask with a laugh.

Ronan groans. "Yeah. Connor was fucking around, and he programmed that for Wolf's number. I haven't changed it yet."

"So, Henry Wolf is messaging you *right now*."

"Give me a sec. Might as well get this over with." He digs through the pocket of his slouching pants.

"You think he's actually going to fire you over text?"

"No, but ..." Ronan's brow furrows as he reads his screen.

"What is it? What did he say?"

"He's reminding me that tee-off is at 7:00 a.m. sharp."

"So you're *not* fired, then?"

"Not yet."

Even after he punched Henry in the eye? In front of a room full of people? I didn't think Henry Wolf's ego would be able to handle that. But maybe that means he realizes how out of line he was. "What did he do? Or say?" I ask.

Ronan seems deep in thought for another moment before tossing his phone on my nightstand. "It doesn't matter."

I sense his mood souring again, and I'm desperate to keep him here with me. I smooth my palm over the thin cotton material of his briefs, reveling in the hard length waiting for me. At least Henry Wolf didn't kill that. Yet.

I steal a glance up to find Ronan watching me with a smirk.

"What?"

"Remember when you insisted we weren't doing this tonight?"

Given we already have, it's a moot point, but if he wants to bring that up ... "Oh, gosh, that's right. Thank you for reminding me." I abandon my fondling and flop back on my bed, rolling and scooting until my head reaches my pillow. "You know how to let yourself out. Good night."

His deep chuckle grates through my body as he turns on my bedside lamp and then backtracks to shut my bedroom door with one hand while his other works on the buttons of his dress shirt.

I admire the well-honed torso peeking out from beneath, the muscle rippling across his abdomen and padding his chest. "You know, you don't have to wait for him to fire you. You could always quit."

"And work for you?"

"Yeah. You'd be *so* good for business," I muse as he saunters back, peeling the shirt off and tossing it on the floor.

"Why is that?"

"Your personality."

He laughs as he kicks off his shoes and then yanks off his socks.

"The tiki captain shirt would look good on you."

"I don't know…"

"*Or* you could go like that. Just don't tell Frank or Jeremy. I make them wear the full uniform, but I'm willing to overlook it for you. Also, you wouldn't mind me featuring you on our website, right? And maybe you could be there to greet all the tourists as they come aboard."

He mock frowns. "Sounds like my job description is quickly growing. Will I get paid for all these additional responsibilities?"

"Yes, with a bed in Palmy Daze. It's nice! Roomy."

He shimmies off his pants and briefs, kicking them

off. I finally have a fully naked Ronan standing before me for the first time, and good God, it is a glorious sight.

"You honestly think you're going to keep me out there when you're in here?" He grabs my ankles and drags me toward him, earning my squeal as my dress bunches up around my waist. Before I know what's happening, my panties are dragged down and off, tossed into a corner. He parts my legs and fits between them, and then, collecting my hands, he pulls me up to a sitting position. "Where were we?" His thumb and forefinger pinch my chin, angling my face. "Oh, right. You were about to suck my dick."

"Was I?" It comes out hoarse, his crass words sending a flurry of nerves through my body.

His fist wraps around the base of it, angling the swollen tip toward my mouth as he waits in anticipation.

I part my lips, teasing the velvety, smooth skin with first a swipe of my tongue, then a swirl, tasting the salty bead of moisture.

"Please, Sloane. Don't make me beg tonight." He winces, as if in pain.

"I think you just did." Replacing his hand with mine, I stroke his length once ... twice ... and then drag the flat of my tongue along the underside before taking him into my mouth.

A strangled sound escapes him as his tip hits the back of my throat. "Fuck, yeah. That's it." His fingers weave through my hair, collecting fistfuls.

I slowly slide him out, only to find a palm on the back of my head gently guiding me back, filling my mouth up with him again.

And again.

And again.

Until he coaxes the hand gripping his base away, forcing me to take him even deeper. His size is overwhelming, but the tempo he's set is perfect, and I settle into a comfortable rhythm, hollowing my cheeks as my head bobs and my hands roam, filling with each side of his perfect, hard ass.

Acutely aware of his intense gaze as he's absorbed by watching the lewd act.

The only warning I get that Ronan is about to come is when his dick swells and his hips make a few jerky thrusts, and then ribbons of salty liquid are shooting into my mouth with his cries.

"Thank you," he whispers, his head tipped back to show off his jutting Adam's apple.

While he comes down off his high, I unzip my dress and shimmy it up over my head, tossing it to the nearby side chair that catches all the clothes I'm too lazy or tired to put away. Scooting back on my bed until my head rests on a pillow, I part my legs and wait.

I'm rewarded a moment later when he opens his eyes, which flare with heat instantly.

"How wet are you?" he asks.

"Wet."

"Show me."

"How?"

He cocks his head. "*Show me.*"

I part my legs wider.

That move earns a subtle head shake.

I finally clue in about what he wants. A nervous

shudder courses through my veins as I slip a hand down between my thighs and slide a tentative fingertip through my slit.

Ronan's lips part with a sharp inhale as he tracks the move like a hawk prowling from the skies above. This man whose sexual encounters could probably rival that of a porn star's résumé is turned on by a simple act. "Again," he demands gruffly, his hand absently fumbling with his still-hard dick.

I do these things in private, not in front of men, and yet the way Ronan's looking at me now, like I'm the most attractive woman he's ever laid eyes on, stirs a feeling deep inside. "Like this?" I do it again, this time dragging my index finger back and forth several times before gently pressing into my center.

His chest heaves, and then Ronan is on his knees on my bed, approaching with clear intent.

"Already?" I ask in disbelief, watching his hard dick throb in eager anticipation.

A devilish grin consumes his handsome face as his hands settle on my knees. "I'm just getting started."

15. Sloane

A blaring alarm cuts into my restful sleep, earning my moan of discontent. "Make it stop!"

A male groans in answer, and then I'm being jostled as the warm, hard body slips away from me. A moment later, the terrible sound is over.

I dare to crack an eyelid. A faint ray of sun streams through a sliver in the curtain. "What time is it?" My words are barely more than a whisper. It was well after 2:00 a.m. by the time I drifted off, my body spent and my head nestled against Ronan's chest.

"Early." Ronan's voice scrapes through the silence, raspier than usual.

I survey his godlike profile lying next to me, sprawled out on his back. He's naked save for the bunched-up bedsheet doing a poor job of covering his morning erection. I resist the urge to reach down and touch it—for the moment.

"You made me sleep in the wet spot," he grumbles.

"I did not. I always sleep on this side," I counter,

adding after a moment, "You shouldn't have come all over my sheets, then."

"*I* shouldn't have?" He rolls his head toward me to shoot me an amused look. "Funny, that's not how I remember it."

Last night is a heady blur. The truth is, it probably *was* me, but it is one hundred percent Ronan's fault. Him and that long, skilled tongue and gifted dick of his. I can still feel him between my legs, thrusting, over and over, bending my body into a dozen ways to get deeper, until I quit fighting against the urge to scream.

I lost count of the orgasms.

"Are you always like that?"

"Like what?"

"An insatiable sex demon."

His dark chuckle fills my ear and the quiet bedroom, sparking my own laughter. "Is that a problem?"

"No, but I might die." I might shrivel up from dehydration, all my bodily fluids leached from me in a nightly sex marathon.

"So you're complaining."

"*No.*" My head flops lazily from side to side to emphasize my claim. "It would be a good way to go."

"Speaking of going ..." He smooths his hands over his face with a curse. The bruises on his knuckles look marginally better. "Tee-off time is in less than an hour."

"Are you sure you want to?" Because I'd like to lock Ronan up in this little room and keep him safe in here, away from Henry Wolf.

"Right now, the only thing I want is to make you come all over my face."

My insides clench with his words. "Sounds like a plan."

"Really ... who's the sex demon now?" He leans over to press a chaste kiss against my forehead. "I have to get home to shower and change." He rolls out of bed, standing with an over-the-head arm stretch that show-cases a web of muscle across his back and a hard, round ass that I had my palms filled with last night.

I watch him as he half stumbles out of my bedroom and to the bathroom. A moment later, the sound of him relieving himself carries.

And I pull his pillow closer to inhale the delicious scent of him. He drives me crazy. I don't think I've ever felt this way about another man. Scratch that, I know I haven't. I could get used to having Ronan here, every day, with me.

Will it always be like this, though? So intoxicating to be around him?

I'm pregnant.

The words force themselves into the forefront of my brain then, and it's like a lightning bolt of reality.

No, it won't always be like this, regardless of how we feel about each other. If I have this baby, *everything* will change. My body will morph, my priorities will shift. Hell, there won't be time for hours of sex when all I'll want to do is sleep!

Will Ronan be onboard for *all that*?

Even Abbi Wolf couldn't say one way or another how Ronan would react, and they're close.

What if Ronan says he doesn't want it? What if he asks me to get rid of it?

What if he just disappears altogether?

Then you don't want him around, Gigi's voice in my head chirps. But is that true? Is it fair to him? Or is it just a matter of it not being the right time? Should I be making this decision *with* him?

I don't know what the right answer is. But I'm pregnant, and Abbi Wolf knows. Will she tell Ronan before I get a chance to?

I wish I could pause time, just long enough to get to know him more.

Ronan strolls back in as my emotions and thoughts are spiraling uncontrollably. "I have another dinner thing tonight, but I'll give you a call after, 'kay?"

I hum my agreement as I watch him collect his strewn clothes.

Is having a family even on Ronan's radar? *Like ever?* Because if it's not, then there's no point continuing this relationship, regardless of my decision about this baby. I *have to* know. "*So,* Abbi's pregnant," I blurt because it seems like the best opportunity for a segue.

"Yeah, only a few more months before she pops." He slips his feet into his briefs and draws them up.

I mock whimper as my favorite new toy is put away.

His smirk is crooked and knowing. "You can play with it again later, promise."

She seems a bit young. Early twenties, at most. *A lot* younger than Henry Wolf. "Do you think she's ready?"

"Who, Abbi?" He frowns. "Yeah, she's happy and in love. And it's not like they can't make it work. Wolf's got all the money in the world to hire nannies and whatever.

Plus, there's no doubt he loves her, even if he's a colossal prick to everyone else."

Love. Is that the key ingredient here? Ronan's mentioned it twice.

But does he want kids? Like, *ever?* I know he mentioned his ex and marriage, but ... *Fuck, fuck, fuck* ... It's too soon to be having this conversation. *Way* too soon. And yet, I have no other choice because I'm here, and this is happening.

I swallow, hesitating before I ask, "What about you? Do you see yourself with a family? *One day?*" Those last two words are tacked on with a wobble.

"Damn, Sea Witch." He chuckles as he pulls up his pants. "It's a little early for this."

"Early in the day or *early?*"

Curious eyes flip to me as he draws his zipper up. "Why're you asking?"

Am I being too obvious? Is he about to piece my secret together like others have? Have a eureka moment and run out my door?

Knots twist in my stomach as he waits on an answer.

I settle on, "Because I'm thirty-one, and I don't like wasting my time." That's the truth.

But not the whole truth.

I hold my breath as Ronan draws his shirt on. Leaving his buttons undone, he grabs his shoes and socks from the floor and sets them on my dresser by the door before backtracking to kneel on the bed. Hard eyes bore into me from above as he rests his palms on either side of my pillow to hover over me. "I'm not wasting your time, Sloane."

A sigh escapes me, even if he hasn't answered my question.

"Are *you* wasting *my* time?"

What? "No."

"Good." Leaning down, Ronan presses a kiss against my lips, one that's gentle and yet full of heat. "I'll call you later," he whispers, kissing me a second time.

I watch his back as he departs from my room. The front door creaks open a moment later, leaving me alone in my house to a flurry of confusing thoughts. What if I *am* wasting Ronan's time by not being completely open and honest with him? By letting this thing between us go on when there's a potentially huge diversion up ahead that I haven't warned him about?

Would I even be weighing my options if Ronan said he was on board?

I've spent all this time worrying that it's not what he wants, but what if it is? What if he knew about the pregnancy and was all in? Would I have made a decision by now?

Yes, maybe.

Which means that maybe I shouldn't be making this decision alone.

A flutter of nerves explodes in my stomach.

Tonight.

I have to tell Ronan tonight.

16. Ronan

Three men loiter by the clubhouse gates when I arrive at two minutes before seven, the golf cart I commandeered to race here coming to a jarring halt. Behind them, Archie and the other caddies wait with the clubs.

I could pick out Henry from a mile away just by the way he stands, like he owns the air we're all breathing. But he seems in a good mood this morning, his deep laughter carrying through the calm morning. It's likely an act. He can fake anything for the sake of his business.

"... it's not every day you get an entire course to yourself," the burly man with a full head of short and curlies says. I recognize his face from the files. That's Jim Harris, CEO of Axis Core, the major consulting firm out of New York City. The other guy is Mark Mancuso, his CFO.

"And here is our fourth," Henry announces, checking his watch as if to make a point.

I knew that punch was going to leave a mark, but

damn, the purple bruising under his left eye is dark. I flex my hand to test the soreness.

The truth is, I almost bailed on this tee time, on this meeting, on this whole goddamn director's charade. I was standing under the showerhead at home—Henry's home—letting the water soak my skin as I replayed my favorite moments with Sloane and wondering why I'd want to be anywhere other than still lying in bed next to her.

When I toweled up, I nearly packed my shit then and there.

But I decided against it. Why make it easy for Henry by quitting? He can man up and fire me to my face.

A part of me is relieved he hasn't done it—yet. If nothing else, it would certainly complicate things for this weekend, given Britt and Dani are staying at the house. And then there's Tasha as well.

I hop out of the cart, smoothing the creases from the dress pants I threw on. It's already balmy out, and sweat is forming around my shirt collar.

"Gentlemen, this is my director of facilities, Ronan Lyle," Henry says smoothly.

We exchange greetings before Henry gestures toward the waiting carts. "Day's only going to get hotter. We're right behind you."

The two men both lament the humidity as they trudge toward their respective chariots, leaving Henry and me alone.

He turns to face me, as if he wants me to get a good look at the damage I caused, but he says nothing. He simply waits. For what?

"Good night?" I ask, knowing how much it'll irritate him.

"For the most part, yes."

More staring.

Finally, I can't stand it. "If you're waiting for an apology, you're gonna miss your golf game."

"Funny, I've been told *I'm* the one who needs to apologize. I'm not sure that I agree."

"No, you wouldn't." I got a text from Abbi late last night, but I'd already silenced my phone, my focus on Sloane and every inch of her body. Abbi wanted my version of events, but I'm more curious about the version Henry told her. "So, does your pregnant wife know you're entertaining the idea of tag-teaming the neighbor, or did you leave that part out?"

"You idiot. Do you honestly think I have any interest in fucking another woman and *that* woman, specifically?"

"Then what was that last night? Were you just swinging your dick around to try and prove it's bigger?" Which it's not. I have it on good authority.

"That was me testing you to see if you're actually serious about this one or if you just brought her to irritate me."

My dark chuckle carries. "Narcissistic prick. You think I live and breathe to find ways to stick it to you?"

He smiles, but it doesn't reach his eyes. "Well, now that I know this isn't a head game, I can see that you're even dumber than I thought."

"You'll have to be more specific."

Henry checks over his shoulder to confirm that

Archie and the other caddie are feigning intense focus on our clubs. He takes a step closer. "What are you going to do, when I unveil our plans and the news reaches her? What are you going to say when she asks you if you knew? Are you going to lie to her?"

The thought has crossed my mind, but the more time I spend with Sloane, the less likely I'd be able to stomach that. Plus, I've never been a good liar. "Leave her out of your plan. Leave the Sea Witch where it is."

He scoffs. "That's impossible. The harborfront footprint will all change."

I expected as much. "Fine. At least leave her home alone."

"That's up to the county, not me."

"That's bullshit!"

Archie turns in his seat, his eyebrows climbing halfway up his forehead.

I temper my tone. I doubt I'll get another pass for hitting him. "You and I both know that if you don't want it to happen, it won't happen. Everyone wants to make you happy, right?"

Henry's lips purse. "Look, maybe I should have gone about things differently last night—"

My loud bark of laughter carries, cutting off his words and earning his glare.

"I've given you an opportunity of a lifetime. Don't throw it away." He turns to leave but falters. "Also, you get one. Last night was it." He holds up his index finger to emphasize it, and then he's marching to his cart.

Did Henry Wolf just apologize to me? It wasn't a

good apology, if that, but it's more than I expected from him.

I dwell on this as I head for my cart.

"Morning, slugger," Archie greets me with his usual Cheshire cat grin.

I slide into my seat, acutely aware of soreness in various muscles. Last night was a workout. "So, you've heard about that."

"You kidding?" Our cart starts with a jolt, and then Archie is speeding down the path after Henry. "I've never gotten so many messages in my life. My phone's been going nonstop. I don't even know half these people. I don't know how they got my number."

"Look at you, popular guy. You didn't tell them shit, right?"

"I don't know shit! But I wouldn't if I did. I know how things work around here."

"Good."

He hesitates. "So, why didn't he fire you?"

I've been asking myself that since last night, and the only answer I can come up with is Abbi. That or he's not as big a prick as I thought. No, it's got to be the former. "I guess I'm just too good at my job to lose."

Archie snickers, but then his eyes widen as if remembering something. "Oh, by the way, I watched *Basic Instinct* last night."

"Connor'll be so proud."

"So, Belinda did *that* to you? The leg ... the skirt ... the thing?"

"Jesus, Archie." He can't even say it out loud. A thousand bucks says my assistant is still riding the V-train. He's probably never even had his dick sucked. "She did, indeed."

"Wow. I would ... *wow*."

He would either pass out or prematurely blow his load. But it's best for his sake that Belinda sticks to abusing Connor.

I reach over to ruffle Archie's hair as we pull up to the first hole. "Now, be a good caddie and don't let me look stupid."

———

"Nice birdie!" Archie exclaims as I retrieve my ball and toss it to him.

"That means one under par, right?" He's been coaching me on the terms and scoring between holes.

"You got it."

We close the distance to where the others wait, having shot their rounds already.

"Did I hear you say you *don't* golf?" Mark calls out, doubt lacing his thick accent. Arkansas, if I had to guess.

"Beginner's luck." Though I've been averaging par or close to it on each hole. If this keeps up, I could walk away with a score in the low eighties, which, according to Archie, is unheard of for a guy who doesn't know how to play and hates everything about the game.

"Seems like Henry's brought in a ringer," Jim muses beside him, equally suspicious.

"Now, why would I do that, gentlemen? He's got no skin in it. Do you, Ronan?" Henry smiles knowingly.

"Not a dime." Meanwhile, these rich assholes have thrown in ten thousand apiece in a private pool, winner takes all. I think that's why they came down here—to golf, gamble, and tell tall tales about women they'll never fuck. I haven't heard a word about Axis Core booking their next event.

"A distraction, then. Another one of Henry's head games." Jim wipes his sweaty brow with his forearm. We're halfway through the round, it's hot as hell out here, and I won't be surprised if we have to call an ambulance for the guy before it's all said and done.

An ear-piercing rooster call sounds then, earning a round of winces.

"Now, *that*'s a distraction," Mark says. "Dang, Henry, where's that comin' from?"

"The neighbor," he grumbles. "We're dealing with it."

No, you're not. I grin at the tree line. Is Sloane over there, poking Ralph to get him to sing? I wouldn't be surprised.

I should call her. I really want to, just to hear her voice. I hated rushing out of her bed this morning. Then she sideswiped me with baby talk while I was putting on my pants. I was not expecting it—that early in the day *and* the relationship.

"So, Henry, we're halfway through the game. I think we've given it enough time." Mark's mischievous gaze darts to Jim. "What's with the shiner?"

"Why? You like it?"

He throws his arms out. "Who the hell punched you in the face? Who'd be *that* stupid?"

Archie bolts for the golf cart with my clubs slung over his shoulder as if to avoid a pending explosion.

"That is a very good question." Henry stalls answering with a long, leisurely sip of his bottled water. "Ronan? You have any idea who that guy was?"

"Nope. No idea." With a shrug, I saunter toward the carts.

17. Sloane

"*Ex-army?* You didn't think to mention that?"

"Why? Is that a bad thing?" Frank hovers over the espresso maker that quit halfway through the early morning rush, turning a tiny screwdriver with his giant hands. I would have had to replace the pricey machine by now if not for him and his uncanny skills with mechanical things.

"No, it's good. It's great. She'll be on time and a hard worker." I scan the dates. Bailey must be in her mid-thirties, at least. She's mature. Another positive.

"Hey, New Girl, more water," Frank hollers, waving an empty pitcher.

I roll my eyes. "Her name is Lara."

She sweeps in with a laugh. She doesn't seem bothered.

"Did Bailey say why she left the army?"

"Nope, and I didn't ask. She said she was looking for something fun and stress-free, and a summer contract on the water would be ideal."

"As long as she wasn't dishonorably discharged. "

Frank tosses the screwdriver to the counter and wipes his sweaty brow with his forearm. "I'm sure you'll find out as soon as you get her in for an interview."

"Who's coming in for an interview?" Skye sweeps past on her way to the storage fridge to replenish the milk and cream before another round of customers arrives. "New tiki captain. *Potential* new tiki captain," I correct. I have to meet her first. "So no one has to be subjected to Frank anymore."

Frank waves his middle finger in the air before snagging a different tiny screwdriver and returning to his work.

"How do such meaty paws handle such delicate instruments," I mock ponder.

Skye returns with two full cartons. "That would be amazing. Then all you'd need is one more, and you wouldn't have to be out there every afternoon."

"And then I could do all the work I'm supposed to do. Wouldn't that be nice." I sigh.

"Thought you hired Lover Boy," Frank mutters, and I can't tell if he's just being Frank or if he still disapproves.

"No. Well, I don't know what's going on there. He went in this morning. Somehow still has a job." Or maybe Henry wants to fire him to his face. "You know, he calls you King Kong?"

Frank scowls as if offended but then pauses to weigh that nickname. "Huh ... I think I like that."

"I had a feeling you would."

He plugs the machine in, and lights ignite. "He ever tell you what Wolf did to make him punch him?"

Skye gasps. "Ronan *punched* Henry Wolf?"

"Yeah. Last night." To Frank, I say, "No, but I have a feeling it had to do with me."

"I was thinking the same thing."

Lara appears with the pitcher. "Who's Ronan?"

"The guy Sloane's banging." Frank accepts the water with a grunt and pours it into the receptacle.

"Oh, wait 'til you see him? He is *so* hot." Skye's blue eyes widen as she nods approvingly.

"Oh yeah, *so* dreamy," Frank mimics, holding his hands together and pressing them against his chest while fluttering his eyelashes.

Skye flicks him playfully in the neck on her way past to restock the napkins. "Sloane's landed a good one. Which she deserves, considering the last one," she adds in a singsong voice, trailing it with a wince.

Lara's focus ping-pongs back and forth between us all, trying to keep up. "He was bad?"

"His name is Cody, and he is rotten. We don't like him."

"He's banned." Frank reaches up and opens a cupboard door to reveal a copy of Cody's mug shot taped to the inside. Above it, in Frank's aggressive handwriting, states "Do Not Serve."

"When did you put that up?" I exclaim.

"Monday. After your run-in with him at Starfish Island. If you see him in here, you come and get me. Got it, New Girl?"

Lara's head bobs up and down.

"And what'll you do, Frank?" Skye's smile is mischievous. She's egging him on for entertainment's sake.

"I'm gonna rip his arms off and beat him to death with them."

Lara's eyes widen as Skye cackles.

Meanwhile, my worry flares. That mug shot was from before Cody and I met, when he got arrested for drunk and disorderly after a bachelor party. The charges were dropped, but the picture remains. "Listen, if Cody sees that up there, he's going to be angry, and Angry Cody isn't good for *me*." I arch my brows with meaning.

"That's why it's on the inside instead of front and center. And you know what's worse than Angry Cody?" Frank hits a button on the machine. "Angry King Kong."

"I've created a monster," I say as a whirring sound announces the newly repaired espresso maker.

"Yes! Thank *you*!" Skye skips past, leaning in to drop a friendly kiss against his cheek on her way past.

"Just keep that door closed," I warn, waving at Cody's stupid face. "And no hitting anyone. Last night was enough for me."

Frank begins collecting tools. "Ronan's got balls to punch a guy like Henry Wolf, I'll give him that much."

"Yeah, he's got those." And plenty more, and he overwhelmed me last night with how thoroughly he consumed my body. But beyond the physical, Ronan has a big heart and fierce loyalty. My attraction to him is quickly growing far beyond the physical, which is dangerous given my situation.

I need to tell him.

No, I *want* to tell him. Because I'm growing hopeful that he might actually be the man I want him to be.

"Sloane?"

"Huh?"

Frank's watching me closely. "You okay?"

"Yeah. I'm just tired. Didn't sleep well, and I have this headache behind my eye." It's likely caffeine withdrawal. I'm normally on my second cup of coffee by now, but I'm still savoring my first, letting it grow cold on my desk.

He's not buying it, though. "You've been out of it the last few days."

"Oh. Yeah. I mean, *no*, I'm good." I'm far from good.

And Frank can always tell when I'm lying. He has the same keen sense as Gigi where that's concerned, and the longer I stay here, fumbling through excuses, the more likely he is to ferret the truth out of me.

"I'm gonna give Bailey a call," I say, waving the résumé in the air as I aim for the doorway between the two sides.

"Hey, New Girl, can you get me ..."

I shut the door to my tiny office, and Frank's voice vanishes. But instead of calling Bailey just yet, I text Ronan. It's midmorning, and I've waited as long as I can.

> Should I save you a tiki, Captain?

There. Quick and playful. Completely unserious. I'm sure he's in the middle of some important ass-kissing meeting, but at least I've given him a reason to reply, if he wants to. And, while I wait for him to, I might as well get this army veteran in here to see if she'd be a good fit.

I'm halfway through punching in Bailey's number when my phone chirps with a text.

RONAN:

Too soon to tell, but that wet spot in
your bed is mine.

My stomach erupts with flutters.

———

GIGI:

So? How was your big night at Wolf
Hotel?

OMG, Gi. Too much to text about. I'm at
the dock now. I'll come by after to fill
you in.

I HOP out of the Cherokee and into the stifling heat, my
floral captain's hat dangling from my fingertips as I stroll
toward the hut ahead, memories of what happened in
there still fresh in my mind.

Skye sits in the window, registering Jeremy's group—
a bunch of twenty-something-year-old couples in string
bikinis and board shorts. A group of older women sits on
a nearby picnic table, waiting their turn, shopping bags
no doubt loaded with booze at their feet. I remember
seeing that booking come in—it's for a sixtieth birthday
party, the ladies from all corners of the country. Those
groups are always a good time.

Jeremy pounces on me the second I reach the dock,
leaving *Tiki Two* to meet me halfway to mine. "So ...
Exciting night last night, huh?"

I hop onto *Tiki One*, tossing my bag onto the floor. Will has come and gone, leaving the coolers and trough well stocked with ice and everything set up. "Yeah, it was something."

"What was that all about?" he prods.

"I have no idea," I lie. Well, it's not entirely a lie. I have ideas but no confirmation.

He leans over the bar on folded arms. "Did Wolf fire him?"

"Not as of a few hours ago, but it's still early." I fish out my sunscreen and, squeezing a dollop onto my hand, begin smoothing over my bare skin. "But if he does, I'm going to hire him to run *Tiki Three*."

Jeremy blinks. "Seriously?"

I know that tone. "Yeah, why not?"

"No reason. It's just, the last time you dated an employee, it didn't go so well."

"This is different. Ronan is not Cody."

"No, I guess not." Jeremy hesitates. "Does he know yet?"

"About?"

"Come on, Sloane."

I look up into a knowing gaze.

Right. "He doesn't know yet. No one does, except for you and Gigi." And Abbi Wolf.

He traces the countertop's woodgrain with his index finger. "Do you know what you're gonna do?" He doesn't have to elaborate.

"I'm not sure, but I think I might have it?" It sounds more like a question than a statement, and it's the first time I've actually said it, not just out loud but even in my head. Almost like a test to see what that sounds like, if uttering the words causes panic. Would it be so crazy? I've been making choices—what I eat, what I drink—as if I've already decided, even if I haven't yet admitted it to myself.

And even if Ronan doesn't want this, I'm thirty-one years old. I have a home and a business. I can do this on my own, if I have to.

I don't want to, but I can.

Raucous laughter sounds from the stairs as Jeremy's group begins their descent.

"I guess that's my cue."

"Yeah, see you out there."

He pauses before stepping onto the dock. "For what it's worth, I think you'd make a terrific mom." With that said, he hops out and greets the incoming group with a dramatic bow and flourish.

18. Ronan

"So, Ronan." Olivia McEowan studies me through thick black frames from across the table of the Coral Cafe like a detective assessing a criminal, deciding how they can best pin a crime on them. "How many years did you say you've worked for Wolf Hotels?"

I didn't. "Close to five." Rounding up, graciously. "At four locations."

"Four locations," she echoes in a soft Texan accent, scanning my bruised knuckles. Her dossier says she's forty-four. Her platinum-blond hair is freshly colored and styled in a chin-length bob that highlights her angular jaw. She's wearing navy pants and a white silk sleeveless blouse that accentuates her thin, lean figure. She's far from a knockout, but she's spent plenty of money filling and smoothing her face into her ideal image. "In this capacity?"

"Various capacities."

She hums, but her pursed lips reveal her skepticism.

I hide my smirk behind a long sip of coffee—my

second this afternoon, thanks to this stupid schedule. Olivia may have stepped into the role of Black Titan's CEO due to her father's untimely demise, but she seems sharp and far from underqualified to hold the position.

Unlike me in my role, I sense she's digging to prove.

Olivia is nothing like Shelby Singer, my first coffee "date." That woman was more than thrilled to educate me on all things duck herding the second I brought it up. I even have an invitation to join her next weekend, but given how many times she stroked my arm, I'm pretty sure she's hoping it'll end with less herding and more fucking.

When I broached the subject of a large-scale event here, Shelby laughed.

Do you know how much that would cost?

My constituents would skin me alive if they found out!

Why I'm entertaining these silly meetings is beyond me. I'd rather be at my desk, going over budget updates. Words I never thought I'd say.

But I'm here, and I'm on thin ice with Henry, so I might as well make the best of it. "I hear you have a future Olympian."

Olivia's eyes soften for a split second. "Maisy. Of all three of my girls, she is the most passionate and skilled."

"Show jumping, right?"

"Right." She pauses. "Are you familiar?"

I could lie. I could regurgitate the crap I learned watching YouTube videos. But something tells me this woman would see right through me, so I decide to be myself. With pants on, per Belinda's advice. "Honestly,

I had no fucking clue that was a thing until two days ago."

The corners of Olivia's mouth twitch. She takes a long, leisurely sip of her coffee—pinky up—before setting the cup down. "Belinda loves her dossiers, doesn't she?"

I chuckle. This is unexpected. "So it's not a well-kept secret."

"What else did she prep you for? Oh, wait, let me see if I remember from the last grand opening." She leans back in her chair, crossing her arms over her small chest. "I was a competitive swimmer in college, I'm divorced, I have three daughters, and my father, the previous CEO of Black Titan, died in a tragic skydiving accident. My brother fought me for the company and even accused me of sabotaging Dad's parachute. I loved my father very much." Pain cuts like a lightning bolt across her face before it's gone, as if it never made an appearance. "I won the company and fired my brother. Does that about cover it?"

"You missed your husband's affair with your nanny."

"Oh, right, we mustn't forget that." Unlike the mention of her father, she seems unbothered by her unfaithful husband. "I know why I was invited here, Ronan. It's the same reason I was invited to the Alaska opening. Henry Wolf wants to wine and dine me and convince me to spend exorbitant amounts of company money at his hotels."

"If you're not interested, why do you come to these things?"

She shrugs. "Because I like being wined and dined? And who knows, maybe one of these times I'll be wowed.

But for now, I can get a few days away from the office and enjoy the quiet of a luxurious new place." She gestures around us with a wave. "And all I have to tolerate is a thirty-minute meeting where you guys pitch Wolf Hotel."

"Like a time-share program."

"Exactly." Her lips twist. "Of course, I expected Henry to greet me."

"And instead, you got me." Lowly operations director. Would she be so stiff if she were sitting across from Henry?

Her blue eyes skitter over my sleeve of tattoos. "I suppose there are worse choices."

Okay, she's softening to me. "You're right. You could have had Belinda."

Her head tips back with a laugh. "Not likely. Belinda knows she doesn't appeal to me."

Huh. Interesting. "So, you know the game she plays."

"The one where a pretty face and money gets you what you want faster than a brain and hard work?" Her eyebrow arches in question. "Tell Belinda to stop recycling research points if she wants whatever reward she gets for my business. Also, there are far more interesting things about me than my ex-husband's infidelity."

"Such as?" Because now I'm curious.

Her attention drags over the giant potted palm tree next to us. "I was the first female CEO of a major oil and gas company. There are a few more now, but I was the first. And I negotiated a multibillion-dollar takeover, which expanded Black Titan's holdings by thirty-five percent."

I'm sure Olivia's used to reciting her résumé and getting impressed responses. "Your company is about as interesting to me as your ex-husband's cheating."

Her mouth hangs open for a beat. "Fine. My equine rehabilitation center is the largest charity of its kind in the state of Texas."

"What's your horse's name?"

She hesitates. "I don't have a horse, personally."

"You have a giant charity, and your children are all competitive riders, and you don't have your own horse." I may not know much, but even I know that's strange. By the way she adjusts in her seat, I suspect there's more to this story. "Why not?"

"Because I don't ride horses."

"Why not?"

She sets her jaw as she considers her answer. "Because I'm afraid of them. Always have been. Is that what you want to hear?"

"Actually, yes." I can tell it's the truth and something she doesn't normally admit to strangers. A slow smile curves my lips. "Now we're getting somewhere interesting."

"AND HERE IS the entrance to the spa." I check my watch. "Right on time."

"I appreciate the escort." Olivia's smile isn't flirtatious, but it's warmer than it was when we first sat down to coffee.

"No problem. It's all a part of my role as liaison. And

I'll let you know what I can set up for fishing." It turns out Olivia may be terrified of horses, but she's a deep-sea fisherwoman who used to spend full days out on her father's boat with him. She hasn't gone since his death. Given she's in the perfect location, I said I'd find a charter for her. On Wolf Hotels' dime, of course, but mostly because, turns out, I like her.

"Oh, you were serious about that." She smirks.

"Weren't you?"

"Yes, but you won't find anyone reputable on such short notice. My assistant already tried."

"That sounds like a challenge." One I'll happily put Archie on.

"Fine. Tomorrow morning." She pauses in thought. "And only if you come with me."

"You want *me* to go fishing with you." And I sense she actually means fishing. Olivia's given no indication that I'd be of use to her any other way, which is a refreshing change of pace for me.

But, fuck, that means my entire morning gone, and my calendar is jam-packed. Plus, I have to get Britt from the airport.

"It'll give you a chance to keep talking me into holding a corporate event here."

"Belinda does need another gold watch." I open and hold the door for her. "Stay tuned. You have my number if you need anything. I'm gonna go take my third time-share pitch for the day. I'll see you at the cocktail reception later." I turn to leave.

"Hey, Ronan?" Olivia nods to my knuckles. "Who'd you punch?"

I stretch my hand out in front of me to regard the discoloration. "Henry."

Her jaw drops in genuine shock. "Seriously? Why?"

"I didn't like the way he was speaking about my girlfriend."

A strange look passes over her face. "You know, you're different than I expected."

"Not the first time I've heard that."

"Well, *I'm* rarely wrong about people, so I'm surprised. Pleasantly so. See you later."

She disappears inside the spa.

I'm halfway to my office to task Archie with chartering a fishing boat when I run into Abbi. She's wearing a tropical-print bathing suit that hugs her belly and shows off her enormous tits, a flowing cover-up, and a wide-brim tan hat to shield her perfect skin.

"Pool or beach?" I ask.

"Haven't decided yet, but I'm meeting Margo out there." She collects my hand in hers to study my bruises. "How are you?"

"Looks worse than it is."

She hums with disapproval. "That's what Henry said too. I know you're both lying. What was it about?"

"Nothing worth repeating."

Her brow furrows. "Look, I tried talking to him about this expansion project of his, but he doesn't seem too willing."

"Yeah, I know. I appreciate it, though. What have you been up to?" I ask, changing the subject.

"This and that. Had some work to catch up on, but then I went to the spa, ate a nice meal. You know, enjoying my quiet time while I still can." Her palm smooths over her belly.

"Still hard to believe there's a whole-ass human growing in there."

"I know, right?" She peers up at me. "What about you?"

I frown. "What about me?"

"You know ... What about kids?"

"Uh ..." Not a subject I've broached with anyone since Tasha, and now it's been twice in one day? "Yeah, one day, I guess. I'm so far away from that, though."

"Maybe not *that far*," she challenges. "I mean, Sloane's in the picture now, right?"

"Jesus, Red. I just met her." I chuckle. "What did you two talk about yesterday?"

"Nothing! Just, you know, stuff." She twirls a strand of her red hair between her fingertips.

It's a dead giveaway when she's nervous. "You're acting squirrelly."

"Am I? I guess it's just my hormones? I go from laughing to crying in, like, seconds. Sorry, I didn't mean to freak you out with that question. I just have baby on the brain."

"Right. Well ... the only thing on my brain is finding a fishing charter so I can convince a very rich oil CEO to sign on with Wolf Hotels."

She holds up her hands in surrender. "Don't let me keep you, then."

"See you at dinner tonight." I give her forearm a friendly squeeze and then take off to find Archie.

19. Sloane

"**Y**ou're coming with us to Siren's Call tonight!" Beverly declares, earning a raucous cheer from the others.

I laugh as I steer us into the harbor, where Jeremy's group is climbing the steps up. After four hours on the water and countless cans of margaritas, these ladies are burned by the sun and pickled by the booze. I've seen this episode before, and I doubt they'll even make it to dinner, let alone out to the bar.

"Would love to, but I have plans, remember? I'm going to see Gigi tonight." They've all heard about her, fascinated by the origin story of the Sea Witch Brews and Cruise.

"Who is *that*?" Samantha pulls her sunglasses down, her eyes glued on the dock.

"Oh, that's probably just Will, here to ..." My words fade as I spot the lone figure standing on the dock with Jer. "That's Ronan." I also told them about him.

My heart rate ticks up.

The spunky woman lets out a low whistle. "Either I'm drunk, or that is one beautiful man you have there."

I grin. "He is that." *And you're drunk.*

"Where? Jesus, I can't see anything that far away." Rhonda roots through her purse to fish out a pair of dark green-framed glasses that she slides on. "Oh, golly gee. Would ya look at that." Rhonda has a two-year-old granddaughter at home and uses words like *golly gee* and *oh, shucks* instead of Beverly's colorful array of fucks and shits.

The other ladies ohh and ahh as we get closer.

Meanwhile, my concern sparks. What is Ronan doing here?

On impulse, I fish out my phone to see that he messaged me.

RONAN:

I need to talk to you. I'm coming by the docks.

The excitement I felt a moment ago withers, replaced by panic as I stare at those words.

I need to talk to you.

About what? It sounds serious, which can only mean ... Did Abbi break her promise?

Is the bottom about to fall out from under our whirlwind romance?

The women are buzzing with appreciation for Ronan as I edge into our mooring spot. There is no way he can't hear their disorderly comments about his tailored pants and fitted golf tee.

All I can focus on is his face. Does that look like a

man who just found out his fun-time girl is hiding a huge secret? I can't tell. He's his usual unreadable self, his mood impossible to gauge, especially when it's partially hidden by those aviators.

The bumpers barely nudge the dock when Tabitha stumbles out, yelling, "Ahoy!"

With lightning-quick reflexes, Ronan dives for her arm to keep her from tripping and falling into the water on the other side. "You look like you had a good time."

"Oh, Lord, that voice. It's so raspy and deep." Beverly drops her own voice a few octaves in a poor but comical attempt to match it, earning a round of unhinged laughter from them all.

"We heard all about you, and it sounds like Sloane's having an even better time," Tabitha purrs, a slur in her words as she gapes up at him.

Oh my God. "Don't forget your things!" I manage as my cheeks burn.

If Connor were here, he'd be strutting like a peacock. But all they get from Ronan is a flicker of amusement across his face.

The ladies step off one by one, each one grinning up at Ronan on their way past, heading for the stairs with careful steps.

"Our ride is four minutes away!" Darlene, who made the reservation and is the least inebriated, hollers before muttering, "It's like traveling with kids." She grabs a towel and a T-shirt from a hook before slapping a wad of twenties into my hand. "It'll be hard to top this day. Thank you so much for everything, sweetheart." With a wink, she hops off.

Up ahead, Tabitha stumbles again while laughing hysterically.

"How about I escort you lovely ladies up to the parking lot." Jeremy trots forward and links his arm through hers.

I should have done that—God forbid one of them tumbles off the dock or falls while climbing the stairs—but I'm too distracted.

With them gone, I turn to Ronan.

When he left my house this morning, he was wearing clothes from last night. Now, he's in a coral-colored golf shirt and light gray dress pants, and I can't decide if I want to admire him as is or peel his clothes off to enjoy what's beneath. "What are you doing here?" Suspicion laces my voice.

"Didn't you get my text?" Ronan wastes no time, hopping onto the tiki and coming around to herd me into my captain's spot.

My back hits the helm. "I did, just now."

Leaning in, he meets my lips in a soft kiss, much like this morning, pulling away just far enough to whisper, "Hey."

"Hey." I close my eyes for a moment to inhale his cologne. "What's up?"

He presses his body flush against me.

"Besides you," I clarify. Whatever brought him here hasn't upset him. That's a good sign, I think?

His chuckle tickles my ear. "I've got to book a decent fishing charter for a rich and important guest, and I figured you'd know the good ones. My assistant found four that can do it. Everyone else is booked."

"A fishing charter? That's what this is about?"

"For tomorrow morning."

I breathe a heavy sigh of relief.

He frowns. "Why? What'd you think it was about?"

"No idea. What are their names?"

He digs his phone out of his pocket and opens it up. "First one is Marlin O'Keefe. You know him?"

"Yeah, and you don't want him. That guy's boat looks like it's a day from sinking every day. How he keeps his license is beyond me."

"Okay. What about Barry Philips?"

"*Barry?*" I scoff. "Did your assistant read any reviews before calling?"

Ronan's brows pucker. "So, not a good choice?"

"Not unless you get off on being verbally abused. He makes Frank look like Winnie the Pooh. That guy is one of the most miserable assholes in Mermaid Beach. Seriously, look him up on Yelp. I think he has a one-star average rating. There's a rumor that he made his crew swim to shore once. I don't know if that's true, but I wouldn't be surprised."

"Shit, I can't bring Olivia out with someone like that."

My stomach clenches. "Your client is named Olivia?" As in, a woman?

"Yeah. Apparently, she's big into fishing."

"Sure she is."

He pauses, studying me. "Why?"

"No reason. How old is she?"

Ronan's lips curl with a knowing smirk. "I don't know, and I don't care."

"Good answer," I mumble, though it doesn't help

much with the knot forming in the pit of my stomach. A woman wants to get Ronan alone on a boat?

Then again, I can think of sexier ways to lure him in without literal bait and hooks.

"Yeah? Well, how about this answer: I have everything I want right in front of me." Ronan reaches into my gaping uniform shirt, slipping his finger under my bikini top to tease my nipple.

It hardens instantly.

Memories of last night flood my mind, and a swell of heat quickly follows. I edge in closer until our bodies are flush once again. I've missed this all day. "Do you have time to come back to my house?"

"Fuck, I really wish I did."

I reach up and slide my bikini cup to the side, exposing my breast for him only.

His eyes flare with heat. "Maybe I can—"

Heavy footfalls sound on the dock then.

Ronan curses under his breath and drops his hand to his side.

My irritation flares while I readjust my suit before turning around.

"Hey, boss," Will calls out. Jeremy is on his heels. "Ran into your group up top. Looks like you had a wild bunch."

"Yeah, those ladies can party." I point to the empty cans in the trash bin, evidence of their afternoon debauchery.

Will jumps onto the boat, casting a "Hey, man" to Ronan before he sets to cleaning up.

Our private time is officially over. For now.

"Who're the other charters?" I prompt. He did come here for a reason besides fondling me.

"Randy Pegg," Ronan reads out loud.

"Randy Pegg," I echo, my face pinched up in thought. "His name is super familiar, but I don't know ... Hey Will, do you know a Randy Pegg? Charters fishing boats?"

He pauses halfway off the dock, his tan arms straining under the weight of the cooler. "Yeah, isn't that the guy who accidentally impaled his brother in the thigh with a spear gun?"

"Oh my God, you're right!" I laugh, even though it's the furthest thing from funny. "He tripped over a rope or something. The brother's fine," I quickly add.

"No to Randy Pegg." Ronan curses. "And let me guess, Nic Wheeler just got out for manslaughter."

"Nic's available?" That's a rarity. "No, he's great! Really reliable. More expensive, though."

"I don't give a shit. It's on Wolf. Let me get Archie to book him." Ronan's thumbs fly over his screen. "All right, thank God that's done. I need to get back."

"I'll walk you out. I'm heading to Gigi's." I grab my bag and throw a wave at the guys. "By the way, the new captain starts tomorrow. Her name's Bailey."

"Is she hot?" Will asks.

Jeremy cuffs the back of his head. "See you tonight at the bonfire, Sloane?"

"Yeah, I'll be there tonight."

His eyes flitter to Ronan, darting to his bruised knuckles. "You too?"

"We'll see how the day goes." Ronan casts a lazy

salute before falling into step beside me, his hand settling on the small of my back. "So, you hired her?"

"Yeah, and I think she's going to be great." We sat on two beach chairs in the shade outside the coffee shop while Bailey filled in details about every aspect of her life, including her honorable discharge after multiple deployments to the Middle East. In my head, I'd hired her within the first five minutes. I hope my gut isn't wrong. "Things around here feel like they're getting back to normal." Except for the whole pregnancy thing, of course.

Ronan's face pinches with discontent.

I reach up to squeeze his bicep. "Don't worry, *Tiki One* is still yours if you want it."

"Yeah, maybe." He chuckles, but the sound is off.

"How was work today?"

"Weird." He tells me about his golf morning and his meetings as we climb the steep staircase, side by side. By the time we reach the top, I'm laughing.

"You have to take her up on it. When else are you gonna get to go *duck herding*?" How is that even a thing?

"I don't think that's why she wants me there." He smiles wryly.

"Right." While I may be drooling over Ronan every time he walks into a room, so is *every other woman*, it seems, including my merry band of drunken afternoon sailors. "And you're supposed to do what with these clients?"

"Make them feel important so they'll spend money with us."

"By chartering a fishing boat." It's a struggle not to sound jealous and accusatory.

"It's her thing." We stop in front of his BMW, the pristine black paint gleaming in the sunlight. "Things are gonna go late tonight, but I'll text you when I'm done." He pulls me in close. "Wait up for me."

"Sure." It's not even a question that he's coming over. I think that's what I love most about Ronan—he doesn't play games. And concern over what his boss thinks about us together? Completely gone, out the window. "How late, though? I might fall asleep." I've been unusually tired these last few days. I can't tell if it's on account of my overactive hormones or suddenly feverish sex life.

"Then send me the code to your door, and I'll wake you up."

A thrill explodes inside me at the thought of the many ways this man might do that. "You're basically asking for a key to my house? Wow, that's presumptuous."

"You're kidding, right? Everyone in your commune has the code to your house. Fucking Ralph probably knows how to peck the digits."

I burst out laughing, earning a rare grin. "Did he shit on your car last night?"

"Has he failed me? Why do you think it's so clean?" Ronan's hand slides down over my cutoffs. "Why are you wearing these?"

"Why am I wearing shorts?"

"Yeah." He palms my left cheek with a squeeze. "They're obstructive."

"Because the last time I captained without shorts, I got manhandled."

"You were with a bunch of deviants." His hand slips under the hem and up between my thighs, working beneath my bikini bottoms.

I gasp as a long finger pushes inside.

A clubby beat begins playing from Ronan's pocket, stalling his explicit touch. He pauses, listening, and then shakes his head.

"What is that?"

"A song from a movie. It's got to be Belinda calling. Connor's been playing with my ringtones again. I need to change my passcode." With a heavy sigh, he says, "'Kay, Gotta go. See you later." His touch vanishes, earning my grumble as he leans in to kiss me. It's over quickly, though, and then he's climbing into his car, his phone pressed to his ear.

I watch as the sleek car pulls out of our parking lot, already aching for tonight.

"So ..." Skye hangs out the guest registration window.

———

"Sloane's got a boyfriend," Rebel says in a singsong voice as Skye describes this afternoon's parting. Thankfully, we were angled away from her, so she didn't get the full view. The view she did get was apparently plenty steamy.

"I don't know what he is." The denial tastes off the second it leaves my tongue.

"Here." Skye holds out a bottle of Sapporo, waving it in the air to and fro, waiting for me to collect.

"I'm good, thanks."

"Really?" She peers down at the full beer in my grasp, now warm. "You nursing tonight?"

Not tonight, but soon enough, potentially. I'm always good for a couple at the end of a long day, so I figured the best cover was to hold a prop. I probably should be dumping periodically.

"Pass that over." Jeremy claps his hands and then deftly catches the fresh beer midair with a "gracias" and a wink for me before jumping back into conversation with the guys on the other side of the fire. Rolland just finished proudly announcing that he carried five beach chairs at one time, earning a round of jesting about his pipe cleaner arms. Every staff member's here, even Lara, and everyone seems to be getting along well, the long, hot days bringing them together quickly.

It reminds me of old times.

While everyone's busy teasing Rolland, I stealthily pour a gulp's worth into the sand.

"Another long day." Frank drops into his customary folding chair next to me.

I jump. "Don't sneak up!"

He makes a point of looking down at his mammoth body, as if the very idea is preposterous, before shooting me a doubtful look. "Get your ears checked."

"It's not my ears. The ground normally trembles upon your approach."

He tosses his water bottle cap at my forehead.

Did Frank see me dumping my beer? Probably not. It's dark. "There's baked ziti and Caesar salad inside. I left the dressing on the side so it didn't go limp." Frank is a notoriously late eater.

"I'll grab it in a bit. You see Mick's report?"

"Yep. Already pulled their deposit and put in a replacement order." People don't read the fine print, especially the part where Sea Witch stipulates charging for damages when people return beach equipment in pieces.

"How's Gigi?"

"Great. She won a hundred bucks playing blackjack with Hank and Larry." Two horny old men who are constantly fighting over her, oblivious to the fact that she'll never give either of them a shot.

"Probably fleeced them both." Frank chuckles through a gulp of water. "I'll bet she loved hearing about dinner last night."

"Did she ever. Her favorite part was how Ronan punched Henry." The gasp and ensuing cackle was priceless.

"And Wolf still hasn't fired him for that."

"Not as of 4:00 p.m. today, but maybe tonight? I don't know, but selfishly, it'd be nice if he did because then I wouldn't have to find a third captain."

Frank grunts, and I brace myself for a lecture. Does he disapprove of Ronan working at Sea Witch like Jeremy hinted at earlier? Given my last foray into "dating the help," I wouldn't be surprised. "Tell him to park on the other side of your Cherokee tonight. I almost couldn't get out this morning."

"Who says Ronan's coming over tonight?"

I get a flat look in response. "Oh, I'm sure he'll be coming."

I snort. *And so will I.* "Bailey's going out with me tomorrow, and if all goes well, I'm opening up bookings for *Tiki Three*. Hopefully, we can fill up the days. I'll keep going out as long as I have to, but maybe we'll get another hire soon." The longer the season stretches on, the less that's likely, given contracts end in October.

I'll be, what—I quickly do the math—five months along by then? Is that right? Definitely showing.

"One down, one to go." Frank raises his water bottle in our customary nightly cheers, and I absently tap the neck of my beer bottle against it, my mind churning through reality. I need to make a decision, but I know which way I'm leaning.

"Does he know yet?" Frank asks, cutting into my thoughts.

"Huh?"

He leans in, dropping his voice. "Does Ronan know yet?" His words are slow.

"About?"

"You want me to say it out loud? Really, Sloane?"

Fuck. My stomach drops. "How did you know?"

"Told you, you've been acting off for days. And I caught you doing *that*." He nods to the dark puddle in the sand where I dumped my beer. "And never, in all the years that I've known you, have you *not* drank after a toast."

"It's bad luck," I echo what Gigi always says. As well as I know Frank, he knows me too.

And now he knows my secret. A wave of relief hits me that I don't have to keep it from him anymore.

"So? Does he know yet?"

I glance around to make sure no one's paying attention to our conversation before I shake my head. "I don't know how to tell him."

"You open your mouth, and you say the words. Simple."

"But it's *not*." That ball of anxiety swells in my stomach. "I really like him, Frank. Like, *really*. But we've known each other for weeks. We barely know each other at all. What if he doesn't want it?"

"You mean, what if he's like your sperm donor of a father?"

"Yeah," I admit after a beat. Never met the guy, but maybe I have daddy issues after all.

Frank is quiet for a moment, his focus on the fire. "Do *you* want it?"

I hesitate. "I think so, yeah." I'm more comfortable with the idea each time I let it wander into my thoughts. "I'm thirty-one. I own my home and my business, thanks to Gigi. I'm kind of set." Except for that one missing piece —a partner to share it all with.

Could that person be Ronan? If it's not, if he runs the moment he finds out, then ... he truly is all wrong for me.

"All right, then you have it."

"Alone?"

"You're never gonna be alone, Parker. You got me, you've got them." He nods at Skye and Rebel and Jeremy. "You've got your village, just like Gigi always says. We can make it work."

I allow myself a few long, calming breaths as his words sink in. I don't know why I was so afraid to tell Frank. He's always been my rock. "And Ronan?"

He shrugs. "He's here if he wants to be."

"And if not ..." I let the thought drift.

"Then I rip his arms off and beat him to death with them."

I burst out laughing at Frank's signature threat.

"Uh ... Sloane?" Mick calls out, interrupting our laughter. He nods to something behind me. "You expecting the boys in blue?"

"What?" I spin around in my chair. Sure enough, two forms in uniform are strolling this way, their flashlights shining their path.

Cops haven't visited here since that time there was an escaped convict on the loose and someone reported seeing them heading down our driveway. Turns out the guy was hiding out in a tent on the vacant property next door.

What on earth could this be about?

I shimmy out of my seat and head to cut them off, Frank on my heels. "Can I help you, Officers?" Not until the beam of light shifts away do I recognize Jackson. "Oh, hey! Long time no see!"

"Hey, girl." His friendly face splits with a wide grin that reminds me of our days back in high school, when he was catching pigskins and I was waving pom-poms. An injury killed his chances of playing college ball—a devastating blow for a running back with a promising career. So, he joined the local police force and has served Mermaid Beach ever since.

The other cop is a stodgy, gray-haired mustache-man whom I've never seen before and, I'm guessing, I'm not going to like.

"What's up, fellas?" I ask.

"Do you have a permit for that?" The stranger cop points to our fire.

"Well, no." I steal a confused glance at Jackson, who sat around this fire more than once back in the day.

"County law requires a permit for all bonfires on the beach."

"But we've never had an issue before." I don't know when the law changed, but no one's ever bothered us about it in the years since it has.

"Now you do." He pulls out a notepad. "I'm citing you for this infraction."

"Are you kidding me?" Frank erupts from behind me.

The cop adjusts his stance and peers over his nose at Frank. "Sir, I'm going to ask you to take a step back and calm down."

"I *am* calm," Frank retorts.

The cop's eyebrows arch in challenge. "Sir, I'm going to ask you one more time—"

"Frank, just ... go over there." I step in between them, waving a hand toward the small, curious crowd. The last thing anyone wants is for Frank to get arrested for being himself.

With a grumble, he saunters away.

The dickhead returns to his ticket pad, his pen jotting quickly under the glow of the flashlight he tucked into his double chin.

"I don't understand. The Sea Witch family has been doing this every night during the season for, like, almost fifty years." Well before my time, anyway. "Why is this suddenly an issue?"

"Got a complaint."

A complaint? "From who?" I look from him to Jackson, who's remained mute in all of this. "There's nobody here except ..." Wait a minute. Of course. "Someone from the hotel called you guys." I glare up at the monstrosity in the near distance. It's not even open to the public yet.

"You're lucky I'm not writing you up for being too close to the grass." The cop tears the ticket off his pad and thrusts it forward. "If you want to have a bonfire on the beach, you can apply for a permit like everyone else."

"But we'd have to apply every day." And pay. "And we're barely on the beach!"

"I don't know what to tell you. Move your pit to your property and call it a cook fire. Keep a pack of wieners nearby."

I can't read the ticket in the dark to see how much I'm on the hook for, but any amount is infuriating.

"See you around, Sloane." Jackson salutes and mouths *"I'm sorry"* before trailing his partner away.

A swell of anger erupts inside me. "You're supposed to be using red light bulbs for the turtles!" I holler after them.

Frank marches over. "How bad is it?

"I don't know." I dig my phone out of my pocket to use the light. And gasp. "*Five hundred* dollars!" I don't have that kind of money to burn!

He curses. "Who do you think called?"

"It had to be Henry or that GM who hates me." The only person I know it wouldn't have been is Ronan. But maybe he'll know who launched an arrow at the target on my back.

I dial his number and wait impatiently as it rings.

20. Ronan

"**B**orn and raised in the Sunshine State, lived here all my life, save for a small stint in Washington. I've been a resident of Mermaid Beach for *forty-two years*, to be exact. Believe me, I've seen the place go through all kinds of evolution," Gayle Anderson says, the twang in her voice indicative of a Floridian. I spotted her speaking to Henry, and I just knew she had to be local government because there was no way this woman, in her high-collared blouse and pleated calf-length skirt, was a high-powered executive. She looks like she spends her afternoons crocheting on the front porch while reporting her neighbors for putting the trash out too early.

I didn't get to Gayle's dossier, but Belinda confirmed she's the county commissioner and plays a key role in how Mermaid Beach grows and changes, which means Henry must be greasing this grandmother's palms to get what he wants.

And I intend to find out exactly how.

A server sweeps past with a tray of champagne then.

"I don't think I should have another." Gayle fans her face with her hand as if hot. Her cheeks are definitely rosier than they were when I cornered her.

"You should *always* have another glass when it's Cristal and you're not paying." I smoothly swap our glasses for two fresh ones.

"You're right." She accepts it with a laugh. "You're *completely* right. But just one more. So tell me about yourself, Ronan? How do you like the area?"

"I love it. I moved to Miami a few years ago, and now I'm here, and I have to tell you, I could make this my home. I mean, look at it." I gesture out toward the gulf ahead. The sky is dark, but Seraphina's is lit up with torches, and the sound of the waves rolling in is unmistakable. Mix it all up with the sea air? Idyllic.

It's not a lie—I honestly could settle down in Mermaid Beach, but that likely has more to do with a certain sea witch than the beaches or the atmosphere. Sloane's offer of a job and a place to live isn't a bad one. I've always liked working with my hands better anyway. But we'd be moving a bit fast. I mean, I'd basically be living with her.

Gayle adjusts her glasses to get a better look at me. "And where did you grow up?"

"Indiana."

"Oh, been there once, in the winter too." She shudders, then laughs. "My grandchildren have been begging us to take them on a ski trip, but I don't know if I can bring myself to do it!"

"You have grandchildren? I would not have guessed

that." I might not be adept at ass kissing, but the longer I spend in this role, the better I seem to be getting at it.

"Oh." She chuckles, patting my arm in a matronly manner. She's nothing like those thirsty ladies on Sloane's tiki cruise today, the ones who looked seconds away from circling me. I'm sure Gayle would label them sinful heathens. "Aren't you sweet. I have six."

"Six!" I force with exaggeration—seriously, whose skin am I wearing? It's chafing. "Tell me about them."

"Oh, gosh, where to begin." She gulps her champagne. "Well, there's Noah, Jacob, and Elijah. Those are my daughter Mary's sons. And then my son Samuel has two girls and a boy: Ruth, Joseph, and Sarah."

"Good Christian names," I note.

"Oh, yes." She nods, her brow furrowed with pleasant surprise. "Henry said the very same thing."

I'll bet he did. He was looking for an angle in, and clearly, he found it. "And which congregation do you attend in the area?"

"Our Lady of the Pines."

"That's the one on ..." I frown, as if struggling to search my memory, letting it dangle.

"Sugar Sand Drive, in Old Town. The big, beautiful white church with the palms on either side."

"Right. I've seen it. Nice place." If I've passed it, I don't recall.

"Yes, Henry and his lovely wife are coming for service on Sunday."

"Are they, now ..." I purse my lips to suppress my smile. Abbi, I understand. She was raised in the church. Before coming to Alaska, she was set on marrying the reverend's son in their small Pennsylvania farming community. But I doubt Henry has stepped foot in a church since he was forced to as a child, and from the snide comments I've caught about the institution and the people who frequent it, I'd half expect him to go up in flames when he crosses the threshold.

"Henry was telling me how his mother-in-law is a devout Christian."

"She is that." I met Bernadette Mitchell in Alaska for the wedding. I've never seen anyone spontaneously cross themselves so often and for seemingly no reason— usually, when Margo was in the room. How she came around to her daughter marrying a man she considered the devil is still a mystery, but I'll bet it had something to do with money. It always does.

As it likely does here. "So, you're an active member at Our Lady?"

"I'd say so." She chuckles, as if my observation is cute. "When I'm not busy running youth groups and charities for the area. And then, of course, there's the work I do for the school board and the advisory council, and ..." She lists all her extracurricular activities, along with awards and recognitions for all her good Christian work.

I listen intently, searching for the hook Henry cast. I know him too well, and he buys his way into everything.

"You sound like a busy lady."

"I don't rest much, that's for sure. Howard—that's my husband—complains sometimes that I don't know how to sit still, and maybe I don't, but I feel like my work is important. I think it's one of the reasons I keep getting reelected."

"It is. Absolutely." My tone, my rapt attention ... Who the fuck am I right now? Surely, I could get an Oscar nod for this.

It goads her on. "My Back to Grace Foundation is especially important. It funds all sorts of events that bring families into the community. I started it nearly fifteen years ago when I saw a distinctive shift in values." Her eyes widen with meaning. "It's concerning, seeing so many young people losing their way. All these *alternative* lifestyles and *ideas* being forced down their throats, especially with social media feeding them nonsense. Every corner of entertainment is pushing their sin-filled agenda these days. Not even literature is safe anymore, aside from the Good Book. They can't change that!"

Clearly, Gayle is a specific kind of Christian—the kind who thinks she has a right to tell people how to live and hides behind bible verses while she does it.

I bite my tongue against the urge to ask if me and Connor fucking a woman at the same time is considered an alternative lifestyle. "So, this foundation, how does it combat these issues?"

"It focuses efforts on providing as many wholesome, faith-based interactions as possible in the community. By doing so, I believe these lost people can find their way back to the Lord."

"Praise be." It's taking everything in me to keep a straight face.

She nods with approval. "The hotel's contributions have certainly helped."

Bingo.

My phone is vibrating in my pocket, but I ignore the

call because I need to learn what I can from this woman. How I'll use it, I have no idea. "So Henry's made a donation to your charity?"

"Oh, yes. Several sizeable ones." She laughs. "I won't lie, when I first heard about plans for this hotel and the area, I was against them. But Henry has helped me see the benefits over time."

How many digits did it take for her to see the light, I wonder.

"What about you? I see you aren't wearing a wedding ring," she notes. "You should come to our Sunday service. There are plenty of young women who attend. I could introduce you to a few."

Old Ronan would accept, like a fox discovering a hen house, and every single one of those young, godly women would end up screaming my name just to prove a point. "I'm not sure what my work schedule looks like."

"The Lord shall wait for no paycheck." She waggles her finger.

My experience at church is limited, but I doubt that's a proverb.

Her eyes wander. "Oh! There's Mayor Wilson."

I follow her gaze to a short and stocky bald man by the fountain.

"I've been trying to get hold of him all day. Henry had me earmark a chunk of money for Theo's son's outdoor adventure club so they can go camping in Idaho this summer. What an experience for those kids."

I struggle to keep my expression smooth. "Does Mayor Wilson know Henry's the one helping out with that?"

"Of course he does! The boys went to Yosemite last year. Theo said the scenery was spectacular." Her smile is genuine. "Henry has been so generous. Councilwoman Reeves' daughter and a few classmates are going to Paris in the fall to study fashion! And Councilman Maher's wife has been trying to start a community theatre, so we're giving her the funds to do it. That's a big one. We've been saving for years. No way we could do that without Henry's help."

"That's *amazing*." What's amazing is that this woman doesn't seem to see Henry's game for what it is. But she can't be this dense ... can she? Either way, two drinks in and Gayle is a fucking canary.

"It truly is. Our community is going to thrive, all thanks to Henry. Of course, he doesn't want credit for it. He's happy to allow the foundation to shine." A hiccup escapes Gayle, earning her laughter. "I think this drink might have put me over the edge. Oh dear, it looks like Theo is leaving. I don't want to miss him before he ducks out." She reaches out to squeeze my forearm. "It was so nice talking to you, Ronan. We'll see you on Sunday?"

"I'll try my best."

Gayle rushes across the room.

"Really great talking to you," I murmur after her. So, Henry is funneling money through Gayle's charity organization to support causes and win votes, and he's buying Gayle's vote by helping her with her mission to save all the lost souls.

"Look at you, schmoozing the politicians." Abbi appears at my side to tease me. She's in a short silk dress that accentuates her belly.

"I think I need a shower," I mutter.

"I met her earlier." Abbi nods toward Gayle. "Reminds me of my mother. Only less fanatical."

And more dangerous. Gayle holds a position of power. Bernadette just likes to gossip and judge.

"She certainly does love her church," Abbi continues.

"I hear you're going this Sunday."

"Oh, haha." She chuckles as if I've made a joke but then sees my expression. "Wait, what?"

"Didn't you know? It's part of Henry's grift to hold her vote so he can push through his big plans for Mermaid Beach. He's tossing money at all of them." I can't help my bitter tone.

"No." She shakes her head. "He wouldn't do that."

"He is. Through her foundation. You know, the one to bring back traditional family values." I sling an arm over Abbi's delicate shoulder and lean in to whisper in her ear, "What would dear, sweet Gayle say if she knew what we'd done in Alaska?"

Gooseflesh coats her skin. "She'd be appalled, but for the right donation would choose to look past it." Even as she jokes, her cheeks flush with the reminder. It always does when I flirt with her. Before, I'd do it on purpose just to get that reaction and remind her of what we had, but now that Sloane is in my life, it feels wrong.

I'm about to pull away when Henry appears. "Is there a reason you're fawning over my wife in front of everyone?"

"Needed a place to rest. There are a lot of people here." I pretend to size up the crowd as I keep my arm on her. "What are you telling them about that shiner?"

"Nothing. No one's asked."

I snort. "Bullshit."

"If you don't move away from my wife right now, you'll have two to match," he threatens in that cool, even tone.

"I hear we're going to church on Sunday?" Abbi cuts our bickering off, ending the issue by stepping out of my reach and into Henry's. Her tone is flat. She's not pleased with his scheming either.

Henry answers it with a smug smirk. "What's one Sunday morning when you spent every single one there for years?"

"Because you hate the church. And it's deceitful."

He sighs. "They get what they want, and I get what I want. Everyone wins."

"Sloane doesn't," I blurt. She's all I care about here.

"I am not altering my entire business plan on account of the woman you're fucking this week," he barks, then glances around as if to make sure no one overheard him. Henry is all about image, after all. "I hear you're taking Olivia out fishing tomorrow?"

Nice diversion. "Yeah, after golf. Can't wait to tell her what an asshole you are." I dig my phone out as it vibrates again.

UNKNOWN:

You better get over here. She's at it again.

I frown at my screen. Maybe it's a wrong number.

Who is this?

How did he get my number?

Three dots bounce, then disappear, and then a picture comes through of a colorful stack of poster board signs piled on what appears to be a shed floor.

"Oh shit."

"What is it?" Abbi asks, worry on her face.

"Did you call the cops on Sloane for her bonfire?"

Henry's scowl tells me it wasn't him before he says, "As if I'd waste my time with that."

Probably not. But I know who would.

A quick scan proves Belinda is nowhere in Seraphina's, but there's no way she left the hotel. "Talk to you later," I say to Abbi.

"7:00 a.m. tomorrow at the clubhouse," Henry chirps after me.

I throw my middle finger in the air as I walk away, not caring who sees me do it.

———

THE PIT IS EERILY EMPTY. Everyone's been working so hard leading up to this week, I'm glad they've gone home for the night.

I head for the executive hallway. If Belinda is hiding, it'll be in her office.

A light glows behind the opaque glass at the end of the hall, confirming my hunch.

I march toward it, anger roiling in my veins.

I'm maybe ten feet away when I hear the rattle, the telltale repetitive thump that I recognize immediately. It could only be one thing. The female moan that carries a moment later confirms it.

Who could she be with in there? The two most likely suspects—Merrick and Preston—were at the bar when I left, so it's not either of them. She would *never* bring one of the media open guests to her office to fuck. So who else …

On a hunch, I dig out my phone and dial Connor's number.

The telltale tune of the *Top Gun* theme song he programmed for my number sounds from behind the glass.

I shake my head. Clearly, whatever Belinda did to him last night wasn't enough to scare him off.

They last another thirty seconds, the grunts and moans and desk creaks increasing in tempo and fervor before the grand finale. If the ringtone didn't give him away, the string of curses that comes with Connor unloading is a dead giveaway.

I lean against the wall as I wait for them to get dressed and emerge. It won't be long—neither of them is the cuddling type.

"You know where to find me for next time," Connor says, close to the other side of the glass.

"There won't be a next time," comes Belinda's sharp tone.

"That's what you said last time—oh, hey, man." Connor pushes through the door to find me there. His hair is standing on end like Belinda had fistfuls of it, and he's red-faced and sweaty from exertion. "You called me. What'd you need?"

"Nothin'."

He shrugs. "Okay, see you at home?"

"Not likely." Unless Sloane takes her anger out on me and doesn't let me in.

"Tomorrow, then. Little Lyle's comin' in, right?"

Shit. I almost forgot. "Yeah, can you pick her up from the airport? I'm tied up here." Or, more accurately, on a boat.

"Yeah, for sure. Just send me the flight deets and warn her so she knows to look out for me."

"Later." Right now, I need to deal with a problem. I duck into Belinda's dimly lit office in time to see her fixing the last button on her blouse. The air stinks of perfume and sex, and paper lies scattered on the floor.

"Did you call the cops on Sloane?" I demand with no preamble. I managed to avoid Belinda all day, but I knew we'd have to do this eventually.

"I did." She says it so matter-of-factly as she collects the condom wrapper from her desk and tosses it into the trash can.

I pinch the bridge of my nose to quell my irritation. "Why?"

She smooths her fingers through her tousled platinum-blond locks. "They have fires daily on the beach, and there's no way they're getting permits for those. I let it go up until now, but we're opening, and I will not have nightly parties outside our ocean-view rooms."

"They're not *right* outside those rooms—"

"They're close enough," she snaps.

She doesn't give a shit about the fires. What Belinda cares about is that not only did I reject her, but I did it because I'm hooking up with the one person who dares to stand up to Wolf Hotels. Then, I strolled into this hotel with Sloane on my arm. I basically threw it in Belinda's face.

But now, she's kicked a proverbial hornet's nest. "That wasn't the best decision."

"I disagree." Her smile is smug.

"I thought you wanted the signs down for the media opening."

"And they are, thanks to you."

"When do the journalists arrive? Tomorrow morning, for that tournament? Plenty of time." I check my watch. "This is gonna be good. Henry will be thrilled."

Her amusement fades. "She doesn't know it was me who called."

"She knows it came from the hotel. Whether she thinks it's you or Henry doesn't matter. But Henry's gonna love being out there on the green tomorrow. We're paired with the editor for *Coastal Luxe Escapes*, right?" A highly influential magazine for the area. "Hope it was worth it."

Belinda's expression has soured. "Given you two are so close, I'm sure you can convince her to uphold her end of the deal."

"I could try, but I don't think I will." I've regretted my part ever since I learned about Henry's plans.

"I don't have time for these games, Ronan."

"Then you probably should have left her alone."

Belinda's thumb clicks the top of her pen repeatedly while she sizes me up. "I strongly suggest you ensure your *girlfriend* behaves. Otherwise, I have no issue digging up the names of those hires we passed on and offering them the positions they should have had. I assume these people still work for her at the Sea Witch?" Her groomed eyebrow arches knowingly.

Someone's been doing her research. Belinda didn't even care to know Sloane's name before yesterday.

The threat has me closing in on her desk, my anger finally reaching its boiling point. "Leave Sloane and her business alone." It'll be bad enough when those officials show up with paperwork behind that eminent domain bid. She doesn't need to lose her staff too.

"I could try, but I don't think I will." She winks as she throws my words back at me.

"Belinda," I begin, restraining my fury but struggling to remain calm as I glare down at her. "Leave Sloane the fuck alone."

"Or?" she taunts.

"Or I will make sure every last Wolf employee knows all about you and Connor, and you and me and Connor. In graphic detail." I can't believe I'm using that as leverage. It's a shit move, and I'm a shit human for doing it, but if it protects Sloane, I'll toss my conscience aside. Henry was right—people are capable of lashing out in unexpected ways.

My palms rest on Belinda's desk as I lean in. "They will know how far down your throat we got, how much you love being on your knees. They'll practically be able to hear you come every time you walk past them in the hall."

Her eyes flash with panic, but they harden in the next beat. "You do that and you can consider your employment with Wolf terminated."

My laugh sounds downright evil. "Do you think I give a shit? I punched Henry in the face last night in front of everyone," I remind her as my phone chirps with another text.

Frank has sent another picture, this one of Sloane balancing on a ladder, her back to the camera as she hangs a bright orange "Fuck You!" sign in a tree.

She's going to fall off the damn thing. Why is Frank allowing this?

"Let me be crystal clear: If even one of Sloane's employees quits on her, I will sing like a fucking soprano on opening night."

Belinda's throat bobs with a hard swallow.

With that threat delivered, I rush for my car.

———

I slow as my headlights catch an opossum scampering across the driveway. There's plenty of wildlife around. The outdoor crew chased a sizeable hog across the parking lot last week. They've also reported a family of armadillos digging up a sand pit near the sixth hole.

Lights glow in the trees to my left, closest to the golf

course. Which version of Sloane am I going to be dealing with? The one who burrowed against my chest while sleeping last night, or the one who left me lying on the beach like a pointless cause?

I pull in next to the Cherokee and hop out, half expecting Ralph to be waiting. But it looks like he and the hens are in the coop for the night.

A large, dark shadow emerges from the woods.

"Good timing. She's almost got the one about the roaches in place," Frank declares in greeting.

"She found that story, huh?" It happened at the LA Wolf location. Turns out the couple who found a dead cockroach in their dinner brought the bug from home in a jar. The idiots were looking for a free stay and some publicity and didn't think they'd get recognized on TV by any of the five other hotels they'd scammed with the same stunt. Even though their claim was discredited, the hotel took a hit.

"It's gotta stop. You and I both know these little signs of hers aren't hurting anyone but *her*."

Still, they'll get a reaction tomorrow. "Belinda's the one who called in the bonfire."

"Does she know what she's unleashed?"

"She knows the signs are on their way back." I drop my voice to a near whisper. "So she threatened to call up all the Sea Witch staff members and give them jobs." Though if I know Belinda at all, my threats of retaliation will be enough to stop her.

Frank curses. "That would be a disaster."

"You don't know the half of it."

"Why?" That distrustful scowl appears. "What don't I know?"

"It's just … there's a lot going on. Things I'm not allowed to share." Then again, I'm sure there are rules against assaulting the hotel owner and blackmailing the GM, and I've broken those. But if there's one thing besides Abbi that Henry will protect at all costs, it's his family's empire. Doing anything to jeopardize it will earn his wrath.

Frank folds his thick arms across his chest. "Does it affect Sloane?"

I hesitate. "Yeah. It does. Big-time."

"Then I suggest you spit it out right now, unless you care more about the hotel than about her, in which case you can get back in that car of yours and *never* show your face here again."

He waits quietly, but he might as well be screaming because I hear him loud and clear. Fuck it, it's all going to be out in the open in two days, anyway. The clock is ticking, and it's too much for me to keep this to myself anymore. Plus, maybe Frank might have advice on how to break the news to her.

In hushed tones, I reveal Henry's plans for the harborfront and this property.

"He can't do that," Frank blurts when I'm done.

"Believe me, if there's a way, he will find it. He's greasing every palm and kissing every baby. In the end, that cocksucker will always get what he wants."

"Jesus." Frank pinches his brow, and I know he sees the truth in my words. "How long have you known?"

"I found out two days ago. He told me on Monday

when he arrived. How long he's had it in the works, I can't say. A while, is my guess. But the big unveiling for media is on Friday, and then it'll be all out in the open. I've been trying to get him to leave this place and the Sea Witch out of it, but I'm not getting anywhere."

"This could not have come at a worse time."

I frown. "Why? What else is going on?"

He shakes his head. "Nothing."

There's definitely *something*, but Frank's not the kind of guy you can push for information. As it is, I have enough to deal with tonight. "How do I tell her?"

"You don't. Not yet, anyway."

"I shouldn't have told you." But I feel lighter. It's not all on my shoulders anymore. This behemoth can carry some of the weight.

"Come on."

I follow him as he trudges through the forest toward the lights, the branches snapping beneath his weight. "How'd you get my number, anyway?"

"You gave it to me. That time you came in looking for her." His tone screams "you idiot."

"Oh, right." I'd forgotten. "And you kept it?"

"How else am I supposed to threaten you?"

If I hurt Sloane, he means. That's the last thing I ever want to do. Odds are good that she'll be the one to crush me.

Multiple camping lanterns line the chain-link fence, casting enough light to illuminate Skye holding the base of a twelve-foot ladder while Sloane teeters at the top. Nearby, the dark-haired coffee girl is threading string.

My palms are sweating. "You let her up there?"

"*Let?*" Frank snorts. "That's funny."

She's going to break her neck.

"Hey there," Skye greets with her Southern twang.

"Hi, we haven't officially met. I'm Rebel," the other introduces herself with a wide smile. "Ronan, right?"

"Right."

"Oh look, Frank tattled on me," Sloane muses, her tone a mixture of grim amusement and annoyance.

"Hard at work on a Wednesday night?" I choose a light, playful tone, even as a voice inside my head screams for her to get down from there.

"We *were* enjoying ourselves by the fire until our asshole neighbor called the cops on us." Sloane loops the string and fastens a knot with force.

"Yeah, that was Belinda." May as well give credit where credit's due.

"I know y'all are swimming in money with your mermaid tanks and thousand-dollar-a-night rooms, but for local folk that Wolf is screwing, a five-hundred-dollar fine isn't chump change. That's groceries."

I let out a whistle. Fucking Belinda. I'm feeling less and less guilty about the dick move I pulled in her office.

"So glad I didn't pitch these." Sloane stretches on her tiptoes, her little yellow sundress climbing high, her calf muscles straining.

"Careful," Rebel warns, stalling on her task, her brow furrowed with worry as she watches her boss. Skye's face doesn't look much happier.

The crazy woman is going to fall.

"Need any help?" I ask, moving in closer.

"Nope," Sloane declares curtly, while Skye and

Rebel chirp, "Yes!" in unison. Even in the poor lighting, I don't miss the pleading look in their eyes, the way their heads bob.

They've strung three signs up already. I shine my phone flashlight on the closest one. "'Wolf Empire Tainted by Death and Scandal.' It's a little broad if you ask me."

"If you're here to convince me to not do this, you're wasting your breath. You may as well go home to your beach mansion."

"I'm not here to convince you of anything." Other than to get off that ladder. "I figured another set of hands will make it go faster." I'm vibrating with energy. It could be the tension, or it could simply be seeing Sloane again.

She pivots on the ladder rung to face me. I wish those eyes weren't hidden by the dark so I could read them. "You want to help me put all my signs back up?"

"I can think of other things I'd rather be doing, but sure."

There's just enough light to make out the corners of her mouth twitch before she returns to tying her knot.

Skye and Rebel share a private glance. They've been roped into this insanity against their will.

I nod toward the house and the trailers.

Skye's head bobs in understanding. "Oh, you know what? I forgot my water. I'm just going to grab it back at my place—"

"Same! And more string!" Rebel adds.

I take over holding the ladder, and with a mouthed "good luck" from Rebel, the two girls trot off through the trees, stumbling in the dark.

"You abandoning me too, Frank?" Sloane asks.

"Yup. You got it from here?" Frank's big, bushy brows climb halfway up his forehead. They seem to say so much.

You won't let her fall?

You'll talk her off the ledge?

You'll take good care of her?

"I've got her."

With one last furtive look at Sloane, he ambles back the way he came.

"Aim this on the branch for me?" Sloane tosses her flashlight down. I have to move fast to catch it, the beam of light inadvertently shining upward, showing off white panties beneath her skirt.

"Not exactly dressed for climbing trees."

"It's not what I expected to be doing tonight."

"That makes two of us." I'd so much rather be peeling those off her in bed. My dick jumps at the thought.

"You don't have to stay."

"There's nowhere else I'd rather be." Even if I'm catering to this insanity.

"I think that one's good." With her last knot tightened, she climbs down. "You can let go now."

"Not a chance. The ground here is uneven."

"Suit yourself." She keeps moving, her ass bumping my face on her way down.

The urge to pin her body and bury my tongue between her legs is overwhelming, but I can read the room—or dark, gnarly treed area—and her mood does not say Enter, so I resist, instead getting some enjoyment from the way her body rubs against mine as she continues until her feet touch the ground.

"You can move the ladder over—"

"Hey." Gruffness laces that single word as I dip down to kiss her neck.

Her body shudders with a soft sigh, and after a beat, she tips her head to give me better access.

I greedily take it, inhaling her scent as I nip at her skin. "I'm sorry," I whisper.

"It's not your fault."

Taking a step back, I seize her hip, guiding her body around to face me. "It was a shit thing for Belinda to do."

Sloane's gaze drifts in the darkness toward the beach. "Gigi built that fire pit when she first moved here. Sea Witch staff has sat around it every night during the season for decades. There are so many good memories, and it's never been an issue until now. Why couldn't she just let us be?" She sounds so defeated.

"She's jealous."

"Of what?"

"Of you." Was Belinda planning on reporting Sloane's fire anyway? Probably, but I helped solidify that decision for her. I hesitate. "She propositioned me yesterday, and I turned her down, then showed up with you at dinner."

Her jaw drops. "She hit on you? She's your boss. That's harassment. You can go to HR. You can have her fired—"

"But I won't. I've crossed more than my share of lines, including with her."

Understanding fills Sloane's face. "You've been with Belinda too."

"Once," I admit reluctantly. "Connor was there."

"Of course he was," she mutters. "You two are like a pair of dirty socks."

I chuckle. "I don't think I've ever been called that before."

"Honestly, is there *anyone* you haven't slept with? Any one attractive woman in your life that you *haven't* fucked." I can see the wheels in Sloane's brain moving quickly as she asks that question. And then she gasps, and I know where this is going before the words are out.

"Oh my God. There was an article about you guys in Alaska. It actually named you. I can't believe I didn't connect the dots until now."

My irritation flares. "That was a shitty hit piece of fabricated nonsense." And it caused months of whispers and turmoil in all our lives. Even my mother heard about it and questioned me. That was an awkward conversation.

"So, it's not true, then? You haven't fucked Abbi?" Sloane watches me.

The denial is on my tongue. I've never admitted it out loud. Only Connor knows—because he was there—and even he doesn't know about that last time, in Abbi and Henry's cabin. "Do you really need to hear me say it?" Because I don't want to lie to her.

She falters, as if taken aback. "So you literally have slept with every woman you've ever met. You know what, don't answer that." She holds a hand up to stop me. "I don't think I want to know." Sloane wanders over to lean against the chain-link fence.

What's going on inside that head of hers? Is she deciding if she can get past my track record?

I've never regretted a second of my life choices. Until now.

I edge in behind her, caging her in with my arms. We listen to the sprinklers watering the grass for a lengthy moment.

"If it makes you feel better, I only loved two of them," I admit.

"It doesn't." After a beat, she asks, "Who?"

"Tasha and Abbi."

"Does Henry know?"

"He does."

"Bet he loves that."

"He does *not*." I rest my chin on her head and slip my arms around her, one hand settling low on her flat belly.

The sound of her breath catching cuts into the quiet night, and then her hand presses against mine, holding it there.

"I'm sorry about what Belinda did. I wish I knew how to fix it." I wish I could fix everything for Sloane.

"You can't. And my stupid little signs won't help, but they make me feel better."

"You want to hop the fence and go fuck on his green?" Because I know that will make *me* feel better.

"He probably has cameras." But humor laces her voice.

"I know where they all are." There's no way I'd let that prick get off watching a video of Sloane and me.

She sinks back into my body. "I wish I had something more than old headlines to throw at him, something to really get under his skin."

A thought strikes me. I hesitate, but only for a second. "I might have something for you."

"Really?"

"Yeah. Something that will definitely gain notice." And likely cement my spot in the realm of the unemployed if Henry figures out I'm the whistleblower.

She twists in my arms and peers up into my eyes, hope shining in hers.

My fingers trace her jawline in the dim light. "God, you are beautiful."

"What is it?" she pushes, undeterred. "What do you know?"

I shouldn't cater to this spiteful mission of hers. Frank's right—it's not healthy. But if she's going to do it anyway, I'll be there right beside her.

"Fine, but you're not getting back up on that ladder."

21. Ronan

BRITT:

On my way! Tasha's on my plane!

Safe flight. I got caught up with work but Connor's coming to get you. Look for the big, blond jock in the red Bronco.

I know what Connor looks like. I've seen pics

Absolutely not. He's off-limits

I'm twenty

And he has fucked at least twenty women since we moved here

Ew

See you soon.

"You seem chipper today." Olivia adjusts her wide-brimmed golf hat while we sit in our respective carts on the path, waiting for Henry and Keegan from *Coastal Luxe Escapes* to finish at the tenth hole. The soft mauve color matches her sleeveless shirt and short skirt and is a stark contrast to her heavy black sunglasses. All in all, a flattering outfit that makes Olivia look young and toned and way less uptight.

And it does nothing for me.

My dick is officially out of commission for all but one woman, and it feels glorious.

"Good night of sleep." If "sleep" means worshipping Sloane's body from every possible angle a second night in a row. "And my baby sister is on her way down with her best friend. I got her a room for a couple of days at the hotel."

Olivia's face lights up with a sincere joy. "That's sweet of you. How old is she?"

"Twenty." I shake my head. "I remember when she was six."

Olivia hums. "My Jenny is turning sixteen. They grow up so fast. You'll see one day," she says with a wink and then returns her attention to Henry and Keegan as they stroll side by side toward us and their carts, their caddies trailing behind.

It's funny, as uncomfortable as our coffee shop meeting was yesterday, I'm oddly relaxed around this high-power CEO.

I peer over my shoulder to spot Belinda and the rest of her team—Lena, Gayle, and a fourth person I can't identify from here—waiting at the start. The good old county commissioner is practicing her swing. Things couldn't be going better if I'd planned them out myself.

"Do you enjoy this?" Olivia asks suddenly.

"What?"

"Golf."

"No, I fucking hate it. If I knew this was part of my job description, I might have stayed back in Miami."

Archie struggles to smother his snickers.

"Well, you're doing very well," she counters. "We're almost even."

"Yeah, I wouldn't brag about that if I were you. I basically picked it up this week."

Her smirk is hard to read—is she amused or insulted? "What about fishing? This charter that you've booked for us today."

"You didn't give me much choice about coming with you, but I actually do like fishing," I admit.

Olivia slips her sunglasses off to appraise me. "I really appreciate your honesty, Ronan. It's refreshing. Equally refreshing is you not kissing my ass."

"I wouldn't insult you by trying."

Henry and Keegan close in on their carts.

"Sure you don't want to throw in with the boys, Olivia?" Henry eases into his cart. His eye looks worse than it did yesterday, but if anyone can carry it, it's this condescending prick. "We're up to two fifty now."

Holy shit. That's a quarter-of-a-million pot. Maybe I should actually *try* to play this game.

Olivia's smile is wide as she slides her glasses back on. "Well, I just don't throw around money like the *boys* do. I like to know it's worthwhile first." Her Texan twang seems intentionally heavy, and the undercurrent in her words is strong—Wolf Hotels isn't getting money out of her that easily either.

Henry's returning smile is tight. "On to the next hole. My favorite one. Ronan's spent a lot of time there, haven't you?" He doesn't wait for my answer, speeding off in his cart.

"Why'd you punch him again?" Olivia muses, though I sense it's a rhetorical question.

"You might be about to see him return the favor. Come on." I take off after him, not wanting to miss the moment Henry rounds the bend.

The old bedsheets Sloane and I repurposed and strung up are impossible to miss, stark white banners against the green trees and clear blue sky, the black lettering legible from way farther than those small poster boards. They are, in my humble opinion, a far better "fuck you" to Henry Wolf.

And they've stopped him dead on the cart path.

I slow down some distance back—no need to crowd him in this moment of glory—prompting Olivia to ease up next to me.

"What does that say?" She squints. "Mermaid Beach council members and their families benefit greatly from funds donated ..."

"—by Henry Wolf to County Commissioner Anderson's foundation." I don't have to see the words. I'm the one who painted them on. "Anderson previously voted against Wolf Hotel Mermaid Beach plans, until change of heart." It took a bit of digging through public records, but with Sloane's help, we found proof of the sudden switch.

Archie whistles but otherwise stays mute.

The one next to it is equally suspect.

Back to Grace Foundation sends Mayor Wilson and son on yearly trips with funds from Henry Wolf.

"Bribery's never a good look," Olivia murmurs.

"No. Especially not when the county commissioner is golfing right behind us." And based on the schedule I scanned this morning, Mayor Wilson is one team behind her.

She looks over her shoulder, as if Gayle's literally there. "You know this commissioner?"

"I met her last night."

Olivia is quiet for a moment, and I can see she's piecing together bits—Henry's black eye, his crass comment a moment ago. "And this person who lives on that property is ..."

"My girlfriend."

Henry's caddy scrambles out of the cart, and then Henry is driving off the path and racing toward the chain-link fence.

"You may want to go save her, then."

"She doesn't need saving." I peel off in my cart to follow him.

22. Sloane

"Is that him?" Frank squints at the golf cart that races across the green toward us.

"Uh-huh." A second cart follows, Ronan behind the wheel. A third isn't too far behind, but the driver in it has stopped and has what appears to be a small camera aimed this way. A reporter, surely. According to Ronan, the green would be crawling with them today for this media open tournament thing.

Anxiety swirls in the pit of my stomach.

"I thought you weren't supposed to drive on the grass," Frank muses.

"He owns the grass. And I guess he's not too worried about it right now."

When Ronan laid out the plan, I balked. I mean, it sounds like a solid accusation. Is it true? Is there any proof to back these claims up? Or have I earned myself defamation suits from two powerful local politicians and Satan, himself?

But Ronan said to trust him. He was adamant this was the right play, and it would land hard and true.

Maybe *too* true based on the stony expression on Henry's face.

He hops out of his cart and strides toward us, his white golf tee pressed and clinging in all the right places. It's 9:30 a.m. and eighty degrees, and I don't see a single sweat stain.

"Howdy neighbor!" I call out through a sip of coffee.

"Too much," Frank warns from his position next to me, arms folded, looking every bit a bodyguard.

"I disagree."

"The stain is a nice touch, though."

"What?" I peer down at my white tank top and note the red splotch over my left boob. "Shit!" Raspberry jam from my toast. That wasn't intentional. Oh well, too late now.

My body is tense as I mentally prepare myself for this confrontation.

"Sloane Parker," Henry says smoothly, stopping short of the chain-link fence, his gaze drifting over my pajamas, stalling on the remnants from my breakfast.

Ralph chooses that moment to let out one of his infamous rooster caws, earning Henry's pained cringe.

"Man, that's a nice shiner," Frank notes. "Who punched you?"

He recovers his composure in the next beat. "I'm sure you already know. It's Frank Hale, right?"

Frank stiffens. He wasn't expecting that from a man he's never met.

I should have warned him ahead of time. "Your investigator really did his homework, huh?"

"What is this?" Henry points to our ode to Gayle Anderson, hanging high up in the trees. An identical one for Mayor Wilson flutters in the light breeze nearby. As sad as I was to lose that set, I will admit it's gone to a good cause.

"Well, I could be wrong, but it appears to be a bedsheet."

His jaw grows taut as he studies me intently. Is it an intimidation tactic? I'm sure it works on others.

I sip my coffee extra slowly, refusing to shy away.

Ronan closes in then, his cart coasting at top speed. It's barely stopped before his shoes are on the grass. "Morning, Sloane. Frank." He eyeballs my outfit and mouths *"Nice touch."*

I purse my lips to hide my smile.

"We were just discussing these libelous claims on Ms. Parker's property," Henry says smoothly.

That word. I swallow the rising panic that swells inside me.

But Ronan smiles. "They're only libel if they're not true."

Henry gives us his back to square off in front of Ronan. "And what do you think you know?"

"Only what Gayle herself told me."

"There is no law against donating to a charitable cause."

"To a county commissioner who was originally against your hotel?" Ronan crooks his head. "I'll bet Councilwoman Reeves' daughter's trip to Paris will be highly educational. And the mayor's son's camping trips? Did Wilson go too?"

Silence meets Ronan's question.

He continues. "Reporters love uncovering a scandal. I wonder what else they'd find if they started digging through those charity records and connect the dots. And hell, bring on the lawsuit. Does that mean I'll end up on the stand? I'll have to speak the whole truth and nothing but the truth, so help me God." A wicked gleam shines in Ronan's eyes. "Imagine the kinds of things that might come out."

"What the fuck are you doing," Henry growls.

Ronan steps in closer.

Are they about to throw punches? Again?

I hold my breath, the tension cloying.

"Just taking a page out of your book and protecting those I care about," Ronan responds, his tone equally lethal. "Doesn't feel too good being on this end of it, does it."

Henry moves in, his chest bumping against Ronan's. Maybe he thought Ronan would step back or lose his balance.

But Ronan stands his ground, not budging an inch.

"I hope it's worth it. You're done. Pack your shit and get the fuck out of here." Turning back to regard the sheet-signs one more time, Henry flashes a cold smile. "Enjoy your home while you still can."

A chill runs down my spine as I watch him march back to his cart and speed away, the wheels drawing divots in the plush green grass.

"Should I finish my round of golf?" Ronan hollers after him.

Henry answers with a middle finger in the air.

"That went well," Frank mumbles.

Ronan wanders over to the chain-link, folding his arms over the top rail. "How's your morning going so far?" His tone is glib, as if he didn't just get fired with an audience.

I move closer, resting my chin on his bicep. His smell —Irish Spring soap and mint-scented shampoo—is familiar and comforting. "You okay?"

"I'm fine. I knew it was coming."

And yet he dove in feet-first and wearing that signature smirk. "Was this a bad idea?"

"No." His mood grows somber instantly as he shifts to free an arm. Reaching up, his fingers are gentle as he strokes strands of hair off my face. "This needed to happen."

"Why?"

"Because Henry is ..." His words fade as his eyes dart behind me, I assume to Frank. "Just because."

Ronan's subtle threat hangs in the air. "What do you have on him?" Because he clearly has *something*.

"Nothing he wants out in public. Look, I've gotta go deal with the fallout from this. It's messy."

"You're coming here later, though, right?"

"Yeah. I'll be the one on foot, carrying all my belongings."

"Oh my God." That's right. He just lost everything. His home, his job, his car. *Everything*.

For me.

"I'm sorry."

"Nah, don't be. Didn't like it much anyway."

"Liar."

He leans in and kisses my forehead. "It might be a bit busy around here today."

"How bad?"

He pulls away and walks backward toward the cart. "There's about thirty teams coming through and reporters in the mix."

"What about them?" I point upward at the banners. I've been to plenty of town council planning meetings. I've spoken to Gayle Anderson and Theo Wilson on numerous occasions. They smiled and nodded and promised that my concerns were valid and would be considered, that the council wouldn't allow Mermaid Beach to be taken over by big corporation. All while their kids and grandchildren will be camping under the stars and planning trips to Paris, on Henry Wolf's dime. "You let them say what they want. Trust me, none of them wants this to go to court."

I watch him drive off. Is he right?

"Lover Boy really just torched his life for you." Frank sounds impressed, which is even rarer than getting him to smile.

"Was it for me, though? Or was this about them?" Ronan has never hidden his dislike of Henry, and after what I learned last night, I'm beginning to think it has more to do with Abbi than anything else.

Is he still in love with her?

"Nah, Parker, I think this was all about *you*."

I frown as I peer at Frank. "Since when do you

defend any guy I'm seeing? And since when have you ever thought my crazy signs are anything but crazy?" When he saw the banners this morning and learned of our scheme, I expected him to climb up the ladder and cut them right down. But instead, he sided with Ronan and abandoned his Sea Witch responsibilities to plant himself in a chair out here, like a sentry.

"A lot of changes are coming."

"Yeah, no shit. It's *my* womb that's hosting a surprise invasion."

"That's not the only invasion." He gestures to the folding camp chairs, signaling for us to take a seat. "There's no good time for you to find this out, but there's something you need to know."

23. Ronan

"Well ... fuck." Connor smooths his palms over Darla's steering wheel as we wait for Britt and Dani to emerge from the airport's front doors. One positive to my newly unemployed status is that my calendar is suddenly wide open.

It took me the drive to the airport to fill him in on everything that's been going on. I got to this morning's grand finale as we were pulling in.

"So, like, you're finished here, at Mermaid Beach?" he asks.

"I'm guessing all Wolf Hotels." I can't see how going back to Miami's Outdoor Crew is an option anymore.

"This sucks!" he explodes. So far, Connor is showing more emotion than I have.

"Yeah. It was a good run while it lasted."

"What am *I* supposed to do? I came here with you." The wheels are churning in his brain. "Dude, we live in his fucking house!"

"Sloane has a trailer you can use."

His flat look makes me chuckle.

"Hey, we slept in bunk beds in a cabin with four other guys for an entire summer. It was basically camp. Don't get all bougie on me now."

"Of course I could handle that. There were hot women sleeping all around us up there."

"Well, perfect, then, because there will be two smoking hot women in trailers next door and the ocean fifty steps away."

"Huh." Connor tips his head with renewed consideration. "Okay, that could work."

"Yeah, I thought so." No need to mention Frank yet. "Look, I'm sorry if this fucks up things for you. I had to do something, though. What Wolf is about to do to Sloane isn't right."

"Yeah, I hear ya, man." Connor drags his tongue over the fading bruise on his lip.

I'm about to ask what Belinda did to him when the glass doors slide open and Britt steps out, wheeling her too-large suitcase behind her as she scans the area, looking for a red Bronco.

"There they are." I hop out and jog forward.

Britt's chocolate-brown eyes light up with her squeal. "I didn't think you were going to make it!"

"My schedule freed up." I collect her in my arms, lifting her small body off the ground and spinning her in the air, like I used to when she was little. She's still wearing the same braids as she did back then.

"Stop! You're gonna make me barf."

"Just do it before you get in his car," I joke, setting her back down.

A familiar freckled face is behind her. "Hey, Ronan!"

"Dani." I pull her into my chest in a hug, resting my chin on the top of her head. "Damn, how long has it been?"

"Three years, I think?"

"You haven't changed a bit. Still pale-ass. You're gonna burn in this sun." I yank on her strawberry blond ponytail, earning her giggle as she pulls away.

"Your hair is longer."

"Yeah." I reach up to push a hand through it. "Might shave it again. It's hot here."

But Dani's head is shaking fervently as she peers up at me. "No, this suits you. It looks good." Her cheeks flush.

It seems her crush has not faded yet.

"Finally, Little Lyle." Connor's deep voice booms behind me

"Connor, this is my sister, Britt, and her best friend, Dani, who is like a sister to me." Even if she's looking at me in a very non-sibling way.

"I've heard so much about you." Britt holds a hand out.

Connor cringes at it. "What? No."

Before Britt can register his words, he has her in a bear hug, rocking back and forth like a child squeezing its favorite stuffed animal.

When she peels away from him, she's laughing.

Dani gets the same treatment.

"All right, all right. Greetings are over." I know Connor too well to be comfortable with his hands all over them.

"Welcome to Mermaid Beach." Connor throws a meaty arm around each of their shoulders and leads them toward Darla. "Gosh, we're gonna have *so* much fun."

"Don't worry, I'll get the bags." I shake my head at his back. He's trying to get under my skin; that's all this is. He wouldn't try anything on either of them.

Fuck.

Would he?

"Ronan!" a familiar voice calls out.

I turn around, and there she is: Tasha, my first love, the woman who crushed my heart.

Holy shit. She's actually here.

She looks the same and yet different. Still tall and willowy, her crop top showing off a hard stomach. That featherlight brunette hair I used to love fisting is cut to her chin. It suits her.

With a wide grin, she leaves her spot by the limousine that her friends are climbing into—I recognize some of their faces—and rushes over, plowing into my body.

It's a beat before I return the hug, shocked to be seeing her again.

"It's *so good* to see you," she purrs in my ear.

"You too," I manage. I used to know this body so thoroughly. She doesn't feel the same, though. She doesn't feel right.

Not like Sloane's body feels right.

With one last tight squeeze, she pulls back but stays well within my personal space, her hands landing on my biceps. "You look amazing. You've been working out."

"Yeah, I needed another addiction since I quit smoking." I've been slacking a bit lately, but now that

I've got more time, I can get back to the gym and running.

"You quit? Good for you." Her hazel-green eyes sparkle. "So, you came to greet me?"

"Giving Britt and Dani a ride." I toss a thumb behind me.

"Oh, right. Of course. I'm so dumb." She laughs at herself. "Well, come and say hi to everyone!" Her hand slides down, fitting into mine as she attempts to tug me toward the limo.

"Actually, how about I meet you at the front of the hotel. I'm heading that way anyway, and these parking attendants are eyeing us." I slip my hand out of hers and move backward toward Darla. "It's a fifteen-minute drive. Twenty, tops."

"Okay? See you there." With a lightning-fast scan of my body, she strolls back to the limo, her hips swinging with each stride of her lengthy legs.

I climb into the passenger side of the Bronco. And groan.

"You, my friend, have a Valkyrie sitch right there." Connor points to the limo.

"Yeah. I'm gettin' that." And the sooner I shut it down, the better, but in front of the airport didn't seem like the right place.

Britt leans in, her arm draped over Connor's seat. "What's a Valkyrie sitch?"

"It means she's making moves to ride your brother's dick—"

"Con!" I bellow at the same time that Britt yells, "Gross!"

With a grin, Connor shifts into gear. "Buckle up, Little Lyle."

"Get moving!" A security officer slaps our hood.

"I'm *movin'*! Don't fucking touch her!" Connor roars before pulling away from the curb, his glower aimed at the skinny man as we pass. Thankfully, his anger fades as quickly as it came. "What are you gonna do about the ex this weekend? Obviously, she can't stay at the house now."

"The fuck if I know."

"Why can't Tasha stay there?" Britt asks.

Connor's eyes flicker to the rearview mirror. "'Cause your bro just got fired, and we have to move out, stat."

Synchronized squeals of "*What?*" erupt from the back seat.

———

THE FRONT ENTRANCE to the hotel is buzzing with activity—cars pulling in and out, bellhops loading luggage onto carts, servers carrying trays with mimosas. No expense has been spared for these next two days while Wolf wines and dines a slew of who's who, reporters, and pretty people who will look good on camera.

And in the thick of it all is Belinda, greeting people with her fake but convincing smile. She's swapped her hot pink golfing outfit from this morning for a sultry coral suit.

"Don't worry. I'll have things sorted by Saturday, one

way or another," I promise Britt as Connor pulls up to the door.

We hop out as a flock of attendants moves in.

"Welcome to Mermaid Beach!"

"Will you be needing help with your bags?"

"Can I offer you a refreshment?"

Britt and Dani fumble over their words, making me laugh. Neither of them has stayed in a luxury hotel before, but they smoothly accept the flutes and cheers each other with a giggle.

I could warn the staff that they're not legal yet, but I won't.

I don't fucking work here anymore.

Belinda's heels click as she approaches.

My shoulders stiffen as I prepare for a confrontation. I haven't talked to her since we squared off last night.

"Aren't you supposed to be working?" She peers down her nose at Connor, which is a skill, considering he's a good six inches taller than she is.

"Lunch break." His blue gaze dips down into her displayed cleavage. "You're looking well."

With a sharp warning glare, Belinda turns her attention back to me. "These are guests of yours?"

"My sister and her friend." If she even thinks of revoking these golden tickets—

"Welcome to the Wolf Hotel. Please, follow Sammy inside, and he'll make sure you get all checked in." She gestures toward the bellhop.

"Call me later?" Britt moves in for a hug.

"Yup. Have fun and stay out of trouble." I jut my chin

toward Dani. "You too." It's a moot warning. Dani lives her life on the straight and narrow.

With excited grins, they skip inside.

"What, you thought I would bar their entry?" Belinda muses.

"The thought did cross my mind."

"Why? To give you a reason to cause another scene? You're becoming so good at it. No, that wouldn't reflect well on the hotel, and some of us care about this place."

"*That's all* some of you care about," I throw back.

"Shouldn't you be getting back to work, Connor?" She scans his uniform.

He takes the hint. "Guess so. Ronan?" He holds up his keys, waggling them once in the air before tossing them to me. "Treat Darla nice."

"Thanks, man. I'll come get you after work."

"See you in your office later, B." With a wink and an air-kiss, Connor strolls away.

Belinda checks around us to see if anyone overheard. "To think, you had it all, and you threw everything away."

"I didn't throw anything away. I know where my priorities are. You should reevaluate yours. When was the last time you saw family? Or went out with a friend?" I drop my voice. "Or didn't choose your fucks based on who's most convenient?"

Her eyes flash with anger.

But I didn't come here to argue with her. "My other golden ticket guests are on their way. I hope you'll show them the same courtesy." I slide on my sunglasses.

Belinda hums. "The ex-girlfriend."

"And her friends, for a bachelorette party. Oh, perfect. Here they are." I nod toward the approaching white limo. The sooner I can be done here, the sooner I can see Sloane again.

Everything after that ... we'll figure out.

The girls spill out in a fit of laughter but are quickly distracted by the hotel's grandeur and a nearby tray of mimosas.

"At least they'll photograph well for the hotel. If they can stay sober enough." Belinda strolls forward to greet them.

"Ronan!" Carrie rushes in and ropes her arms around my neck, nearly choking me. If I had to guess, she's had a few cocktails on the flight down.

With a chuckle, I peel her off. She looks the same as she did the last time I saw her. "Congratulations." I tug on the bride sash hanging crookedly over her torso. Tasha and two girls I don't recognize wear ones marking them as bridesmaids.

"Thank you!" she squeals. "Did you ever meet Hank?"

"Doesn't ring a bell."

"He went to Grayson High too, but he was a few years older. He played football. Wait, did you play football? You guys would have gotten along. Well, maybe you still will! God, you look good." She pauses in her mile-a-minute rambling to ogle my face first before she moves on to my body. "Tasha has been talking nonstop about you since you guys reconnected. It makes me so happy. Honestly, she was such an idiot for breaking up with you. I tell her that every day—"

"Okay!" Tasha rushes in, grabbing Carrie by the biceps and gently guiding her to face the hotel entrance. "Follow them so we can get checked in to our rooms. I'll be there in a second."

"Okey dokey. See you later, Ronan." She skitters away.

"Oh my God, I'm so sorry." Tasha hides her face under her palms for a beat. "We got no sleep last night and started the party early."

"Give her some water. You don't want to miss dinner tonight. It'll be one of the best meals you've ever had." I can give Wolf credit for that much, at least.

"I don't doubt it. This place is even more incredible than the pictures." Her eyes trail up the storied facade. "You'll have to take me for a tour. When are you going to be done for the day?"

"Actually, I don't work here anymore."

Her jaw drops with shock. "What?"

"Yeah, as of this morning."

"Seriously?" She pouts. "What happened?"

"It's a long story. Don't worry, it's all good. But I'm losing the house. I'm on my way there now to pack up my shit. Which means I don't have a place for you to crash this weekend." I wince with apology. "Sorry."

"Oh, right. Of course. Don't worry about it. I'll figure something out. But what are *you* going to do?"

Perfect segue ... "Crash at my girlfriend's until I can figure out my next move."

Tasha's mouth makes an "oh" shape. "That's—a relief, that you have a place, I mean." But the disappointment in her eyes says otherwise. "Does she live around here?"

"Yeah, right next door."

"Nice." Her head bobs slowly. "Has it been long? I mean, did you know her before you moved here?"

"No, I met her when I got here."

"So, it's still new."

I know that pitch in her voice. It's hopeful. She's hoping I'm going to say "nah" or "we're just having fun" or any combination of words that means she still has a way in.

There might have been a time when I would have felt satisfaction with crushing that hope after the pain Tasha caused me. Now, I only wish her well.

"Yeah, but it's serious." At least it is for me.

"Well ... I'm happy for you. Truly. Kinda shitty for me." She smiles sheepishly. "But I guess I realized what a good thing we had too late."

From the corner of my eye, I spot Olivia strolling toward a black sedan, dressed in a business suit, pulling her suitcase behind her. What the hell? She's supposed to be on that fishing charter. *Shit.* "I gotta go."

"Oh, yeah, go, do what you've gotta do. I hope I see you around so we can catch up." Tasha takes off in a rush to rejoin her friends.

And I jog over to reach Olivia just as she's about to climb into an airport taxi. "Hey."

She stalls. "Ronan."

"Why aren't you out there reeling in a grouper or some shit like that?"

"Because I lost my fishing partner. Some man with a broom for a mustache showed up at my door to replace you. I turned him away."

"That's Darian." I chuckle. "Damn, has Belinda already promoted him into my position?"

"I have no idea. I stopped listening the moment I opened my door. So, that's it for you here?"

"Looks like."

She slides her sunglasses off to reveal concerned eyes. "How are you doing?"

"I'll be fine. Sorry if the back half of your game wasn't as much fun."

"I wouldn't say that. The eleventh hole was *something*. And then Henry triple bogeyed, *twice*. It was a spectacular fall from grace. I doubt he's ever played such a terrible round in his life."

"I guess he won't be claiming that pot."

"I'll say." She grins. I think I've finally met someone—other than Sloane—who truly dislikes Henry. "That county commissioner and the mayor left their rounds and hunted down Henry to speak with him at length. Stalled our abysmal game, and then he drove off after the fifteen hole without so much as an apology. They were definitely *not* happy. I noticed a few carts with people holding cameras whizzing by."

"Rushing to get their shot before the evidence vanishes." I don't know what it is about Henry Wolf, but he attracts headlines like flies to shit.

"Those bed sheet banners will be on the front page of state and local news by Saturday." Olivia nods in agreement.

"That's what we're hoping for." Because a lot of questions will inevitably follow.

She studies me intently. "Was it worth it?"

"I guess we'll find out soon enough." Breaking a confidentiality agreement is the least of my worries now. I give her the thirty-second rundown about Henry's plans.

She hums when I'm finished. "You must really like this woman to go to all this trouble."

"I do. But I also don't like Henry demolishing people's lives so he can get richer. How much money does one person need?"

"You do know which industry I play in, don't you?" Her laughter is soft.

I shrug. "What can I say, Gayle's lips flapped like a flag in the wind after a glass of champagne, and she gave me ammo. I decided to use it. Nothing else has been working."

"Some people really shouldn't drink." Olivia shakes her head. "To be fair, though, I was dead sober when I admitted my unhealthy fear of horses. I suspect you have an unusual skill for getting people to say and do things they normally wouldn't."

"Yeah, I've heard that once or twice." I jut my chin at the open trunk, where the driver patiently waits for Olivia to release her grip on her bag. "So? You going home early?"

"Yes. A few issues have come up that I need to deal with in person. Plus, I miss my girls."

"Belinda will be *displeased*."

Olivia snorts. "She's been circling. I told her that the only interesting person at Wolf abandoned me. Let her stew in that." She reaches into a pocket in her purse and produces a business card. "If you need help, you give me a call. Henry's not the only one with friends in high places."

I stare at it blankly for a beat before accepting it. "I might take you up on that."

"I hope you do. And if you're ever interested in working for me, I'm sure I can find you something."

"I don't know shit about oil and gas."

"You're smart. You can learn." She nods to somewhere beyond me. "Henry Wolf's wife is not waiting for *me*."

I peer over my shoulder to see Abbi standing by the Bronco, wearing a short tan sundress and a pained expression. Clearly, she's heard the news. A heavy sigh escapes me. This is going to be an uncomfortable conversation.

Olivia pats my arm. "Take care of yourself, Ronan."

"You too, Olivia."

"Ollie to my friends." She winks and then climbs into the back seat of the car.

I ease the door shut and then head over to where Abbi waits, my chest tight with anxiety. "Hey, Red."

She cocks her head as she peers up at me through a lens of sadness and disappointment and something else I can't discern.

"I'm sorry. I had no other choice. I can't sit by and let him do this to her. At least now, maybe she'll have a fighting chance." If people start poking around to see how much truth there is to these claims that Henry's buying votes, what are they going to find? How many trips and projects have been funded by "the foundation"? And is it enough to reverse whatever plans he's shoehorned into the city development agenda?

Or maybe I'm deluding myself.

"I wish you'd talked to me about it first."

"Why? So you could talk me out of it?" I scoff. "It was a spontaneous, late-night decision. And don't worry, he'll be fine. Henry's not stupid enough to leave incriminating evidence." He probably has something on every single one of them in his back pocket, courtesy of his PI.

"You really disappointed him."

"Yeah, well, I wish I could say the same, but Henry is exactly who I knew he was. A callous prick that I should never have risked my life to save."

She winces. "I tried. Honestly, I did. I talked to him after dinner on Tuesday and then again last night. I even brought up Wolf Cove and his grandparents' history and all that. But you know how he can be about business."

"This isn't on you." I smooth my hands over her biceps—delicate but deceptively strong, thanks to all those years on the family farm. "Look, I'm not trying to make your life difficult. And I had every intention of staying here. I was actually starting to enjoy the job, I think. But there's no fucking way I can work my ass off every day for a guy who says he's doing all this in memory of his father, who built an entire resort in Alaska to honor his grandparents and personal connection there, but then fucking destroys everyone else's lives." I take a deep, calming breath.

"I think that's the most number of words I've ever heard you speak in one string," she muses.

It earns my laugh, despite my anger.

"Is it just about protecting Sloane's property and business?" Abbi asks gently. "Or ... is there another reason you're doing all this?"

"Well, yeah, it's because I care about her."

"But is there any *other* reason?"

"I don't understand what you mean." She's fishing for something.

"So, you don't know?" She studies me intently, as if searching for my lie.

"I don't know *what*, Abbi?" I can't remember the last time I used her actual name, but I'm not in the mood for games.

She lets out a frustrated groan and glances around us. "Okay. I have to tell you something. I promised her I wouldn't say anything, but I think you need to see the *whole* picture. You have a right to know."

Unease slips down my spine. "Know *what*?"

24. Sloane

I trace the faded turquoise lettering on the stone's surface.

I remember this rock.

I was twelve, and my mom had just passed. Gigi and I were walking along the beach at sunset, as we did most nights, and we came upon this flat, round rock at the shoreline, where the waves lapped and the warblers foraged for bugs. It was far too heavy to wash up on shore overnight, and yet it seemed like it had done just that.

Gigi insisted that Mom had placed it there for us and that we should move it to sit among our chairs. That way, Mom would always have a spot with the Sea Witch crew as they huddled around the fire each night. It was a silly tale, and I knew it, but I went along with it anyway.

The two of us lugged it all the way back, struggling and stopping for breaks. Once we got it there, we spent all night deciding on the right spot.

Did Mom like to look out on the ocean or at our home?

Did she sit closer to the fire or farther away?

We must have rolled this thing around ten times, but once we settled on a place, I painted "Mom" across it in her favorite color. And that's where it's stayed ever since.

"We'll move it," Frank says. "I'll build a new pit right over there, and they can shove their fire permits up their ass. Hope they get paper cuts."

"I'm pretty sure the permits are digital now," I mutter, feeling defeated. If what Frank just told me is true—which I have no reason to believe it isn't—then is there even any point? They're going to force me out and pave over everything.

"We'll fight it, Parker. You're good at fighting."

"Yeah, and what has that gotten me? I fought that place for years, and there it is." I throw a hand toward the great looming building. "So, what, I'm going to fight the town this time? You know how it goes when they start talking about needing new roads. They can claim just about anything they want. Remember Seaglass Way at the edge of Old Town? All those big, beautiful, hundred-year-old houses?" The homeowners argued for historical significance, and everyone thought they had a good shot. The Mathers house was the oldest home in the entire county. But they lost, and the bulldozers moved in. "All that effort and money and time that I'd spend, and it'd be a waste. I don't have it in me anymore, Frank." I drop into a chair. "I should just enjoy this while I can." Will we even be here next year? How long before they'll expect me to vacate the premises?

His forehead furrows. "There's still a good reason to fight. Wolf's fingerprints are all over this, and that's not okay. He's a private corporation, and he'll benefit. All those businesses around the Sea Witch aren't going to take this lying down. You're not alone in this. This will go to court."

But the same fire that drove me for years hasn't ignited now. "I know I'm not alone, Frank." I look pointedly at him. "Now, I have someone *else* to think of. How am I going to bring a baby into this world when it's taking everything from me? My home, my livelihood. How long before Gigi's gone too? Oh my God, Gigi." I press my hand against my stomach as it roils. "This is going to kill her." How long can I keep the news from reaching her ears?

Frank's heavy frame hunches over the back of the Adirondack chair as the weight of this seems to settle on him too.

We sit in silence for a lengthy moment, as the faintest sound of laughter carries from beyond the trees. It's a woman. Likely enjoying an early cocktail on that glamorous patio, reveling in the picturesque gulf and balmy heat, oblivious to the turmoil the owner of that hotel is causing countless people.

Even Ronan got caught up in it.

"He really did try, huh." Things are beginning to make more sense now. He insisted I meet Abbi; he hoped she'd love me. Maybe enough to persuade her oligarchic husband to back off? He punched Henry in the face! Did that have anything to do with this? Even if not specifically, I imagine knowing this didn't help.

"When did Ronan find out?" I ask.

"He said Monday."

"When Henry came in." That's the evening he surprised me after my swim. That troubled look on his face ...

He knew, but he didn't tell me. I can't decide if I'm angry or not. Would I have any right to be, though, given I stood in that shower with him, holding my own giant secret?

I *need* to tell him.

The alarm chirps on my phone, signaling the coming afternoon cruise schedule. "I've got to go. Bailey's training with me today."

"I can do it," Frank offers.

I pull myself out of the chair. Sitting here moping isn't going to change anything. "No. I don't want her scared away on the first day." Though something tells me she doesn't scare easily.

He snorts at my poor attempt at a joke.

Somberness quickly takes over again as I pause to admire the view from our little slice of heaven, the water rippling, a pelican soaring above, the oat grass swaying in the slightest breeze. "It all feels like it's crumbling, doesn't it?"

Frank reaches out to gently squeeze my shoulder. "We'll figure it out. We always do."

I force a smile to try and quell the voice screaming in my head.

Not this time.

This time, I'm pretty sure we're about to lose it all.

25. Ronan

The Bronco jolts and bumps as I hit the countless potholes racing up Sloane's driveway. Connor would be screaming if he could see me abusing Darla like this, but I don't give a fuck about his vehicle or my unemployment or anything else.

Sloane is *pregnant*?

How the fuck is she pregnant? I mean, I know *how*, but she said she was on the pill. It had to be that first time, here at the house, during our big seasonal hiring weekend. That embarrassingly quick, twenty-second fuck against the wall.

How long has she known?

When did she find out?

She definitely knew on Tuesday. She spat that pricey champagne out, suggesting it had gone bad. As if we'd be serving spoiled Cristal. How did *I* not figure it out then?

Probably because I'm twenty-six, I've been living the rake life, and fatherhood is the last thing on my mind.

I'm not going to lie, the moment Abbi uttered those

words was a gut punch. I nearly doubled over in shock. It was quickly followed by frustration—that Sloane hasn't told me. She's had plenty of time and chances. I've spent the last two nights in her bed with her.

But she's afraid to tell me because, according to Abbi, she thinks I'll bail.

She literally watched me torch my career this morning—for her!—but she thinks I'm *that* guy? She thinks she needs to deal with this without me?

Why, is it because we barely know each other?

Or is it because this whole thing means way more to me than it does to her?

Fuck that. I need answers. I feel like I've shown her all of my cards, and she's shown me none of hers.

My hands curl tightly around the steering wheel as I reach the house. Her Cherokee is gone, but Frank's truck is here. Hopping out of the Bronco, I charge for his Airstream, the hens scurrying away as loose gravel scatters with my steps.

A loud thud draws my attention toward the beach, and I quickly change course around the house to where Frank stands next to a pile of rocks, shirtless and wiping sweat off his brow with his forearm.

"Where's Sloane?"

He peers over his shoulder, his tanned brown skin red-tinged from the heat. His perpetual scowl fades a touch when he sees me. I guess that's progress. "She's already at the dock. Probably about to leave."

I check my watch. "Shit." Now I'll have to wait three hours until she's back in to get answers.

Frank rests his elbow on a propped shovel. "Why, what's going on?'

"Nothing. I need to talk to her."

I get a head-to-toe appraisal of my board shorts and T-shirt. The first thing I did when I got to my office to clean it out was change. "So, you know." It's not a question.

"I know what?" I ask warily. Does Frank know?

Wait, of course he does. When I told him about Henry's plans last night, Frank said something along the lines of this being the last thing she needs right now. *This* is why. Because he knows she's pregnant.

He shrugs.

I'm not getting anything out of him unless he wants to give it.

Frank ambles about thirty feet over to the fire pit and, after adjusting his work gloves, collects a small boulder with a grunt, his giant, muscular arms straining under the weight.

"You're moving the fire pit."

"Figured I'd do it while Sloane's not here, seeing as it'd break her heart to watch."

I study the pile of soot-coated rocks. This pit's been in that exact spot for decades, Sloane said last night. Home to gatherings every night of each high season. Countless memories formed.

If I'm learning anything about Sloane, it's that she values tradition and family—both blood and found—above all else.

He lugs it over, dropping it next to the others. I hadn't noticed the orange spray paint before, with lines marking the new pit's location and whatever else he has planned. He's marked x's in the sand around it. I assume to gauge space for chairs.

"Not like we have a choice, unless we want to pay five hundred bucks a day every time your general manager reports us."

"She's not my GM anymore." Which reminds me, I need to grab that ticket off the kitchen counter. I did get a few fat paychecks. The least I can do is cover it while I still can. "I heard there's been some activity on the other side of the fence? Reporters and things?"

A slow grating sound carries. So, King Kong *can* laugh. "You should've heard the sound that commissioner lady made. Thought she was gonna drop dead."

"Yeah, that one thinks she's doing the Lord's work."

Frank heads back over to the old pit, where Ralph pecks at scurrying ants, their homes disturbed.

I follow him and collect a few of the smaller stones.

"The mayor tried scaling the chain-link," Frank goes on, hauling another hefty boulder. "Just after Sloane left."

That makes me chuckle. "What was he gonna do? Climb the tree?" The guy is, like, five foot three. I'm over six feet tall, and I stood on my tiptoes on top of that wobbly ladder to tie those sheets up there. In the fucking dark. If I never see a ladder again, it'll be too soon.

"I don't know what he thought he was doing, but when he noticed me there, he slipped and got his pants caught on the chain." The ground indents as Frank drops the rock into the sand. "Basically hung himself on his balls."

I wince at the visual. But wait— "He missed *you* sitting there?"

"I got it all on video."

"You're kidding me."

Frank gives me a look. I doubt the guy knows how to kid.

"Do me a favor and text it to me. It could be useful." I doubt Wilson wants a video like that going viral on social media, which is where it belongs.

"Yeah." He rolls his shoulders against the strain of his labor. "I told Sloane about the new harborfront. And the new road."

"*What? When?*" My anger flares. I didn't tell Frank so *he* could be the one to deliver that news. I wanted his advice. *I* should have been the one to tell her.

I guess Sloane and I are even, then.

"This morning, right after you left. She's got a lot going on right now, and she needed to see the full picture so she can make the right decisions for her."

Abbi basically said the same thing to me. "You mean, because she's pregnant?"

He pauses mid-reach. "Who told you that?"

"*Not* Sloane. When'd she tell you?" I don't know why it bothers me that he knew before me, but it does.

"She didn't. I figured it out 'cause I know her, and I'm not an idiot."

I roll my eyes at his dig. "Is she gonna keep it?"

"You need to ask her that."

"That's why I came here. To talk to her."

He tugs off his gloves and wipes his brow again. It's too hot for this type of manual labor, and yet something tells me he'll walk through a lava-spewing volcano for her. "And say what?"

"Just …" Good question. What *will* I say? I was so focused on hearing the words from her mouth that I didn't think about the "and then" part. "That I'm here, no matter what she decides?"

"Is that true? Are you?" Frank challenges, an edge in his tone.

"Of course I am!" I throw my hands out. "Haven't I proved that I'm in her corner by now?"

All I get in response is a grunt as he treks back toward the old pit.

I follow him. "Is this not something I planned on happening? Sure."

"You and her both," he mutters.

"Yeah. Well … she *should* have told me."

"You *should* have worn a condom," he throws back.

A wheelbarrow sits nearby. I grab the handles and push it over. "Would you believe me if I told you it's the first time I haven't?" Not including Tasha.

"No."

"I've always seen myself having kids, but not until my thirties."

"Shit happens."

"When's she going to be done?"

"Four." He hoists a boulder, his arms straining. "Are you always this chatty?"

"No, actually, not at all." I begin tossing smaller rocks into the steel tray. "Do you know which way she's leaning?"

"Nope." It's more of a grunt as he struggles the last

few steps, maneuvering around Ralph before letting go of his cargo.

"Come on, man."

He chugs his water, wipes his mouth with his forearm. "What's your plan? To stay here and annoy me until Sloane's done working?"

"Probably. Might take a break to grab a bite." If I can stomach food. I toss more stones in.

Frank sighs heavily. "We're not doin' this. I have a better idea."

26. Sloane

"We always anchor on this side and leave over there for the families." I point to the various parts of the sandbar. "Plus, it's easier to move in and out of Starfish Island with the current. It can get jammed up around here on those hot summer days. We've had upward of a thousand vessels pack in."

Bailey's full lips pull together as she whistles. "I've heard about this place for years, but seeing it in person for the first time is a whole other experience."

"Where are you from, again?" I don't think I asked that yesterday.

She grins, showing off pearly white teeth. "Born in Arkansas, but my dad was military, so we were all over the place. Berlin, South Korea, Australia. My mom's from Dublin. I guess that's why I sound the way I do. Picked up a little bit of this and a little bit of that and never been able to lose any of it."

"I was wondering." She has a slight accent—an oddly elongated vowel here, a dropped letter there—but I was unable to pinpoint it. Now that she says it, though, there's definitely a slight Irish twang.

"Don't know why. My brothers sound like they're from Arkansas, like my dad." Glacial blue eyes shine as she regards the display of pontoons, speedboats, and Jet Skis. They're a stark contrast to her lengthy black hair that flutters in the breeze.

"I hear Midwest accents all day long. Yours is way more interesting." I steer us in toward Jeremy, where the other half of this party of twenty-something-year-old girls is cheering and waving, ready for an afternoon of waterside fun. Sorority sisters, in town to celebrate a birthday and staying in one of their parents' gargantuan beach houses.

"You made it!" Jeremy's waiting with the tethering hooks.

"Because these guys are technically one group, we'll connect and make one big floating bar. Normally, though, we anchor fifteen, twenty feet apart," I shout over the music and laughter.

"Got it." Bailey nods as if making a mental note.

"Have you ever anchored before?"

"Plenty. We had a big ol' fishing boat for years. Took it out on some rough waters."

"Then this should be a breeze. 'Kay. Toss it in, and make sure it's fixed. The current here is deceptive. You'll be getting pushed out, and you won't even know it."

Bailey moves with ease to the outside of the tiki and, hauling out the anchor from its storage spot, throws it in, giving it a good tug to ensure it won't drag along the sand.

"Nice." Jeremy nods approvingly. He hasn't taken his

eyes off her since I walked her down the stairs to show her the tiki.

I can understand why. Bailey's beautiful and fit, with an angular face and a hard body. She told me she's thirty-four, but she's in better shape than any of these twenty-somethings we're shuttling around. More importantly, she seems easygoing and up for anything, and she laughs a lot.

"She's a natural." She'll make a fantastic addition to the Sea Witch team.

Until I'm forced to close up shop.

It's taking *every ounce* of my energy to hold a positive attitude. Maybe Frank shouldn't have told me about Henry's grand plans. I'd rather live in ignorant bliss for as long as possible.

Then again, I know why he did. It changes things for me. Before, my biggest concern was raising a baby as a single parent, when all the other elements of my life—my home, my business—were a constant. I've been starting to picture myself holding a baby in my arms, and every time, it's always against the backdrop of the back porch or the coffee shop. Now, suddenly, when I try to imagine my life in a year, I can't see anything clearly.

My path ahead leads into dense fog in unfamiliar territory. That's terrifying.

And what was possible yesterday no longer seems possible today.

"Go forth and enjoy!" Jeremy hollers as the two groups merge. He cranks up the volume on his speaker, the summer tunes carrying as bodies drop into the waist-deep water with splashes and laughter.

With them gone, he swings his lanky body over his bar and hops aboard *Tiki One*. "So, Bailey, how's it going so far?" His eyes trail her toned arms and the tattoos adorning them. The uniform shirt I gave her is a bit big—it was meant for AJ—and it reaches halfway down her thighs. I'll have to put in an order today.

She checks the latches on the cooler. "Well, Jer, it's been fifteen minutes since you saw me at the dock, but I think it's going okay. Sloane, what do you think?"

"Yeah, the first fifteen minutes have been good."

"Okay, okay." Jeremy waves us off as we tease him. "If you ever need any help or advice, I'm here. Seven days a week, sometimes. Just a text away."

"Damn, Sloane works you to the bone around here, huh?" But she winks at me to offset the barb.

We're going to get along well.

"It's a grind, yeah, but she treats her staff well. I haven't paid for a coffee in years, even during off-season."

"Hallelujah, I was *praying* for that perk." Bailey holds her hands together in mock prayer.

He grins. "You stayin' in Rainbow Alley?"

"Uh ... no, I'm staying with my aunt in her cramped one-bedroom in Old Town until I find a place."

"Oh man, Sloane ..." He nods toward me as if to say, *go on, tell her.*

I hadn't before now because I wanted to be sure Bailey was a keeper. "I have a few trailers on my property that I rent out to staff for the season at a low price," I explain. "It's on the water."

"Wow, seriously?" Her eyes light up. "Do you have any available?"

"Come on, hook a girl up, boss!" Jeremy goads.

I chuckle. "I've got one. You can come check it out tonight. I will warn you, it's tiny, but the bigger one has been spoken for, and you don't want to bunk with *that guy*."

"Did you hire someone else too?" Jeremy scans our passengers in the water while chatting.

"No. Well, sort of?" Do I call Ronan a hire? But the trailer's not even for him because he'll be in my bed. "It's for Ronan's friend, who needs a place to crash because Ronan's losing his house."

"And Ronan is ..." Bailey prompts.

"Her man," Jeremy offers before I have a chance to answer.

"I don't normally have non-Sea Witch staff staying there, but there's a lot goin' on right now."

"Oh. Right. *The hotel*." Jeremy nods.

"You've already heard? You weren't even there today!"

"I got a few texts," he admits.

"And? What'd you hear?" What is the staff saying about the crazy rooster commune lady?

"That you accused Henry Wolf of a bribery scheme."

I cringe. "It was a little softer than that." Not much, though.

"And Wolf fired Ronan."

"Yeah, that part's true."

"Ronan, your boyfriend," Bailey says, trying to piece our conversation together.

"Yes. He's a director there. *Was* a director."

"At this hotel."

"Uh-huh. Next door to my house, and the bane of my existence." Though it's beginning to feel more like Henry Wolf is the problem. The giant building beside me is suddenly tolerable.

"Was it because Ronan punched him?" Jeremy asks.

"No, though that didn't help."

Bailey's head ping-pongs back and forth. "Wait, so Ronan punched this Wolf guy?"

"In the eye." Jeremy points to his own eye. "Henry Wolf owns the hotel."

"Where Jer also works," I throw in with an accusatory tone.

"Only two days a week." He gives me a pointed look that might as well say out loud that I sabotaged his career aspirations.

"Where you'll be full-time after you abandon me in the fall," I remind him.

Bailey's forehead furrows. "So Ronan and Jeremy work for this hotel, and this is an issue."

Jeremy chuckles. "Man, you're so new. Okay, let's take you back to the beginning."

While Jeremy gives Bailey the CliffsNotes version, I keep watch of the people and boats around us. Everyone is enjoying the sun and water, blissfully unaware that my world is falling apart.

One of Sander's dinghies is heading this way, the colorful banners peddling ice cream and boiled peanuts fluttering in the breeze.

I groan when I spot the driver. "I can't deal with him today."

"Who is he?" Bailey asks.

"My ex." I give her a flat look. "He's a cheating, lying ball sac masquerading as a nice guy."

She hums with understanding. "I've had a few of those."

"He keeps away from us mostly, especially since Ronan threatened him." If he's coming around now, he must have a reason, and I'm sure it's not a good one.

"Gosh, there's so much drama here."

"I know. Please don't quit on me," I whine.

"You kidding? I love drama." Her eyes dance with genuine excitement.

"Then you are in the right place. Here, lemme run interference." Jeremy hops around the bar and positions his tall, lanky body on the outer edge like an easygoing bouncer.

"Thank you. I don't have it in me to be civil. Today has already been a day." And it's barely one o'clock.

"Ladies! Who wants ice cream!" Cody hollers. "It's the best in all of Mermaid Beach." His skin is bronzed from weeks in the sun, shirtless. I've never seen him so dark. The idiot's going to get skin cancer.

But our group of girls falls for his charming act like ... well, like *I* did ... waving their hands in the air as several scramble back to our little barge for their cash.

It gives Cody an excuse to close in, his little motor rumbling. "Hey Jer, how's it goin?"

"All good," Jeremy says. He doesn't know how to be an asshole even when he's trying to be.

"Yeah? How's working at the Wolf?" Cody swaps cash for ice cream bars, sparing several grins and a wink for a blond in a hot pink string bikini.

"Still early days, but no complaints."

Cody's eyes skim past me to land on Bailey. "You're new."

"I am. First day." Bailey leans over the bar. "And you are ..."

"Cody. Want one?" He holds up a vanilla bar. "On the house."

"How can I resist." She holds her hands up, beckoning him to toss it to her, which he does.

Ripping open the wrapper, she slides the long bar into her mouth in a suggestive manner and then moans. "You're right. You *do* have the best ice cream."

What is she doing? Why is she flirting with him? This is what he wants.

A smug smile fills Cody's face. He thinks he's won her over. "So, first day, huh? I guess you haven't heard about Sloane yet."

"What do you mean?" she asks innocently.

"I mean, you wouldn't have taken this job if you knew what it's like to work for her. She's fucking certifiable. I would know, I almost married her."

My stomach clenches as I struggle to tamp down my temper. All the while, the horde of sorority sisters listens and watches intently. He's trying to embarrass me in front of my customers.

"If you want, I can put in a good word for you over at Tiki Wiki. I know the owners. That's them right over there." He points to a cluster of knockoff tiki floats about fifty feet away. "They pay better, too."

"No, they don't," I snap before I can stop myself.

"Wait a minute. *Cody*. Right! You're the guy with the micro penis!" Bailey says it loudly.

Gasps and giggles sound all around us.

Cody's smile falls off.

"Hey, come on, ladies," Jeremy scolds, getting in on the childish game. "It's not his fault he has a nubbin. He was born that way."

"There's nothing wrong with my dick!" Cody yells, his cheeks turning red at the unwanted attention, as gazes inadvertently drift downward over his shorts.

There isn't, I can attest to that, and I told him regularly, when he fished for validation. I also caught him holding a tape measure to it once, so I know it's a sensitive subject for him.

"Of course not." Bailey adjusts her tone to sound like a mother placating an upset toddler. "It's just as good as all the other dicks."

The tiki cruise sorority sisters must have clued in to the bad blood between us by now because they suddenly break out in a chorus of Lady Gaga's "Born This Way," a few at first until the others join in. Their voices carry over the sandbar, attracting spectators.

"Fuck you all." Cody steers his boat away from us.

"Where are you going?" Bailey hollers after him, a devilish gleam in her eye. "Thanks for the ice cream!"

He revs his engine in response and cuts out, heading back toward shore.

My hands are pressed against my mouth. "I can't believe you just did that."

"You kidding? I've spent a lot of time around men. I know his type, and he deserved it."

"He did." Normally I would *never* condone mocking a guy like that, but it's Cody. There is no level low enough to sink to with him.

More loudly, she calls out, "We ladies stick together against cheating ball sacs, am I right?"

The sorority girls let out a cheer before returning to their conversations.

I throw an arm around Bailey's shoulder. "How would you like a promotion?"

"Hey! What the hell! All I had to do was make fun of Cody's dick?" Jeremy exclaims, feigning offense.

"You're both getting a promotion. You're now officially tiki boat admirals." I mock salute.

"Finally!" Jeremy holds his hand up for a high five, which Bailey meets with a slap. "What's our bonus?"

"Free scones?"

"Yes!" he hollers in triumph, earning my laugh.

But his amusement fades in the next beat as he spots something behind us. "Hey, did you book *Tiki Three* for today?"

"What? *No.* What are you talking about?" I spin around to see what he's talking about.

That's definitely *Tiki Three* approaching us. The Sea Witch logo is front and center. Frank's behind the wheel. What's he doing? Why is he coming all the way out here? He could have just texted me.

And is that ...

My pulse speeds up, as it does every time I spot Ronan. I didn't think I'd see him again until tonight.

But why is Frank bringing Ronan here?

Unless ... there's only one reason I can think of that they wouldn't text me, and that's to deliver bad news.

"What's that about?" Jeremy's worried frown says he's thinking the same thing.

I edge toward the other side, watching them approach, my heartbeat now a slow, repetitive thump in my ear.

They're twenty feet away when Ronan leaves his seat and comes around to stand on the edge, his eyes hidden behind his sunglasses.

"Grab the line!" Frank calls out.

Jeremy makes to move for it, but Bailey's faster, swinging around to the far end to catch the rope Ronan tosses her.

In seconds, Frank has the engine cut and is hopping out to link the tiki to ours, *Tiki One* rocking under his weight.

"What's going on?" My gaze flips from Ronan to Frank and back to Ronan.

"I'm taking over. You're going back with him." Frank jerks his head toward Ronan.

"Is it Gigi?" My voice cracks on her name.

"*What?* No. Gigi's fine. Just got a text from her."

A wave of relief bowls over me. I smack him in the arm. "Don't do that to me!" Today is already soul-crushing. But losing Gigi too? That, I couldn't bear.

Realization dances across his gruff expression. "Oh, yeah, sorry, didn't think. But you two need to talk."

"About?"

"*You two need to talk*," Frank repeats, giving me a high-browed look.

"Oh."

Oh.

Ronan leans against the tiki bar, waiting. His golf attire is gone, swapped out for board shorts and a worn gray T-shirt clinging to his chest.

"Who told him?" Was it Frank? No, he'd never do that. It had to be Abbi. Why, though? Is she angry for me trying to sabotage her husband's plans?

"No idea."

I guess the *why* doesn't matter, though.

"And? What'd he say?"

"Oh no, I'm not doin' this with you too." Frank's resolute head shake brooks no argument. "You go figure it out with *him*."

I swallow. Moment of truth. Is this the end of things with Ronan? Is this the part where he says this isn't what he signed up for? That he's out? Will this be a repeat of my mother's short-lived romance, when my father told her to "get rid of it" so they could continue with their sordid affair?

What if he wants me to have it?

I swallow against the ball of anxiety that's erupted in my throat. "You remember Frank, right, Bailey?"

"Oh yeah, we go way back."

"Another smart-ass in my life. Just what I needed," Frank grumbles, earning her grin.

I drop my voice. "Listen, I've got something I need to do, so he's going to take over training you for the day."

"Yeah, no problem. Do what you've gotta do."

Louder, I announce, "Okay, ladies! I have to head

out, but the very capable Captain Frank is going to get you back to shore safely."

Half of them wave to me; the other half are too focused on ogling Ronan.

For his part, he's not paying them any heed, his focus glued on me.

"Good luck," Jeremy whispers as I pass him to grab my bag from behind the bar.

With a forced smile, I skip over to *Tiki Three*, dreading this conversation. "Hey."

"Hey."

I wish he would take off those sunglasses. Maybe I'd have a clue as to what he's thinking.

"I got this." Bailey reaches down to unfasten our link.

Brushing past Ronan's body, I scoot to the helm and start the engine. "'Kay!"

Bailey undoes the ropes, tucking ours into the compartment before hopping back to the other side. "Rainbow Alley tonight?"

"Sounds good." I ease us away from the cluster of boats and people. Daring to steal a peek over my shoulder at him, I warn, "You should take a seat. We're about to start moving."

Ronan doesn't take a seat, though. He comes around the bar and steps in behind me, his hands settling over mine, his fingers filling the space between each of mine.

Okay, at least he doesn't seem angry. "Abbi told you?"

"Yup."

Awkward silence hangs as we motor toward land. I know I have to address the elephant on the tiki boat. He's waiting for me to do it.

I watch the channel ahead as I admit, "It's the last thing I expected to happen. I wasn't trying. And I don't know what I'm going to do yet." I bite my bottom lip with hesitation. "But I was thinking that I want to keep it."

I feel his chest lift against my back with his own inhale. "Okay."

Is that a good okay or an *oh shit* okay? I can't tell.

"I'm thirty-one years old. My mom died around this age from ovarian cancer, and that can be hereditary. That's something I think about. You know, what if I don't have as much time as I think I do to start a family. What if this ends up being my only shot."

"Okay."

"Stop saying okay. What does that mean?"

His hard swallow fills my ear. "It means I'm good with whatever decision you make."

I abandon my line of sight ahead to peer over my shoulder at him. "*But what does that mean?*"

He reaches up to slip his sunglasses off his face, revealing his beautiful eyes. "It means, whatever decision you make, I'm here for it, and I'm all in."

"But this is a baby, Ronan. A whole human."

His handsome face splits with laughter. "And here I thought it was going to be a sea witch."

"Shut up." I chuckle as I check the water ahead.

Another beat passes, and then he leans in to whisper in my ear, "I'm telling you that I'm all in with this. With *you*."

My heartbeat pounds in my chest. Am I hearing this correctly? "So, if I have this baby ..."

"It's gonna have an incredibly annoying uncle named Connor in its life."

I laugh, but it morphs into a groan. "We barely know each other."

"I know *enough*." He dips his head down to feather-soft kisses over my neck. "I know I wouldn't want this to be happening with anyone else but you."

I hesitate. "Not even Abbi?"

A finger slips under my chin, turning my face to meet his hard gaze. "No. Not even Abbi."

I can't say why, but I believe him. Stretching up, I graze my lips against his before returning my focus to the waters ahead, where a slower boat moves. I adjust our speed. "Frank told me about the harborfront and the access road."

He sighs. "I didn't want to tell you until I had no other choice. Until I'd tried everything I could to get Wolf to change his mind."

"And what are the chances of it happening?"

"You saw him this morning. He's serious. Which means we need to fight him every step of the way."

"That's just it. I've been fighting for the last five years, and what did that get me? Nothing. He took my peace, and now he's coming after my home." The high of hearing Ronan's words, his unwavering commitment to me, gets a cold splash of reality as I admit that. "I don't know. This changes things."

"What do you mean?" he asks warily.

"What kind of mother will I be if all my energy is tied up fighting Henry Wolf, who has endless resources? Who always gets what he wants? And if I don't fight, my house is gone, my business is dismantled. Sure, I can try to restart, but it won't be the same. *I* won't be the same. How do I manage *all that* and a baby?" Not to mention the fact that Ronan just lost his high-paying job. Good luck finding anything similar here. "I don't want to leave Mermaid Beach. It's my home."

"You don't have to. And this bullshit with Henry shouldn't be part of this decision."

"It shouldn't be, but it is."

His body tenses against my back. "Just ... give it a few more days before you decide one way or another."

"That's about all the time I have left."

Ronan's strong arms wrap around my body as I steer us into the harbor, the silence heavy but not uncomfortable, as we each digest the situation. At least everything's out in the open now, and no one is running anywhere.

What are the odds that the fuck boy who strolled into my shop one afternoon has turned out to be everything I needed in my life?

When we reach Sea Witch's slip, Ronan hops onto the dock and grabs a line. He begins tying us up.

I rest my elbows on the bar and watch with amusement. "Have you never tied up a boat?"

"Huh? Yeah, once or twice."

Coming around the bar, I leap off to join him there. "If you want to be a captain, you're going to have to learn how to do proper marine knots."

"Yeah?" His lips curve with a smirk. "Are you gonna teach me?"

"Someone has to. Gigi would be appalled by this mess."

Soft laughter carries as he steps aside, hands out. "Go ahead, then, Sea Witch. Give me that lesson." His molten eyes drag over my bikini. "And then I'll give you one of my own."

27. Ronan

A young woman in a housekeeping uniform watches me as I pass by her, but I keep my focus on the suite at the end of the West Tower hall, pretending that I belong here.

She's not the first staff member to do a double take as I strolled through the hotel lobby and into the elevator. Someone really should tighten security.

I hesitate for only a second before I knock on the door.

Muffled voices sound behind it.

After a lengthy pause, the door swings open.

"Ronan!" Margo holds a champagne glass in one

hand as she backs up, allowing me past her bikini-clad body. "What a lovely surprise."

"Where are they?"

"In the bedroom." Her smile is downright playful. "Are you here to join us?"

"Don't start. Today is not the day."

"Yes, I heard." She mock pouts. "I know Henry can be difficult, but you are proving to be equally so."

"I'm only protecting what's mine."

"Sloane," she purrs, trailing me through the spacious place like a cat on my heels, waiting for any opportunity to rub up against my leg.

I heard this suite was big, but you could host a party for thirty people in here without batting an eye.

Voices draw me down a hallway in the back and through double doors.

"Oui. Just like that." Joel aims his camera at Abbi, who leans against a wall near the bank of windows in a lace bra and underwear, a gauzy, see-through robe draped over her body, parted at her protruding belly. The afternoon's rays give her an angelic glow. She's had her hair and makeup done and looks sexy as hell.

Sloane is going to look like that.

She'll have a swollen belly too, and inside, she'll be carrying *my* child.

It hasn't sunk in yet. I might need a few more days for that to happen. Maybe an ultrasound or two. And while this isn't how I ever planned for it to happen, the longer I sit with the thought, the more welcome it becomes, because the one thing I am sure of is that I care about

Sloane. Deeply. Hell, I probably love her, but I'm too chickenshit to admit it to myself yet. The last two times did not end well for me.

This time? I'm not letting anyone get in the way.

"For a guy intent on trying to destroy this hotel, you sure can't seem to stay away." Henry peels himself from the wall he was leaning against and stalks forward. "Do you have any idea the PR nightmare you've caused me? What it's going to cost to make this go away?"

I don't have the bandwidth to dance around words with this guy. "Sloane's pregnant."

That slows him in his tracks. "It's yours?"

"Yes."

"*You sure?*"

"Do you want a matching black eye?" My fists clench.

"Can we take a break?" Abbi offers an apologetic smile to Joel.

"I need to use the toilet anyway." He sets his camera down and ducks out.

Margo follows him. Thankfully. I don't need an audience for this.

"It's his." Abbi collects a silk robe from a nearby chair and slips it on, covering herself up.

Henry's surprised gaze shoots to his wife. "How long have *you* known?"

"I figured it out at dinner on Tuesday."

"And you didn't tell me?"

"Why would I?" Her tone is sharp, and the look she tosses is disapproving.

He sighs heavily, taking a swig of his scotch as he

wanders over to the window to look out on the water. "Okay. *And?*" There's a clear *what do you want from me?* ring to the word.

I had no plans to face off against him again today. Not until I listened to Sloane explain the reasons why she wants to keep this baby, followed closely by the reasons she thinks she can't—all stemming from Henry fucking Wolf.

I grit my teeth and mentally prepare myself to do the one thing I never pictured myself doing. "Look, I didn't ask for this job, or the car, or the house. You're one of the richest bastards out there, and I've never asked you for a dime. I *could* have, after that day in the mine."

Henry's jaw grows taut.

"I've never asked you for anything, but I am asking you now: stop pursuing this project. Leave Sloane and her home and her businesses alone. That is all I'll ever ask from you. Let her live her life the way she wants to."

"You think it's that easy? You think I can just flip a switch and end things?"

"You can make anything happen if you want to."

A strangled sound escapes his throat. "I *told* you to stay away from her. I *fucking told* you that getting involved with her would be a bad thing."

"For who? You? Because as far as I'm concerned, she is the best thing that's ever happened to me. She's *every-thing* I've always wanted, and now she's pregnant, and she wants to have it, but she thinks she can't because of *you!* Because she can't be a good mother *and* fight you to save what's hers, what's been in her family for fifty years." Maybe I shouldn't be sharing this, but I'm scraping the barrel here, searching for some shred of humanity in this guy.

"Then I guess she shouldn't have it."

Abbi's sharp inhale cuts into the room, her palms smoothing over her pregnant belly as a horrified look morphs her pretty face. "*Henry.*"

"*No*, this is not on me!" He holds up a finger. "I warned him."

"Yeah, you did, and I didn't listen. I fell for her hard, and now I will do *anything* for her. So what do you want me to do, Henry? Beg? Do you want me to get down on my knees and beg?" I drop down to the hardwood floor and hold my arms out wide.

"You look ridiculous," he growls.

But I ignore him. "Here I am, on my knees, begging the great and powerful Henry Wolf to back off."

"We're done here." He storms out.

"You owe me!" I roar after him, his rushed footfalls a hollow echo in the suite. A moment later, the door slams shut, and the silence that follows is deafening.

I sink back on my haunches. Let those words haunt him while he sleeps.

"Valiant effort," Abbi says softly, sympathy painted across her face.

"Worth a shot." I haul myself to my feet, my spirits heavy. "I better go find Connor so we can get to the house and pack up before he changes the locks."

"He wouldn't do that."

My laughter is bitter. "No offense, but if you believe that, then you don't know who you're married to."

Her brow furrows, but she doesn't answer.

"If you need me, I'll be at the commune next door." I stroll toward the bedroom door.

"She's definitely the one, huh?" Abbi calls out. "The one who saved Ronan Lyle from himself?"

I smile. "Yeah, Red. She's the one."

28. Sloane

Connor trots down the steps of Palmy Daze, wearing swim trunks, his brawny chest on display.

"It's not a four-story beach house, but it's okay, right?"

"You kidding? Bed, shitter, TV, AC, beach." He marks each one off on a finger. "*And* I can literally stumble to work every morning. It's perfect."

Skye and Rebel stroll past in their bikinis, towels draped over their shoulders.

"You comin' for a swim before dinner?" Skye calls out over her shoulder, her Southern twang heavier than usual. A dead giveaway when she's flirting.

"Hell yeah." Connor takes off after them, the three of them passing Frank on their way to the water.

And so it begins.

Frank ambles toward me, covered in dust and dirt from the task of moving the fire pit. "You sure that's a good idea?"

"No, but it's too late now. I'll warn them." Rebel and

Skye may be close, but not *that* close. They won't be up for sharing Connor's body parts.

"He's paying his fair share. So is the other one."

"Yes, sir." I mock salute.

He rolls his eyes. "Come and see what we've done."

"I'm allowed?" I drifted off after Ronan left to get Connor, exhausted by the last few late nights, and woke up to Rebel clattering in the kitchen and strict rules to stay away from the back because Frank and the beach crew were at work. I was in no hurry to watch them dismantle five decades of history, so I helped finish dinner, and then I freshened up the trailers in anticipation of Bailey and Connor.

"Come on." Frank jerks his head. "Everyone helped. Even the pipe cleaner."

I hold my breath and follow him around back to where a sweaty group of Sea Witch staff lingers, chugging water. Nearby, Jeremy flips burgers on the grill, the smell of BBQ permeating the air.

"Wow."

What used to be just sparse grass and sand is now a small oasis. They leveled the ground and spread screening, setting patio stones to form paths toward the stone fire pit, from both the house and the beach. In each corner, the soil has been churned and small palm trees planted.

"My uncle owns the garden place out in Old Town. He'll sell plants to us at cost. You just gotta tell me what you like." Rolland leans on his shovel, his tanned arms smeared with dirt. He doesn't look so scrawny anymore.

"I can't believe you guys did all this today."

"It took, what, three and a half hours?" Ron says, checking his watch. "Had some old materials in storage at the compound that we hauled over."

"The pit looks the same." It's like they picked it up and carried it over in one piece. Same sooty stones, same size, same shape.

"I had the power washer ready, but Frank said he'd aim the gun at my nut sac if I touched that dirt," Brock, a quiet guy, says.

"And he knew I meant it," Frank adds, as the others laugh.

"But look, see? We're still close to the beach. It's just over there." Will waves his hands in the direction of the water, where Connor and the girls lounge, waist-deep.

"Yeah, now the hotel can go fuck themselves if they call the cops on us again." Mick studies a fresh scrape on his knuckle. "And we can keep having our fires like we always do."

"Guys, this is incredible." They worked their Sea Witch jobs all day in the hot sun, and then they came here to do this. "Thank you." It seems inadequate.

"We're the Sea Witch fam." Jeremy appears then, throwing an arm around me. "We're always here for each other."

Would they be here, though, slaving for me, if they knew how I'd sabotaged them?

"How much longer for the burgers, dude?" Mick whines.

"Five minutes. Ten, tops," Jeremy promises. "Just enough time to jump in the water, you filthy pigs."

A chorus of curses sounds, and then the guys are

abandoning shovels and work gloves, their sights set on cooling off.

The guilt that's been gnawing at my conscience for weeks finally erupts. "I've got to come clean," I blurt. Might as well get everything out in the open today. "I know you guys applied for seasonal at the hotel."

Wary glances dart around. Rolland appears utterly confused.

I rush on before I chicken out. "I blocked your hires. Well, Ronan did. For me. I couldn't lose you all. Not like that. Not to them. But I know it was wrong." I hold my breath as I study their faces, waiting for their reactions.

"Yeah, we know," Mick admits with a shrug. "Cody came by the compound and told us."

"What? When?" Frank demands to know.

"Yesterday afternoon. You were out at the sandbar."

A muttered curse, followed by something unintelligible—likely a threat of bodily harm—slips from Frank's lips.

I knew Cody had it out for me, but I didn't think he'd be *that* motivated. If I felt any shed of sympathy after Bailey skewered his ego, it's gone. "Okay, so ..." What do I say next except "I'm sorry, and I'll understand if you want to quit."

"If you ask me, you did us a favor." Ron shrugs. "I talked to Dave, and it doesn't sound like he likes it over there. Too stuffy, too many rules. Plus, he misses livin' here."

The little olive branch he holds out is worth more than he knows. "How can he not?"

"Speakin' of, when's Bailey showin' up?" Will grins.

"Settle down, you don't have a shot in hell at that," Jeremy tosses back as he returns to the grill. According to his version of events, Will was tripping over his tongue when the tikis sailed back to the harbor and he got his first look at the new captain. Or, should I say, admiral.

I chuckle. "Soon, actually."

The group disbands toward the water in a flurry of laughter, taking some of the weight from my chest with them. Even Frank, never much of a joiner, trudges after.

"Feeling better?" The steps creak as Ronan takes them down. He must have witnessed that whole spectacle from the back porch.

"Bless me, Father, it has been—" I mock squint in thought. "—*six hours* since my last confession?"

"You're not fully absolved yet. That thing we did earlier is considered a sin in some cultures."

"Dude." Jeremy holds his hands out in a *what the fuck* manner before returning to his burgers.

Ronan's lips twitch, the only sign of his amusement.

"Settled in all right?" I emptied a few drawers to make room for his clothes.

"All good." He sidles up behind me, curling his arms around my shoulders. "The new pit looks professional."

"Yeah, they did a great job. I wish they didn't have to do it in the first place." I pause. "You sure you're okay?" I could be projecting, but his mood has been ominous since he returned with Connor and his duffel bag of belongings. Is he already having doubts? Regrets?

His hand grips my chin, angling my head back to meet his intense gaze, just like he did in my bedroom this afternoon, when he took me from behind. "You and me are perfect."

How does he read me so well?

Leaning forward, his lips meet mine in a tender kiss that makes my chest swell and my heart race. Even though my entire world feels like it's crumbling around me, somehow, Ronan gives me the strength I need to face it head-on.

A car door slams.

I force myself to peel away. "That must be Bailey."

We walk hand in hand toward the parking lot, my attention veering toward the trees and the golf course beyond. "Do you think they're still out there taking pictures?" Rebel said she spied several sets of legs near the fence line this afternoon while she was in the garden. She couldn't say if they were curious golfers or media people, or maybe Wolf staff.

"Doesn't matter. It's out there."

"How long before lawyers show up in my driveway?"

"Let them. Can't wait to hear what they have to say." He says it with such confidence.

Bailey stands in the middle of the parking lot doing a slow, circular turn as she takes in the trailers, the cluster of cars, and Ralph.

"You're gonna have to put a leash on Connor," Ronan murmurs as we approach.

"I'm not worried. She can handle her own." Tight black workout shorts and crop top show off a honed body, layered in hard muscle. Envy swells inside me as I call out, "Welcome to the Sea Witch commune!"

"When can I move in?"

"You haven't even seen your trailer yet."

"I don't need to." She slides off her sunglasses, revealing an eager twinkle. "This feels like home."

———

"PUT YOUR FOOT *HERE*." Bailey demonstrates, pointing to a spot on the sandy ground, her hand on Jeremy's shoulder. At the crew's relentless whining, she's been giving basic combat demonstrations for the past half hour.

"Like this?" Jeremy follows the instruction.

In a lightning-quick move, she flips him over her leg, and he lands flat on his back with a dull thud. "Yeah, exactly like that."

"Ow," he groans as laughter explodes around the fire.

"Ron. Toss another one." Mick holds his hands up, and Ron throws a hot dog, narrowly missing Lara's cheek.

"Keep your wieners away from our faces!" Rebel scolds, earning several hoots.

I lean back in the seat I'm sharing with Ronan and hold my Sapporo against his lips. "We need more chairs." A few of the old Adirondacks were not keen on the move and lost pieces along the way.

He takes a sip to help me keep up appearances that I'm drinking. "If only we knew someone who owned a beach chair rental company."

"If only." I rest my head next to his and admire the blanket of stars above. My problems are only just beginning, but for tonight, surrounded by my Sea Witch family, cradled in Ronan's arms, they seem a galaxy away.

Skye trots past then, changed out of her bathing suit and into skimpy cotton shorts and a fitted T-shirt.

"Took you a while." I note her matted hair and the lazy, crooked ponytail—she rarely walks around without an artful top bun to tame the frizz. And the fact that Connor is still not back from changing either.

"Someone had to clean up the mess in the kitchen. Here, figured you'd be ready for another cold one." She holds out a fresh beer.

"Thanks." I accept it.

Ronan's soft curse tickles my ear. "I'm gonna be wasted if this keeps up."

I nuzzle my face into the crook of his neck. "Good. Easier for me to take advantage of."

His phone lights up with a text then, and Tasha's name appears on the screen.

A dash of discomfort burns in my stomach. For an ex he only just reconnected with, she messages him a lot. "Didn't you say she was here this weekend for a bachelorette party?"

"Yeah. I saw her at the airport when I went to pick up Britt." He says it so offhandedly.

I hesitate, not wanting to show my insecurities. Cody used to do that all the time, dismiss frequent texts and meet-ups from female "friends." When I'd question why, he'd gaslight my concerns, tell me to stop being so jealous.

Turns out I had reason to be then.

Do I have reason now?

"How was seeing her again after so long?" A woman he was in love with, the one he thought he'd marry.

"Weird. But also good. Validated what I already knew, that she's in the past."

"Does she know that?" Because I can only think of one reason why a girlfriend is messaging her ex so much.

The firelight casts just enough of a glow for me to see the truth in his eyes as he says, "She does now."

"Good."

His answering smile is crooked. "By the way, are you sure it's okay for Britt and Dani to crash here this weekend?"

"Yeah, as long as they're okay with sharing the spare room."

"They won't care. They're like two peas in a pod. It's just for two nights, anyway. But I can put them up in a hotel—"

"No, don't be dumb. The more, the merrier. Besides, I can't wait to meet her." What is Ronan's sister like? And his mother and father? Will they like me? Will I like them?

"Yeah?" He toys with a strand of my hair. "And when do I get to meet the original sea witch?"

"Soon. I promise." First, I have to figure out how to break the news to her that everything she poured her heart and soul into building is going to be gutted, paved over, erased. My stomach tightens with dismay. "Tomorrow? That's when he's rolling out his big plans?" I don't have to spell out Henry's name.

Ronan's expression hardens. "Yeah."

How long before that news reaches Palm Oaks? It's better if Gigi hears it from me.

Heavy footfalls sound from behind us, and a moment

later, a bare-chested Connor strolls up, dressed in gray track shorts and holding Ralph like a football under one arm, a bag of potato chips dangling from his free hand.

Jeremy's jaw hangs. "How did you catch him?"

"Easy. Found him sittin' on Darla's hood. Guess he likes her."

Frank snorts.

"Watch this." Connor holds a chip out between two fingers.

Ralph's bird neck stretches as he snatches it away with his beak.

"I have been trying to catch that guy for *years*, and you got him on your first night here," Rebel admits with astonishment. "That is amazing."

"That's because *I'm* amazing," he counters, winking at her.

"Yeah, Connor's a regular cock whisperer," Ronan mocks.

Frank's head tips back with a deep bellow of laughter. It's so surprising and so boisterous that everyone freezes for a beat before joining in.

We're all still laughing when two figures materialize from the darkness next to the oat grass.

29. Ronan

They approach from the beach like ghosts emerging from the shadows.

"You have got to be kidding me," I mutter as Sloane's body goes rigid in my lap. What the fuck is Henry Wolf doing here? Tension cords my muscles as I watch him step onto Sloane's property, Abbi at his side. They're dressed for whatever dinner function they came from—she's in a gauzy white dress, he's in a pale green linen suit. They practically glow in the dark.

Heads turn, one here, two there; someone turns the music down to a lull.

Frank sets his ukulele on the ground next to him, his brooding sights set on Sloane's nemesis like a guard dog deciding how far it should allow an intruder in before it lets them know they've made a terrible mistake.

He'll have to beat me to Henry if he's here to threaten Sloane in any way.

The tension is choking.

Ralph decides that's the perfect moment to peck

Connor's bare chest. A flurry of wings and a howl of pain later, Connor's ribs are clawed, and Ralph dines on the scattered bag of chips.

"Bad boy," Rebel scolds, even though Connor's the idiot for carrying the damn rooster around in the first place. She abandons her seat to inspect the angry-looking, red scratches. "Let's get those cleaned up right away. There's a first aid kit in the house."

"I'll help!" Skye chirps, trailing them away and inside. I'm not sure if it's because she wants to avoid the impending confrontation or if Connor's already fucked her and she's staking her claim. Poor girl if it's the latter.

Abbi moves in while Henry hangs back, closer to the beach, his hands tucked into his pockets as he sizes up the little beach house.

"This might be the best slice of cake you'll ever try in your entire life." Abbi holds out a plate wrapped in foil. Sympathy etches her face. "I hope you like chocolate."

Sloane hesitates. "I do."

"If it's poisoned, we're all witnesses," Mick mumbles, loud enough for everyone to hear.

Sloane climbs to her feet. "Thank you." Her voice is cordial but strained as she accepts the offering. How does she feel about Abbi now, after she betrayed her confidence? Now that Sloane knows our history? Will they ever be true friends? I hope so.

"Ronan? Henry would like a word."

"Would he, now ..."

Abbi's eyes shift to me, and I see the pleading in them.

May as well get this over with. Heaving myself out of

the chair with a stretch, I take my sweet-ass time crossing the property to where the prick waits. "What do you want?"

"Walk with me." Henry turns and heads back toward the beach without waiting.

"Sure, why not." I follow, on guard for whatever threat he plans on serving up next, across the sand until we're mere feet from where the water laps at the shore.

Behind us and to the left, the hotel looms, lit up and full of life as its first guests drink and eat like gluttons who aren't paying a dime. But out here, the silence takes center stage, neither of us saying a word, staring into the darkness for several long moments.

"I will not be unveiling the harborfront plan tomorrow," Henry finally says.

"Probably smart, until you can buy off whoever you have to."

"I will not be unveiling the harborfront plan *at all*." His tone is cold and calm, and full of displeasure. "Not in its current design and scope, anyway."

"And what *exactly* does that mean?"

He sighs. "It means you've won."

"Won *what*?"

"Sloane's home and business are safe."

I abandon the view of the dark, foreboding water to take in the little I can see of his profile. "Is this for real, or are you feeding me bullshit? Because if you are, so help me fucking God, I will—"

"It's real," he cuts my threat off before I have a chance to utter it. "There was an emergency closed-door council meeting this evening to discuss the accusations brought forth. All current revitalization plans for Mermaid Beach's harbor and surrounding area are suspended until further notice."

"Already?" Doubt mars my voice. "That was fast."

"Yes. It seems Wilson got a call from the state governor, asking if there was any truth to the rumors after Olivia McEowan contacted him, expressing her concerns over corruption in Mermaid Beach's government."

"*Seriously?*" Olivia called the governor? There's no way she gives a shit about Mermaid Beach's mayor trading trips for votes, so either she hates Henry Wolf *that* much and wants to flex her arms, or she did it for me, which might be even a more bizarre reason. I don't know the woman at all.

"Yes. *Seriously.* Clearly, you made an impression. I truly hope it wasn't with your dick, after all your theatrics."

"Shut the fuck up. I didn't sleep with her." But my mind picks through his words. "You said 'until further notice.' That means they can wait until this all blows over and start up again."

Henry's already shaking his head. "This was always going to be an uphill battle. I knew that, and I was prepared to make it happen. But now, a few heads will have to roll, and then elections will bring new faces. Wilson's done. Future development plans will be put under a microscope." He pauses. "One day, Sloane's going to realize things can't stay the way Ruby Parker started them. There *will* be development. Residents will demand the chains and boardwalk upgrades, I promise you that. And when they do, I will be there to make sure it benefits my company." He doesn't falter a beat with that admission. "But she won't be fighting against me anymore. Not in the short term, anyway."

"What about with the council and the mayor?"

"They won't come after her. I'll see to it." His jaw clenches, and I have to wonder what that means.

"And the access road through *here*?" I jerk my head toward the little bungalow.

He follows my gaze, settling on the lights from the window. I can just make out Abbi's and Sloane's silhouettes inside the kitchen. "I've expressed my opposition to it."

He says it as if that's enough to halt plans. It likely is because when Henry fights, it's never fair, and he always gets what he wants.

Until now, apparently.

"So, that's it." Just like that.

"Yes, just millions of dollars lost in design later," he mutters under his breath, but then he exhales, as if trying to expel his bitterness. "You were right. I do owe you for what you did in Alaska. For risking your life for me. And you've never asked me for anything. So, I will make sure Sloane's interests are protected with any future plans, and you can play house or whatever the fuck it is you plan on doing with her. But consider us even."

"Fair enough." I guess my groveling made an impact after all.

"I need to get back to people." He peers up at the house again. "But I think Abbi would rather be with her friends than listening to Shelby Singer describe in excruciating detail the intricacies of herding ducks."

A bark of laughter escapes me. "I am *not* going to miss that."

"Get her back safely, please."

"Of course."

With one last glance to his wife, Henry trudges back the way he came.

And I move swiftly for the house, barely able to contain my excitement to share the news with Sloane.

A cringe-inducing caw screeches into the night.

"And get rid of that fucking thing!" Henry's voice booms in the darkness.

I laugh. "Can't. Ralph stays. He's family."

30. Sloane

The hefty green wing chair is against the window facing out, and all I can see is an elbow and a ball of yellow yarn on the floor beside her.

Hey, Gigi," I call out as we step into her room.

"Sloane? I wasn't expecting you today."

"I know, but I got off work early."

A wrinkled hand reaches out to collect a wad of bills from the table beside her. She waves it in the air. "I won a hundred and fifty bucks off those feckless twats, Larry and Hank. I let them think they're sharks, but *I'm* the real shark."

Behind me, Ronan chuckles.

"Is that Frank?"

"No, it's Ronan."

A pause and then, "Well, don't just stand there. Help an old girl out. They pushed me in here too close, and now I'm trapped!"

Ronan swiftly rounds me. "Hold on tight." Seizing the top corners of the headrest, he tips the chair back just enough to swivel it around on its hind legs, earning a whooping sound from Gigi.

"There, that's better." She abandons her knitting project and smooths her hands over her pale blue slacks. Someone's pleated her hair today and secured a small yellow butterfly clip above her left ear. "Now, where were we? Let's get a good look at you, young man." Her blue eyes lift to appraise Ronan's face. "Huh. You are as handsome as in the pictures Sloane showed me."

"She showed you pictures of me?" Amusement laces his voice.

"Yes, from the Henry Wolf file."

Ronan's eyebrows pop as he regards me. "She has a *Henry Wolf file*?"

"*Had*. Hush, Gigi." I dangle the small paper bag of scones in the air before setting it on the small table beside her.

"I think my granddaughter is trying to buy my silence." Her bony fingers peel open the folded top enough to lean forward and inhale the fresh-baked scent. "It's working."

I laugh. "Okay, officially, Gigi, this is Ronan. Ronan, this is Gigi."

"The Original Sea Witch," Ronan says, and a wave of déjà vu hits me then, bringing me back to the day he walked into the rental shop.

"Now, just an old witch." A mischievous spark ignites. "I've heard a lot about you."

"Not as much as I've heard about you," he counters.

"Well, pull up a chair, and let's compare notes, then." She gestures toward a nearby stool. "Hope you brought a scone of your own because I don't share. Not unless Nurse Ratched shows up, and then this is all yours."

I can barely contain my excitement as I reach forward and collect his hand. "He will, but first, Gigi, there's something we want to tell you."

October

"Frank, can you bring the ladder around back when you have a sec?" I holler, knowing he can hear me from his trailer's stoop where he sits, scattering corn for the hens before work.

"For what?"

"Just bring it, please?" The shed is behind Rainbow Alley, and the ladder is long and awkward.

Heavy footfalls sound as he trudges around to find me standing at the foot of the porch.

"Where's the ladder?"

"Where it belongs until I know why a pregnant woman needs a ladder to do yoga," he throws back, nodding to the mat stretched out on the sandy ground.

I point up. "Because that siding looks loose." The hurricane that came through west of Mermaid Beach last week brought plenty of rain and wind with it. The guys have been cleaning up downed branches around the property for days.

He follows my aim. "Okay, so then *I'll* go up and take

a look at it when I'm back later. Or get Ronan's ass up. Does he know what you're doing out here?"

"He went for a jog." I add in a sullen tone, "And I don't have to run everything by him. Or you."

"*Stay off* the ladder."

"*Fine.*"

His brown eyes drag over the turquoise walls of the house, the rich color noticeably faded. "You should start thinking about when you want us to paint. I know we usually do it in the spring, but next one's going to be hectic."

"I know." I smooth my hand over my growing belly. I'm due in February, and it'll be all I can manage to keep up with preparing for high season with a newborn. Nothing will get done around here. "I was thinking maybe next month? Storm season will be over, and it's always quiet then." It's already quiet now. Skye and Rebel left for their last year of college in August, and Lara stepped up in a big way to allow me a break. So big that I'm trying to find a way to keep her on even part-time. The beach chair crew has mostly packed up and left, leaving Rolland to manage the few chair rentals until Frank and Ronan haul everything into storage. Even Ron is gone. The inflatable banana boat was a hit and paid for itself *many* times over, but the kids are back at school. Plus, Bailey has her USCG Captain's license so she can cover the odd last-minute weekend booking.

I officially let Jeremy go to his full-time bartending position at Wolf last week, but he's already talking about how he can swing both jobs next summer. We'll see if he feels the same way when the time comes.

Bailey's turned into a fan favorite, her five-star reviews nearly canceling out the bad ones Frank's earned us. Her seasonal contract with us is coming to an end too, but she's asked if she could stay in the trailer off-season, and I've agreed. I love having her around, and I'll need every extra pair of hands in the coming months.

Ragged breathing draws our attention to the beach, where Ronan saunters up, bare-chested and skin glistening, his hat on backward as he chugs the last of his water bottle.

My body responds instantly, craving his touch, even though I had it not an hour ago.

"Hey," he says through pants, his eyes drifting over my little black yoga shorts and matching crop top. "What are you two doing?"

"She asked me to bring the ladder over so she can look at loose siding," Frank announces.

"Tattletale!" I accuse.

"*What?*" Ronan groans with frustration. "Come on. I thought we agreed, no ladders for now."

"I was just going to—"

Bailey's howl of laughter cuts in to my poor excuse. "Play with the bull and you get its horns!"

"Just wait until *you* lose a bet, Bails," Connor warns, always one to hand out a nickname.

"That's Admiral to you."

The sound of gravel crunching is the only warning we get before Connor trudges past in nothing but a paisley floral swim thong and his running shoes, muttering to us, "No big deal."

My jaw drops.

"Tongue back in your mouth, Sea Witch," Ronan scolds.

"I wasn't!" But there is *very* little left to the imagination, as his bare ass cheeks lift with each step, covered only by the fluorescent orange T at the top.

Bailey jogs past in her running gear, her phone aimed to record the entire sordid event. "Rebel and Skye are gonna *love* this." They became fast friends the day Bailey started. They talk nearly every day.

"Tell 'em to eat their hearts out."

"Yeah? I'm sending it to Britt, too. What should I tell her?"

Connor groans. This buffoon has never shown a shred of embarrassment, but he might actually be close this time.

Meanwhile, Ronan's jaw clenches, as it does every time there's any conversation that involves his little sister and his best friend.

"Where are you going?" I'm unable to keep my laughter at bay. These two have struck up a strange friendship.

"To grab a coffee at the Sea Witch," Bailey says.

"He's not coming in the shop like that!" Frank bursts.

"That's okay, he can wait outside and greet your customers!" Bailey grins as she rushes to catch up.

"That's about four miles each way, and Connor's not in shape for running," Ronan muses.

And it's past the hotel. I check my watch. It's early, but there'll be people out. "He's going to be hugging his knees by the time he gets there."

"Great, because Connor's hairy ball sac is what

customers want to see when they come for their morning coffee," Frank mutters, marching away. "No fucking ladders, Parker!"

"O-*kay*." I roll my eyes as I resettle in a butterfly pose on my mat. "What do you have planned for today?"

Ronan stretches his arms over his head, his gaze drifting out to the emerald-green water—still warm despite the cooler temperature. "I was going to get *Tiki Three* out of the water this morning so Frank can do his thing before we put it in storage. Then I have a meeting at the county office."

"Yeah? How's that looking?"

"They seem *very* open to reconsidering the limited vendor licensing for Starfish Island."

"I'll bet." Bedsheet Gate has earned us notoriety around town. The last thing Councilman Sanders wants is a new banner strung up, highlighting his company's monopoly of the sandbar concession business. The town is doing *everything* they can to appear unbiased and honest, now that people know the councilmembers have been personally benefiting from Gayle Anderson's charity. Mayor Wilson resigned a week after the infamous day, which tells us there's dirt to uncover, and it likely goes beyond the Wolf Hotel.

Gayle Anderson, on the other hand, still hasn't admitted to any wrongdoing, and every time the question comes up, her go-to response is to list every unfortunate soul who has ever benefited from her charity. She is careful to never speak about the Wolf Hotel organization.

A few of the other councilmembers have posted weak statements of their own, claiming any benefits their family may have seen from funds donated by Henry Wolf are strictly a coincidence. At the same time, Councilwoman Reeves' daughter's trip to Paris was quietly canceled. Reeves has since launched a PR campaign to focus on keeping Mermaid Beach's small-town charm.

Of course, none of the shit splatter has landed on Henry, his publicity firm and lawyers spinning it far away from him.

We took the bedsheets down the morning after Henry came to declare his losses as a show of good faith. The damage had been done. True to his word, no lawyer has so much as breathed the word *lawsuit* in our direction.

Repositioning myself on my hands and knees, I stretch my neck and angle my body into a cat-cow pose. "What do you think the chances are that we'll have Sea Witch vendors at Starfish next year?"

"Almost guaranteed," comes the raspy answer, confidence in his voice. "I'm still running numbers and poking around to see what sells, but I think we can turn a profit within the first two months. After that, it's all gravy. And Henry has agreed to have the concierge staff recommend our cruises. Belinda's head will explode if she's still around next season and hears about it."

I smile, listening to Ronan. He might have felt clueless in his position at the hotel, but he's stepped up at Sea Witch, looking for ways for us to expand and make money. "Thank you, Director." It's an honorary title, much like Bailey's Admiral status. Ronan gets a chuckle out of it.

And when I think about the career he gave up for me,

for us, my heart swells with love and gratitude. I can't believe there was a time that I thought Ronan was wrong for me, that trusting him would be a mistake. He's everything I hoped he might be and more—loyal, reliable, protective. He still draws attention from women wherever we go, but he only has eyes for me.

And for our unborn son, spending evenings with his ear pressed against my belly before his mouth is pressed against every other part of me. He's been to every doctor's appointment and didn't waver a beat when we flew to Indianapolis in August to meet his parents and tell them the news. Ronan Lyle may not have seemed like father material when we met, but I couldn't imagine doing this without him.

"How much convincing did Abbi need to—do." My voice falters as I roll over onto my butt to face Ronan, only to discover a tent in his shorts. "*Seriously?*"

"What?" He scoffs, as if the question is ludicrous. "You thought you could put your ass in the air like that and *not* get a reaction from me?"

"Yeah, because I'm so sexy right now." I rub my expanding belly. I was barely showing until a month ago —more bloated than anything—and then suddenly, I popped.

"This clearly says you are." He slips his hand in to the front of his shorts, pushing the material down far enough to reveal his hard length in a lewd display.

"Ronan!" There are beachgoers walking along the shoreline at all hours of daylight.

"Relax, no one can see, Sea Witch." With a lingering stroke, he tucks himself away. "I need a shower. You coming?" He doesn't wait, sauntering toward the side of the house, where the outdoor stall waits. I can't count how many times we've had sex in that thing since he's moved in, often with the curtain wide open, as if it feeds his salacious tendencies. In fact, I can't remember the last time I *just* showered in it.

I hold off for a few beats, pretending I have an ounce of self-control around that man, before I climb to my feet and run after him.

Just starting this world?
Don't miss the scorching hot forbidden romance between
Abbi Mitchell and Henry Wolf.
TEMPT ME (The Wolf Hotel #1)

Tempt Me Excerpt

One

February

"I didn't mean for it to happen, Abigail. I swear!"

"You didn't mean for it to happen! You didn't mean to put your..." My words fall apart with my sobs. I can barely see Jed's face through my tears. Tears that haven't stopped since I ran for my dorm room earlier today. Tears that have left my skin raw and tight. And every time I think I'm all cried out, the image of Jed and *her* flashes inside my head and a fresh wave hits.

I wipe my dripping nose against my sweatshirt sleeve. I'm far past the point of caring what I look like. "Who is she, anyway?"

"Nobody important." He brushes his own tears away with his palm and then reaches for my face, cupping my cheeks. "You are my whole life. You've *always* been my whole life. Always! You know that, right? Tell me you know that!"

I swallow against the sharp knot lodged in my throat but it doesn't budge. I *knew* that. Up until today. "Then why would you break my heart?"

His handsome face flinches as if I'd slapped him. Something I wish I had the nerve to do. "You weren't supposed to find out."

Oh my God! "That makes it better?"

"No, that's not what I'm saying." He hangs his head for a moment. "Look, we're getting married next year and then it's just you and me. It's been just you and me for *all*

347

these years. And," he swallows, hesitates, "this is something I've been thinking about. A lot, lately."

"About cheating on me?"

"No! About, you know..." He winces. "Sex."

That's what this is all about? "Why didn't you tell me? I would have—"

"No, Abigail." Jed's face is suddenly stern. "You and me, we're doin' it the right way by waiting until we're man and wife. You're so innocent. So pure." He leans forward, pressing his forehead against mine. "It means everything to me that you'll give that to me on our wedding night. But"—a sheepish look overtakes his face—"I'm a guy. It's different for me."

"How is it different?" Who is this person sitting in front of me?

"Because we're weak! This is something I need to do. I need to get this out of my system, or I'm afraid I'll make a mistake down the road, when it *really* matters. Trust me on this one. You don't want me straying later on, when we have kids, do you?"

I'm listening, but I'm not believing these words coming out of Jed's mouth. "So we're breaking up?"

"No." He frowns. "Not exactly. We're taking a little breather, okay? Just until I can get my head on straight. But we're meant to be, you and me." He brushes strands of hair off my face, like he's done a thousand times. "I'll come back to you. I promise."

I'm so angry and hurt, I can't even face him anymore, so I fix my eyes on the small gumball machine promise ring he gave me on my sixteenth birthday, my sobs drowning out the rest of his words.

April

"Look directly into the camera when you answer the questions," the woman commands, her cold blue irises piercing behind a pair of trendy horn-rimmed glasses. Between those, her honey-blonde bun, the fitted black business suit and four-inch heels, she could pass for one of those librarian/strippers instead of a corporate recruiter.

I adjust my practical gold-wire-framed round spectacles. "Okay."

She readies the iPhone sitting in the stand for taping while I fidget on my stool, tucking wayward strands of my ginger hair behind my ear and smoothing the wrinkles from my shirt. I didn't come dressed for a videotaped interview. I figured this job fair would be like any other; I'd wander by some basic booths, collect a few pamphlets, and talk to representatives who want to be anywhere but a Chicago library on a Saturday.

For the most part, that's what it is. But the booth for Wolf Hotels is different. It's three times the size as of the others, with sharply-dressed recruiters and an on-site interviewing station behind a screen, to help speed up the hiring process for those who meet the basic criteria.

And the only reason I made the basic criteria is because I lied on the paper application that I filled out twenty minutes ago. Now I'm petrified of getting caught.

"Full name, please."

I've always hated being on camera. I clear my throat nervously. "Abigail Mitchell. But I go by Abbi," I'm quick to add. My mama calls me Abigail, and everyone else from my hometown calls me Abigail because of my mama. I've never liked it.

The interviewer is stone-faced. She doesn't care what I go by. "The role that you're applying for?"

"Outdoor Maintenance and Landscaping?" I think that was the official title on the application form.

"And please describe your experience that will be invaluable to us, Abigail."

"It's Abbi." I force my biggest smile and hope my annoyance doesn't show on video when they play it back later. "Sure. Well, first off, I love the outdoors. I grew up on a farm and have spent years baling hay, throwing bags of grain, and hauling buckets of water for the animals. So don't worry, I'm plenty strong." People don't believe that I am. My slim five-foot-five stature is deceiving, but one look at my body in shorts and a tank will attest that I'm feminine but honed with muscle from long days on the Mitchell farm.

I've already provided all of this information on the handwritten application form, but I guess they want the live version as well. "I've run my own landscaping company for five years, operating out of Greenbank, Pennsylvania, maintaining commercial properties with excellence." I've been pulling dandelions and cutting grass around my podunk town every summer since I was fourteen. To call what I do "landscaping" is a farce. But if it gets me this job, far the hell away from my life, I'll say anything.

"Were any of these properties hotels?"

"Yes." Never say "no" in an interview. Always find a way to spin it into a yes.

"Please tell me about these hotels."

Crap. And there it is. I've never been a good liar. "It was just one, actually. It's called the Inn. It's...an upscale bed-and-breakfast." Three rooms in an old Victorian house, run by Perry and Wendy Rhodes. I hear one of the rooms is decorated with a cat theme. Cat wallpaper, cat pillows. Cats, everywhere.

By the way the woman's painted red lips are pressed together, I'm pretty sure my answer is not the one she was looking for. "Okay. Thank you. I also see here that you worked weekends serving customers at a place called the Pearl for several years."

"Yes. That's my aunt's restaurant. I'd help her out during the busy season." I hesitated about using Aunt May as a reference. I can't be sure she'll give me a glowing recommendation if it means I won't be coming back to Greenbank for the summer. Mama would have her skin if she ever found out she helped make that happen.

"What type of establishment is it?"

"A family restaurant."

"So, not fine dining?"

I sigh. "No. I wouldn't call it that." Slapping together hot turkey sandwiches and pouring Cokes from a fountain does not make for fine dining.

"And have you ever cleaned houses professionally... No," she says, seeing me shake my head fervently, my face twisting with disdain at even the suggestion. That means dealing with fitted sheets all day long, and that sounds like torture to me.

"I see you've also done receptionist work."

Finally, something I can answer truthfully and positively. "Yes. I've worked part-time in my church's office for years. I still do, when I go home for the summer."

"What exactly did you do for them?"

"Answer phones and schedule appointments for the Reverend. I also balance the church's books and organize the annual Corn Roast weekend charity BBQ for our parish." Something I can't bring myself to do again this summer, but will be guilted into doing by my mama and the reverend, should I go back to Greenbank.

She scans my application. "I see you're in school right now." She pauses, and I realize that I'm supposed to answer her.

"Yes. I have one more year in a Bachelor of Arts degree." The right side of my face is burning from the heat of the lamp. I imagine this is what an interrogation feels like. How much longer is this going to take?

"Are you able to commit to the four-month contract, from May through August?"

"North Gate College starts in September and exams finish at the end of this month, so that won't be a problem."

She smiles. "Good. And what are your plans for after college, Abbi?"

My face falls before I'm able to control my expression. That question catches me off guard. She's talking about next summer, and all I can focus on is getting through today, tomorrow, and this summer. Ideally in Alaska.

Is this where I'm supposed to lie and say that I aspire for a career with Wolf Hotels? I debate my answer for a few heartbeats, and finally decide on the truth. "Honestly, I'm not sure anymore. I was supposed to get married and help run the family farm, but my fiancé and I are—" I stop myself with a deep breath and then an embarrassed little smile. So inappropriate for an interview. "My personal situation is in limbo," I say instead, my voice growing husky, my eyes burning with the threat of tears. It's all still too fresh, too raw. "I'll probably go back home. My family's there."

"And help run the farm?" Her eyes graze over me—over my thick braid that I can't help but toy with when I'm nervous, over my favorite royal-blue button-down that's probably been washed one too many times, over my generic jeans, and down to my Converse—and I know she's judging me. I sit up straighter, feeling more self-conscious than I already do being in front of a camera.

I look nothing like her, or any of the other recruiters here. They're all put together, with smooth, richly colored hair and perfectly painted faces. I don't wear much makeup; just a little lip gloss and, on occasion, shimmery pink nail polish. I don't use hairspray and not a drop of dye has ever touched my hair for fear that it'll make the color worse than it already is.

"Yes." That has always been the plan. But now I feel like I need to defend myself. I'm not just another farm girl, getting ready to bake pies and pop out little farm babies. "I started a side business making soaps, moisturizers, and essential oils a few years back. It's called Sage Oils. I'm going to focus on expanding that." Sage, after my favorite herb, though my products involve everything from mint to lavender to lemon. Up until this point, the bulk of my sales have been thanks to the annual Christmas bazaar and summer fair. I can't complain though; that money will pay for my flight to Homer, should Wolf hire me.

"My, you're quite the enterprising young woman. And so busy. Landscaping and soapmaking businesses, college, farming..." I can't read the woman's tone to tell if she's genuinely impressed. "And what do you do for enjoyment, Abbi?"

I bite my bottom lip to stop myself from saying "Umm" while I think. Wolf Hotels is one of the most posh lines of hotels in the world. I need to sound smart if I have a hope in hell of getting this job. "As you have noted, I'm quite busy with work and school. When I have free time, I spend it with my family, and with my church, solidifying my faith." Which is in some dicey water as of late. "I also volunteer at the local animal shelter, both here in Chicago as well as at home."

"So you like animals?"

"Yes!" I nod emphatically. "I'm excited to see Alaska's wilderness."

She offers me a tight smile. "Right. Last question. Why should we hire you to work at Wolf Cove in Alaska?"

I look down at the pamphlet in my hand—pictures of white-capped mountains and vast wilderness, glacier valleys and volcanoes.

Thousands of miles of serenity, of nothingness.

Thousands of miles from my current life.

They don't want to listen to my sob story, and it's sure as hell not going to get me hired. I struggle to smile as I stare into the camera, silently pleading with my eyes to whoever is making the hiring decisions. "Because I'm smart, hardworking, diligent, and ethical. I respect people and I love a challenge. Plus, I've always wanted to visit Alaska, and this looks like an incredible once-in-a-lifetime opportunity." I clear my throat. "I have nothing to distract my focus. I will give Wolf Cove *everything* I have to offer this summer."

She presses a button and steps around. "Great. Thank you. We'll be in touch."

"When will you be making your decisions?" It's the beginning of April; I'd be flying out in four weeks if I get hired.

"Shortly. We've already filled many of the positions from our pool of current Wolf employees who are interested in the Alaska location. We're just plugging some last-minute holes with outside recruitment." She sticks my application into a red file folder. Is that the reject file?

"Do I have a chance? Honestly." I can't believe I asked that, but I have nothing left to lose.

"We tend to hire people who already have luxury hotel chain experience. But we'll be in touch." She stands there with her arm leading the way to the exit.

My shoulders sag. I force myself to leave before I beg her to put in a good word for me.

There's no way I'm getting this job.

May

I inhale deeply, reveling in the crisp ocean air as land approaches ahead. Chicago was in the seventies when I left this morning. Two layovers, a flight delay, and fifteen hours later, the fifty-five degree day's high has dipped to low forties and I had to dig my winter jacket out of my suitcase.

"Have you ever been to Alaska before?" the captain, a soft-spoken white-haired man named John asks, his hands resting easily on the ferry's wheel.

I shake my head, my gaze drifting over the sea of evergreen and rock as far as the eye can see. We left the dock in Homer thirty minutes ago. It didn't seem like it would take that long to cross, but Kachemak Bay is vast and wide and unlike anything I've ever seen.

And on the other side of it is my home for the next four months.

I'm so glad I remembered to pop an Antivert an hour before boarding. I'd be puking over the rails by now had I not. Boats and I have never coexisted well.

"So, what made you come?" I can tell John likes to talk, as much for conversation as to assess the foreigners coming to his homeland.

"A brochure," I answer simply, honestly.

He chuckles. "Yeah, it'll do that, all right. Lures plenty of folk our way."

I smile, though his words resonate deep inside. It "lured" me. Yes, that's exactly what it did.

Frankly, the brochure didn't need to work too hard.

When things take an ugly turn, people are always saying they're going to pick up and move far away. Australia, France, anywhere that puts an ocean between them and their problems. Most don't ever act on that. I certainly had no intention of doing so.

And then I went to that job fair in the city library, more than a little panicked about what I was going to do this summer. Recruiters were peddling administrative and counselor positions, trade internships, day care. Nothing I was interested in. Plus, they were all local Chicago-based positions. The last thing I wanted to do was stay in Chicago for the summer. I needed to separate myself from it and its bitter memories, if for only a few months until school started again in the fall.

But the idea of going back to Pennsylvania, where everyone including the cows had heard the nitty-gritty details about my breakup with Jed, was even more unappealing.

That's what happens when you grow up in a small town and then go away to college with your high school sweetheart, who's also the reverend's son, who you were supposed to marry the summer after you both graduate college.

Who you've been saving yourself for.

Who you caught with his pants down and thrusting into some raven-haired jezebel.

And, while in the depths of despair, though you know better, you tell your upstanding, churchgoing mama, who is known around town as much for her raspberry pie as for her big mouth.

That scandal sure gave the folks of Greenbank something to talk about during Pennsylvania's long, cold winter. It's been months since D-Day, or what I like to call Dick Day, when I caught him. February 2, to be exact.

I'm sure tongues were wagging across pews during church service. When I visited over Easter weekend though, I got nothing but sympathetic nods and pats. Jed, sitting in the pew directly across from us, earned more than a few glowers. Not everyone shared those feelings, though. His father, Reverend Enderbey, decided that giving a sermon on man's weakness for carnal flesh and the need for forgiveness and understanding would be more appropriate than discussing the resurrection of Christ that day.

Much like Jed promised me, Reverend Enderbey has promised my parents that this is just a momentary blip in Jed's faith; that he's feeling confused and needs to sort out his priorities. He'll come back to me, after he's done sowing his wild oats.

Why do they all think I'll want to take him back?

He broke my heart that day, and has continued breaking it daily, every time I see him walking hand in hand around campus with *her*.

He's not just sowing wild oats. They're *dating* now.

So when I passed by the Wolf Hotels booth at the job fair a month ago and spotted the pamphlet with a beautiful vista of snow-capped mountains and forest, I immediately stopped and started asking questions, and within ten minutes I knew that Wolf Cove was my ticket away from sadness, temporarily at least. I just needed to get myself to Homer, Alaska. They'd provide transportation to the hotel, subsidized accommodations and meals onsite, and weekly transport to Homer, if needed, and in turn I'd work like a dog and keep my mind occupied.

The best part? It was almost 3,800 miles from everything I know.

It sounded perfect. And unattainable. I walked out of that interview feeling hopeless, assuming that there was no way I'd get the job.

And yet I'm standing here today. I call that divine intervention. God knew I needed this miracle.

It came in the form of a phone call a week after the interview, with an official offer for a position in the Landscaping and Maintenance crew. I screamed. I even shed a few happy tears, which was a nice change from all the sad tears I've spilled since February. Knowing that I could avoid Greenbank, Jed, and my family, that I would be leaving my dorm room the day after my last exam and hopping onto a plane... that's the only reason I've held it together this long.

The ferry turns left to run along the coastline, farther into the bay.

"What are those places, over there? Do people live out here?" I point toward the little huts speckling the shore, camouflaged within the trees.

"Nah. They're mostly lodges and cabin rentals."

I study the structures, like yurts on stilts overlooking the water. "They're nice. Rustic."

"They are, indeed."

"Not like Wolf Cove, though."

John chuckles softly, shaking his head. "Not quite."

If the pictures in the pamphlet are at all accurate. My

mama's convinced that it's all computer generated, that nothing that luxurious would exist up in Alaska. That I'll end up contracting West Nile from the thick fog of mosquitoes, or I'll wake up in the rickety shack that I'm sleeping in to find a bear gnawing on my leg.

To say Bernadette Mitchell is unhappy about this Alaska job is an understatement. At first she flat-out told me that I wasn't allowed to go. I hung up the phone on her that night, the first time I'd ever done that. Probably the first time *anyone's* ever had the nerve to hang up on a woman like her. I half expected her to drive the nine hours and slap me upside the head.

Two days later, after she'd cooled off, she called and tried to persuade me. I was making a grave mistake, leaving Greenbank and Jed. We'd be away from the chaos of Chicago and the temptations that made Jed stray. We'd have each other, day in and day out, and I could remind him of why we're so perfect together.

I know it's not going to be that simple.

So I dug my heels in. I've been "good girl Abbi" all my life, sitting next to my parents at church service every Sunday, keeping company with like-minded people, staying away from the "bad kids" who drank and smoked pot and had sex. Always listening to Mama.

Maybe if I'd just spread my legs for Jed, my heart wouldn't have been smashed into a thousand pieces.

While she's my mama and I know she wants what's best for me, she, too, thinks that Jed and I belong together, and that our reunion is inevitable, once he gets "the devil" out of his system. I had to bite my tongue before I pointed out to her that the girl currently sucking Jed's dick is a significant obstacle in this imminent reconciliation of ours.

I scan the approaching buildings, my excitement triumphing over my exhaustion. "Where is it?"

"Wolf Cove is just around the bend."

Wolf Cove Hotel in Wolf Cove, Alaska. "How do you go about renaming a cove, anyway?"

John chuckles softly again. He's such a pleasant man. "The cove has been Wolf Cove for hundreds of years now. The Wolf family has a lot of history up here, with the gold mines. That's where they made their first fortune. Though I'm sure they could afford to have it renamed, if it came to that. They're a successful lot. Generous, too."

Man, to be a part of that family. They must have a lot of money, to risk opening a location like this all the way up here, and set their employees up the way they're doing for us, and all the benefits. "Hey, thanks for coming back for me. I didn't want to stay in a motel." It's just John and me on the ferry, and a deck full of crates and supplies. He was kind enough to make another trip across the bay and pick me up after my flight delay. Apparently he carted a full load of college-aged employees over hours ago.

"We didn't want to leave you stranded. 'Specially on the first day. I woulda had to come back for the supplies first thing in the morning, anyway."

I glance at my watch with dismay. "I've missed the orientation session." It started at seven, almost an hour ago. The skies are deceptively light for this time of evening. "I can't believe how bright it still is."

"Wait 'til June."

"Less than five hours of darkness on the equinox, right?"

He grins. "Someone's been doin' her homework."

"I like to be prepared." The day I applied for the job, I ran home and researched Alaska late into the night instead of studying for my exams. The further I dug, the more excited I became, and the harder I prayed that I'd get the job.

"Well, I'm sure one of the ladies will be kind enough to fill you in on what you missed. They seemed like a nice group. Polite youngsters like yourself, for the most part anyway."

At twenty-one, it feels strange to be referred to as a "youngster," but I guess next to John, who's got to be pushing seventy, that's exactly what I am.

The ferry rounds the crop of small islands and turns toward the cove. John points to the massive building ahead. "And there's Wolf Cove Hotel."

My eyes widen. "Whoa. The brochure pictures weren't fake." And they don't do this place justice.

John chuckles again. "No, they certainly weren't."

I stare at it quietly, mesmerized. The main lodge towers over the water. Even from this distance, I can see that the lodge is grandiose in its design and massive in size. I can't make out the details to appreciate it yet, but there's no doubt it's something to be admired.

"They just made the finishing touches two weeks ago. Been working on it for almost three years, now."

"Is it still opening on Sunday?" Belinda, the woman who called to formally hire me, said that these first few days would be focused on training and last-minute preparations.

"I'll be ferrying in the first guests at noon. I've been bringin' employees in by the boatload over the last two days. There are a lot of you. A high staff-to-guest ratio, I heard someone say."

"How is the Wolf family going to make any money?"

"I'm guessing the twelve-hundred-dollar-a-night price tag will help."

My mouth drops open. "Who can afford that?" I barely scraped together the eleven hundred I needed for my plane ticket here.

"What's that famous line from that movie? Oh, shucks. You may be too young to remember. The one with the baseball and all those cornfields. 'If you build it...'"

I smile. It's only my dad's favorite movie.

He winks.

We fall into a comfortable silence as we approach, and I realize that I've been rolling my promise ring around my finger unconsciously this entire time. It's been three months since Jed and I broke up and I haven't been able to bring myself to remove it. Now, I slip it off, letting the cheap metal rest in the palm of my hand. A part of me —the hurt, angry part—wants to toss it into the water and be done with it. A symbol of my faith in Jed.

But I can't bring myself to do it just yet. So, I slip the ring into my pocket and try to focus on the months to come.

Also by K.A. Tucker

The Wolf Hotel Series:

Tempt Me (#1)

Break Me (#2)

Teach Me (#3)

Surrender To Me (#4)

Own Me (#5)

The Wolf Hotel Mermaid Beach Series:

Release Me (#1)

Empire Nightclub Series:

Sweet Mercy (#1)

Gabriel Fallen (#2)

Dirty Empire (#3)

Fallen Empire (#4)

For K.A. Tucker's entire backlist, visit katuckerbooks.com

About the Author

K.A. Tucker writes captivating stories with an edge.

She is the internationally bestselling author of the Ten Tiny Breaths and Burying Water series, He Will Be My Ruin, Until It Fades, Keep Her Safe, The Simple Wild, Be the Girl, and Say You Still Love Me. Her books have been featured in national publications including USA Today, Globe & Mail, Suspense Magazine, Publisher's Weekly, Oprah Mag, and First for Women.

K.A. Tucker resides outside of Toronto. When she's not writing, you can find her reading recipes she'll never make or chasing rabbits away from her hostas.

Want news about upcoming books, sales, and other exciting things? Sign up for K.A. Tucker's newsletter. Visit her website at katuckerbooks.com.